Jemima Jones has had a career in public service working to make a difference for the environment and its communities across New Zealand and Australia. She has two grown daughters, and Jemima lives with her husband, with two labradors and three cats on a very windy hill in Lower Hutt, New Zealand. Jemima loves to write stories about real life and to develop characters that are relatable and identifiable in all communities. You will definitely see elements of your family or your neighbours in her work.

For my husband—my eternal love.

For my beloved daughters—you inspire me daily.

For my parents, my dad for feeding my desire to tell stories and my mother for believing I had more to give.

Jemima Jones

Death Comes With Secrets

AUSTIN MACAULEY PUBLISHERS
LONDON * CAMBRIDGE * NEW YORK * SHARJAH

Copyright © Jemima Jones 2025

The right of Jemima Jones to be identified as author of this work has been asserted by the author in accordance with sections 77 and 78 of the Copyright, Designs and Patents Act 1988.

All rights reserved. No part of this publication may be reproduced, stored in a retrieval system, or transmitted in any form or by any means, electronic, mechanical, photocopying, recording, or otherwise, without the prior permission of the publishers.

Any person who commits any unauthorised act in relation to this publication may be liable to criminal prosecution and civil claims for damages.

This is a work of fiction. Names, characters, businesses, places, events, locales, and incidents are either the products of the author's imagination or used in a fictitious manner. Any resemblance to actual persons, living or dead, or actual events is purely coincidental.

A CIP catalogue record for this title is available from the British Library.

ISBN 9781035899180 (Paperback)
ISBN 9781035899197 (ePub e-book)

www.austinmacauley.com

First Published 2025
Austin Macauley Publishers Ltd®
1 Canada Square
Canary Wharf
London
E14 5AA

Huge thanks to my husband and daughters for their support of my writing and believing in me without question.

Special thanks to my mum for being my unofficial proofreader and reviewer.

Special thanks to my dad for sharing his stories to fuel my own.

Thank you to the many who have been part of this journey. There is a piece of your encouragement, inspiration and heart in my writing and I am grateful for all of your support and kindness.

Table of Contents

Lucy The Day James Died	14
Claire	22
Lucy	25
Pippa	28
Jade	32
The Christmas Party	35
Lucy	41
Pippa	44
Claire	47
Jade	50
Church	51
Lucy	55
News Travels Fast	59
Jade	62
Lucy	65
Jack	68
Lucy	71
Sam	74
Lucy	77
Jade	80

Pippa	85
Claire	90
Lucy	94
Jade	98
Lucy	103
Claire	105
Lucy	109
Pippa	114
Claire	119
The Funeral	124
Pippa	137
Jack	139
Claire	143
Jade	148
Pippa	152
Claire	158
Lucy	164
Midnight Mass	169
Lucy	174
Claire	176
Pippa	180
Lucy	184
Claire	188
Mark	191
Lucy	194
Claire	198

Pippa 201

Lucy 204

James Smart was tired and hungry. He thought his truck was probably a couple of kilometres up the road and he almost wanted to nap right in it when he found it. It was warm enough to do that in the early summer, and he had slept in his truck a heap of times.

It was like that in the country; sometimes, you just slept where you parked, too tired or too drunk to get home. James was thinking about doing that now like a sensible person, but he wasn't always sensible.

James had been out shooting. He had some small-time jobs from local farmers for the summer, while he was home from studying veterinary medicine at university. James loved animals. Yet, he was also a farmer's son, so he was practical when it came to animal pests.

He knew the damage to the land and cost of a rabbit population on a farm, so he didn't let emotion cloud his judgement when it came to getting rid of them. Over time, he had become quite the shot, so his services were sought after, and he was able to make a fair bit of money to fund his next university year and his beer consumption.

James marvelled at how this summer, shooting rabbits was almost like taking candy from babies. The rabbits were overrunning the farms, like plagues of locusts. James could clap his hands and three hundred rabbits would spring from the grass and run.

All he had to do was shoot, almost without aiming and he would knock down a fair number. Child's play, James smiled to himself, just a little too confidently.

James wore camo pants and brown work boots lightly laced, as he preferred. His t-shirt was partially covered by a plaid flannel shirt, long worn and missing more than one button. His light brown curly hair had grown longer over his time at university, and he liked the way the curls bounced down over his face.

Girls often liked to twist it through their fingers or ping it like a spring when he was out drinking, and he liked that too. Yawning and feeling the weight of his gun, James could see the shadows of the trees lining the road on the asphalt. The moon was full and low hung in the sky and the glow of it made the butt of his weapon glint.

He was thinking about the bacon buttie he would have before bed and the heat of his mum's spicy tomato relish, the way it hung there on his tongue after the other flavours had melded and passed. He wondered if he might fry an egg as well, as he was feeling extra hungry after all the walking and the chickens were laying well, his mum, Lucy, had said.

As he walked, car lights came into view from behind James and the light grew larger the closer they got. He knew that it was probably about the time that the Christmas Farmer's Cooperative 'Do' was finishing and that it would be some friends or neighbours making their way home.

He waved out, because that's what you do in the country, and the car tooted at him as it drove carefully past. James smiled because he recognised the car as old Mr Jarrett and his wife, Betty. Mr Jarrett had a small farm up the valley and had been the school bus driver for a time too. Betty was the organist at the local church and knitted big thick woollen jerseys that Mr Jarrett wore winter and summer.

James was passing the swampy part of the roadside, where the water pooled in the winter months and dried out slowly over the summer. Not wanting to get wet feet, he stepped sideways onto the asphalt, walking in a close track as near to the edge as possible without twisting an ankle.

The county roads were narrower than the city ones and he knew that there wasn't a lot of room for him and two cars passing each other, not that he expected that would happen at night so much.

James popped an ear bud in and rock music played from it. The beat of the music was strong, and he elevated the volume to compensate for wearing just the one bud. *This will wake me up a bit,* James thought, as he plodded on step after step towards his truck.

James nodded his head slightly to the beat and played a bit of air guitar with his gun, eyes shut as he sang. And then, it was over. There was a small bump and James was dead, music still playing.

Lucy
The Day James Died

Stoney Hollow was abuzz with activity as preparations were underway for the night of the year. The Farmer's Cooperative Christmas 'Do' was the biggest event of the district. The community centre was all done up with real Christmas trees inside and out, bunting and a big blow-up Santa that could move up and down the chimney stack.

Lucy Smart was marshalling the troupes and could be heard at the top of her voice, shouting, "I said to put the red bows in the trees, Pippa, not on the tables and Claire, take those wee snowmen and put them where the bows are."

Claire and Pippa shared knowing looks and hustled off to do as they were told. Lucy was the bossy one on the committee and it wasn't worth opening your mouth to argue.

Lucy was married to Jack, a sheep farmer who quietly longed for a different kind of woman in his life. Lucy might have known it but if she did, she never said, not to anyone. Mind you, she was very busy. She filled every possible minute with church and community groups, always in charge and never shy from telling you how things should be.

She was a well-built if not slightly short woman, with an untameable fringe and penchant for sensible shoes. Sturdy, you might call her, not athletic but strong and not unfamiliar with physical work.

She was just the kind of person all communities needed but didn't always value. In command, organising, confident and everywhere. When the children had been in school, she was the PTA mother, bus monitor, newsletter writer and swimming pool key keeper.

As they got older, she was the swimming coach, librarian, Sunday school teacher and justice of the peace. And then, of course, there were her farming related duties, winter ball, Farmer's Cooperative Chair and Wool and Shearing

Award judge. Never a dull or empty moment in Lucy's life, but plenty of harried and harangued community folk as a result!

Lucy was a boarding school girl and a good church-going lass. Her Bible was well-worn with pages curled and her school chums always knew she would turn up to everything, from a wedding to a funeral or the opening of an envelope, they often joked.

After school, she had gone to university and trained in accounting but, after a couple of years in the family business, she found herself a fish out of water, too loud and busy for the seriousness of managing other people's money. Lucy's mother had taken her aside and had one of those wee chats, the not so private and humiliating ones that everyone knew was coming but her.

Her mother told her she wasn't really suited to an 'indoor' job and suggested she marry that nice Jack who had been coming around to the house. *You will do better there,* her mother said, *out on the farm with the sheep to talk to.* Her mother said, *have some babies, dear and get involved in the community.* So that is what Lucy did. She put her tail between her legs, quit her job and told Jack to propose and she would accept.

And so, there she found herself. 4000 sheep and land as far as the eye could see with bad internet and kids that couldn't wait to move away. Jack was a good husband and she wanted for nothing. Over time, he seemed to have learnt the art of switching off to her continued chatter at volume and they got on rather well, except if he challenged Lucy's way of doing things or told her off.

On those occasions, Lucy sulked terribly. He wasn't fussed on church or sport or much else other than farming but he enjoyed her cooking and her sense of family and that was good enough for him, for a long time.

Three children, grown now, had come along in quick succession and Lucy was a harried and often time, poor mother. She did a good job of building robust stock with good levels of independence and strong work ethics. The children didn't always appreciate that she was 'that' mother, the one who was always in amongst it, organising, shouting and telling off their friends but she was kind, if not a little emotionally detached.

The elder two children, daughters, had husbands of their own now but didn't continue the farming line and lived in the city. One was a successful lawyer in the environmental field and the other a teacher at the same school that Lucy had gone to. That had left Lucy feeling very chuffed indeed.

Pippa and Claire laughed as some other poor soul was getting the Lucy treatment. "No Kate, they just won't do, I am afraid, I said recyclable and these are not, tut-tut!" Lucy exclaimed.

Pippa, who was in charge of the red bows, was another farmer's wife. She came from farming stock and the family farm was handed down over the generations. She had married into a similar family, and many in the district thought them the ideal couple, her with her farming roots and pretty features and him with his family holdings and handsome looks.

Pippa was a kind person, tolerant and unflappable. She was the person who always brought people closer together and kept the peace in Stoney Hollow. She smoothed the rough of Lucy's rub and people confided in Pippa and sought her advice often.

She had brains, was a fabulous cook and pianist and had the most delightful twin boys, Archer and Hunter, who had matching mops of blonde floppy hair and green eyes like their dad.

Pippa's husband, Duncan, was a lovely kind man who loved his wife and children. They were a tight knit family and spent a lot of time taking the children out and sharing new experiences. Pippa and Duncan both agreed that living in Stoney Hollow shouldn't be all their children knew and so, they made a big effort to show them the world beyond the farm and expose them to different kinds of people and communities.

The children loved going to the Turkish place in town for kebabs or to the Indian for curry and poppadums. They had been to Japan on a family holiday and to Italy to stay in a villa over the summer months when they were smaller. Yet, nothing they saw changed the fact that the boys loved the farm, raising lambs and calves, running over the fields and finding frogs and riding their ponies and tiny motorbikes.

Pippa was dutifully placing the bows on the trees and making sure they were symmetrical and straight, for she knew if they were not, Lucy would be on her tail. She didn't really mind Lucy, knowing her heart was in the right place, even if she did bark the orders just a little much.

Her husband, Duncan, couldn't abide Lucy, he called her 'that woman' and 'the foghorn' but Pippa tried hard to see the good in most people and Lucy was good in her own spirited way. She did wish at times Lucy didn't always shout and on the odd occasion, could have done without her cheery good morning when things weren't going well.

If she was going to be super nasty, God, did she detest those bloody sensible shoes, all similar and looking like those worn by a spinster nursing sister or nun, for that matter.

Claire was a different soul to both Lucy and Pippa. She wasn't very clever, in a sophisticated way and she desperately wanted to be more like Pippa and a little like Lucy. The shame was she just didn't have the smarts to get herself together.

She was organised but harried, good with the children but fast losing track of them and great fun for a cuppa and a natter. Her house was always a state of organised chaos, partly because she was petrified of forgetting things. So, to combat that, Claire had a habit of writing absolutely everything down and sticking it to the fridge, and the walls, and sometimes, the cupboards.

She couldn't bring herself to throw a single kindergarten painting out, hence the paper piles were all over the house, and this was even if the picture consisted of two bits of dried macaroni and some non-toxic glue. So, as a consequence, the house was messy, full to bursting and nothing had a proper place or order of any kind.

Claire had almost black hair that was sort of in between long and short with a poor cut that she got from the oldest hairdresser in living memory in the local shop. It was shorter in the front with longer layers in the back, almost mullet like. She had a keen sense of fashion but somehow, she never quite looked put together, often with clashing colours or outrageous shoes that didn't match with her outfits.

She did have a good curvy figure and could chat along to anyone, which meant she was popular with many. Claire was kind, always digging in her overloaded and beaten-up handbag for a sweet for the snow plough driver or a peppermint for the school bus monitor, dusting off the handbag fluff before smiling and handing it over.

What Claire lacked in intelligence, she made up for in spirit and she gave everything a damn good try. She was on the PTA; she helped in the classrooms at school a couple of mornings a week and she fed her family very well. She knitted and darned poorly but persistently and if asked, would clank along on the piano at family dinners.

She sung a little but would rather be in the kitchen, cooking up some good hearty farmer's food for hungry men. Well, that was if she could find the kitchen under the post-it notes and children's art!

Her husband was the envy of many farmers in the district, not for any other reason that Claire did everything. Apart from the work on the farm that her husband did, Claire managed everything else. She paid the bills, did the paperwork, plainly but accurately, organised the contractors and the shearing and she fed everyone while she did it.

There may have been washing everywhere and homework on the dinner table, but she worked until she dropped and most nights that was about midnight or 1am. Claire's husband, Mark, knew he was lucky, but he wasn't the type to say so.

He was a quiet chap who was happy to listen to Claire whittle on but didn't say much back. He liked his home comforts, wasn't a natural farmer and was secretly waiting for the day his son might take over.

Claire and Mark had two children, son Francis and daughter Flora. Francis was a family name passed down the generations, but Flora, Claire had chosen because flowers made her happy. Francis was a thin pasty boy and failed to thrive as a baby.

Flora was more robust and highly likely to be a better farmer than her brother, who was more interested in computers than lambs and wool. Next year, both Francis and Flora would be away for school and Claire was dreading it. She had no idea what she would do with her time and boredom scared her more than death.

As she put the 'wee snowmen' as Lucy had called them, on the tables, she wondered if she should measure them to ensure they were even and to Lucy's regimented standards. That was Claire, never 100 percent sure of herself and always glad of a compliment or smile from a man, whether her husband or otherwise.

Claire's thoughts were interrupted as Jade came in, dragging her bag behind her as the strap had broken as she jumped out of her car. Jade was beautiful. Green eyes and black hair, skinny black jeans and heels. Her black hair glossy and full all the way to her waist with gentle waves giving it body and shape. Everyone saw Jade's beauty, from the preacher to the butcher to the little girls waiting for the bus. She was simply divine, and out of place in Stoney Hollow.

"God, sorry Claire," said Jade and she swished her hair over her shoulder. "Bloody cows in the road had me stuck for ages and I was already late. Nelson had a bad night with his back and we slept in, love. Only just had my smoothie from breakfast and it's nearly lunchtime!" She gasped.

Jade was English. She had arrived in Stoney Hollow on a backpacking trip and got a job at the pub. It was meant to be a short-term thing for some pocket money, but she met Nelson, a forty-something bachelor with a large sheep and beef operation and that was it, they were in love in a heartbeat and married in two.

Jade didn't do farm work with the animals, but she had her Maltese dog, Poppet, and her horses and she was a city girl to her core. She didn't cook or even drive until she had been married a year. Her arrival certainly sent the tongues wagging in the district and plenty of people said Nelson had taken leave of his senses when he married her so quickly.

Five years on and Jade was happy. She had found her place and Nelson didn't mind that she didn't work on the farm or in the house. He had plenty of money and was happy to keep her in style and to pay for her hair appointments, fake nails, lashes and spray tans. Jade said she loved the bones of him, and it seemed that was true.

Jade was habitually late and always glammed up. In keeping with the season, she had had her nails done with snow scenes for Christmas and spray tan freshly applied. Claire was dumbstruck for a second, caught between snowmen and the vision that had walked in. She blushed and smiled.

"No problem, Jade, I hope Nelson's back is feeling better this morning. My Francis hurt his back a while ago and it can take some time to come right. Is he doing exercises? That's what the doctor told Francis, do your exercises, Francis and you will be back on the horse in no time. My Francis is allergic to horses, so I did think that was an odd thing to say, he knows he doesn't ride," said Claire.

Jade laughed out loud. "Oh Claire," she smiled, "you are a funny one."

"Never mind Nelson, he gets plenty of exercise," Jade explained, winking. "Now, give me something to do before I get distracted, and all the hard work has been done."

With that, Lucy appeared, tapping her watch. "Yes, well, Jade, some of us might think you wanted the work to be done, coming in at this time. Well, make yourself useful and grab those fairy lights, Pippa is getting the ladder and we need to string them up over the door outside. Not any old way though, swoop them into small loops like bunting," Lucy ordered.

"Yes ma'am," said Jade with a cheeky salute that made Claire giggle out loud.

Lucy had arranged the catering to come in and been very specific about the menu. She didn't want any of this fancy city nonsense because she knew there would be hungry farmers to feed and alcohol to soak up over the night. She chose big sausage rolls, club sandwiches, chicken legs wrapped in bacon, roast lamb shoulder, jacket potatoes with butter and sour cream, coleslaw and lots of bread.

For dessert, she had gone for fruit salad, Pavlova, cream-filled brandy snaps, trifle and Christmas cake. Last year, she had left the catering to Pippa and while it was lovely, it wasn't really men's food and there had been some complaints about people going home hungry or not being familiar with some of the things dished up.

Pippa had said she wanted to try some new things when she took on the catering last year. But afterward, Lucy had told her in no uncertain terms that fancy food like baba-what's-its-name and chickpeas wasn't for farmers, and she should have known better.

Pippa had been offended and left, feeling a bit stupid. She should have known that something new wasn't going to be flavour of the month. She had lived in Stoney Hollow her whole life, so why she thought people might be open to new things was stupid. Plain dumb.

She knew that it had been a mistake to model her menu on Duncan's open-minded views and tastes. How easy it was to forget that not everyone was like him, so willing to be shown new things and to try new things whether food or farming practice.

Lucy was clapping her hands. "Gather round, gather round," she shouted at Pippa, Claire and Jade as they came into the main hall. The smell of real Christmas trees was strong, and Pippa sneezed, the most gentle and petite sneeze the others had ever heard.

"God," said Jade, "where is that pixie sneezing, as it sure didn't sound like a fully grown human did that!"

Pippa laughed and her face flushed. "Pathetic, isn't it?" She said, smiling. "I just could never do one of those dramatically loud sneezes like some people do, right from when I was small."

"Right, right," muttered Lucy very loudly. "Time to sort these costumes out. Now, Jade, yours is the smallest, of course, no curves in that one and then, Claire, yours is the biggest. Mine is at home already, so the third one is yours, Pippa. Now, make sure you each get a wig and a hat and a pair of ears. The shoes are pinned to the stripy tights."

"Now, make sure you have these on before you arrive, so just come dressed in them. Jade that hair is going to have to be tucked up somehow, so I brought some bobby pins and a hair net, in case you don't have any. Pippa and Claire, yours should fit nicely under the pixie wig," Lucy explained.

"Thanks Luce," said Pippa. "These are really cute outfits."

"Yes," said Claire, "but I am not sure I have the right knickers for them, what colour would you wear?"

Jade laughed. "Love," she said, chortling, "don't wear any. You can be the naughty elf!"

Claire's face reddened but she smiled back. "Oh Jade, you are such a tease, Mark would have a blue fit if I did that. How could I go to church in the morning!"

Lucy stiffened. "No one is going without underwear. Claire, just wear something light coloured, and you will be fine. Now, the food is here, so let's get locked up and home and the caterers can take care of things in the kitchen."

Claire

Claire pulled into the driveway. Its leafy green elms lining either side before the grassy hills rolled gently into the distance. She wasn't much of a gardener but luckily, Mark's mother lived in the cottage down the lane from the main house and she still had a green thumb.

She made sure Claire knew it though, chastising her often for the lack of care she put into the house and the garden, compared to her high standards. It was Mrs Green's hard work, or Nana Green as they now called her that showed in the flower beds, thick with roses and annuals. The gladioli and the dahlias, sweet peas and lavender standing proud behind box hedging.

As Claire pulled up in her trusty Toyota, the dogs yapped around the vehicle, and she noted that Francis had not opened his curtains and the washing was still on the line. Dragging her costume, handbag and the mail along with her, Claire scooped the billowing sheets up, unpegging them as she walked towards the concrete steps near the back door to the house.

Once Claire made it inside, the sheets were unceremoniously dumped onto yesterday's washing in the easy chair in the dining room, covering the underwear and flannel shirts. The dogs rushed in behind her, one chewing on a dead rabbit and another with full breasts from a recent litter of pups. The breakfast dishes were on the table and the remains of the attempts the children had made at lunch littered the bench.

"Francis, Flora," Claire yelled to the children. "Come and help me get this place tidied up a bit. Nana Green will be here soon; she is going to look after you tonight and give you your dinner. She will have a blue fit if she sees the house like this, you know how she is."

Flora bounced into the room, hay in her hair and her face bronzed from days outside in the elements. "Mum!" She huffed. "Do we have to have bloody Nana Green again? She is SOOO old and grumpy. Can't we just stay here by ourselves?"

Claire smiled in a manner of sympathy for the pleading of her youngest. "Hey, what is the swearing about?" She questioned her daughter, before adding, "Sorry darling, I am afraid Nana is coming and that's that. She isn't too bad and she might teach you to play 500 if you ask nicely."

With that, Francis came into the room, rubbing his eyes, tired from too much time on the computer. "I hate Nana Green," he grumped.

"Francis!" Claire said. "You're lucky lightning didn't strike, talking like that about Nana. She loves you, even if she is a bit strict, and she is coming, so let's make a start on those dishes."

Never to be admitted to her children but Claire's thoughts of her mother-in-law were not so far from theirs. She wasn't a particularly maternal woman, except when it came to Mark, and she put Claire to shame in many ways, not just her home making and gardening but in her knowledge of the Bible, the district and the farm.

Claire just couldn't compete, and she gave up trying, for the most part. She knew that Nana Green found her a disappointment and that she thought Mark could have done better. That was common knowledge in the family and Claire was humiliated by it.

God! That reminded her that she needed to deal with her car. It was a complete mess and Nana Green had complained, last time they went to church, about the state of it and the animal hair on her coat. She had a right go about how she looked like she had been rolling with the dogs and that it wouldn't surprise her if the pastor refused her entry on account of the state of her.

Disrespect to God, she had said, disrespect to God. Claire had wondered at the time if God really would care about her coat. Claire didn't really think God was like that, but then of course, Nana Green would know, wouldn't she?

Mark came in from cutting hay and looked like a scarecrow with bits of it sticking out of his clothes and hair. His cheeks were red and his nose sunburnt. Claire wondered what had happened to the sunblock she had put out for him and where he left his hat.

"Mark," she said, "look at you all covered in hay and dragging it through the house. Next thing, your mother will have the vacuum out and I will be in trouble. Quick sticks, get yourself out of those clothes and into the shower, I need to go shortly, and I still haven't folded the washing."

Mark shrugged and looked at Claire curiously. "Ah Claire, after all this time, you're still fussing after my mother. You know it doesn't matter a jot; she will always find fault. Give it up, woman and just leave me be. That's the last of the hay for now and I am bloody glad of it. Damn stuff gets everywhere, and my throat feels like a desert. Next summer, Francis can give us a hand and start learning the ropes, perhaps he will do better than I at tolerating the damn stuff."

"Mark, get out of that chair now please and get clean. I need to go soon because Lucy wants me there for last-minute chores, and you need to settle the kids with your mum, feed the dogs and be at the community centre for 6pm. Chop chop, Mark, chop chop," said Claire and she clapped her hands together and gave Mark her best attempt at a stern eye.

Lucy

Lucy had been home for half an hour. The dogs were fed, Jack's shirt ironed, and the house was still except for Jack in the shower and the water pump humming. Lucy had dirt under her fingernails from digging some fresh carrots and beetroot and was tying together bunches of foliage with white berries supposed to resemble mistletoe that she planned to hang in strategic places in the community centre when she arrived. It was her last flourish for the evening, and she smiled as she thought about its romantic suggestiveness.

Jack's clothes were laid out on the bed, checked shirt, denim jeans and navy suede lace-up shoes that Lucy had bought from the high-country store that sold everything from butter to cotton and shampoo to weed killer. For fun, Lucy had pinned a pair of little gold bells with a red bow to Jack's pocket front as a nod to the season, and his socks had little green Christmas trees on them.

As Jack emerged from the bathroom, rubbing his hair dry and without a stitch on, Lucy wittered on about her day. "Well Jack, you should have seen Claire, a complete fright, another dreadful haircut and do you think she could keep those wee snowmen straight? Well, no, she couldn't."

"Honestly, not a brain in her head sometimes. And then, I gave her the elf costume and she literally came out and said she didn't know what underwear to put on with it. Dear lord, the girl has air in that head, as sure as I stand here. And Jade, well, I ask you, talk about late, late I said, well, I just wonder what Nelson puts up with."

"No work in her, I say, nothing. All nails and lashes, good for little but sitting around. Heavens, Nelson must wonder what on earth he married. Not a decent meal on the table, nor a child in sight. No, no, Jack, those socks on the bed, not those ones in your hand, and it's the brown belt not the black. That's it, tuck the shirt in, no, not that far, just pull a little bit out, pull I said."

Jack, completely accustomed to Lucy's ways, did as he was told and said nothing. Lucy didn't notice. She never did.

"So, I told James, bacon butties in the fridge and the hens are laying plenty, so cook an egg too when you get home," Lucy was saying. "He's out shooting again down the main road tonight, he said. Says there's just hundreds of rabbits around now and the breeding season has them increasing all the time."

"He reckons he will make his university money before Christmas at this rate. Of course, I told him. Well, don't count your chickens. Don't you think he needs a haircut, Jack, yes, he does. I must get him into town for a good one, not like that dreadful cut of Claire's, good grief, it's awful."

"Might take him to town next week, he can get a haircut and we can buy him some new socks and jocks and some of that nice slice he likes at the Happy Kitchen, yes, you know the one, it's got the thick caramel and the chocolate. And I can get some knitting needles that I have on order and the cranberries for the sauce on Christmas Day and some mint tea for your mother."

"Yes dear," said Jack finally, when Lucy took a breath. "Sounds a nice idea."

"Good that's sorted then. Now, I am going in my truck tonight because I have to leave in ten minutes, but you can follow in your truck because I will be later than you from packing up the hall," Lucy explained as she pulled on the stripy elf's tights, wondering if they actually were a little too tight, now she had them on.

"Now, make sure you have some cash for the raffle and don't drink too much because you are driving and of course, we have church in the morning and then, your parents are here for lunch. Your dad wants to see the new tractor and your mum is bringing some mending with her."

"Amanda and Anna will be here Tuesday for Christmas with hubbies, of course, so I have made up two of the spare rooms and cleaned the guest bathroom but I think you might need to check the water tanks in case we need some extra. If you do that before they get here, then that will make it easier and save any embarrassment if we run out."

"You know their city ways now, not a consideration in the world for water use, just turn on the tap and magic, no care at all about water, not at all," she whittled as she fixed the wig and pixie ears to her head, shoving her mad fringe up underneath with gusto.

"Yes dear, water tanks," said Jack.

"And I was thinking, Jack, you really need to talk to Joe Clements, try and get him to reconsider his membership at the pool. I know the kids are grown but his arthritis could benefit from some exercise and he could walk lengths if he doesn't want to swim."

"The school needs the support, Jack, so make sure he knows. Carl Bond will be there tonight and he will tell him, pool did wonders when he had his knee surgery, he swears by it, tells me all the time, Lucy, it was magic, he says, magic, Jack!" Lucy shouted in her loud voice as she squeezed a slightly too small elf hat on her head and bent down to do up her sensible shoes, flat-soled Velcro-fastening ones that were practical but not particularly stylish.

"Phew," Lucy said. "That does it, I'm all set. Now, don't go to sleep in the chair, Jack, I need you on time with a smile on your face to make people feel welcome. And no overdoing it on the drink because you need to drive home and those bloody rabbits are a hazard."

"I told James he was doing public service tonight on his night shoot, helping us all get home in one piece. I saw three squashed rabbits just on the drive home. God awful things, breeding like, well rabbits and did you see what they have done to Joss Tait's Garden?"

"All that time in hospital and they have run it into the ground, she's going to need a lot of help to get that back in shape," said Lucy, tut-tutting her way to get the mistletoe bunches off the hall table.

"Right then, I'm off," she said, bustling out the door with her felt elf shoes in her hand, jingling as the little bells on their tips moved with her steps. "See you soon, Jack, and don't forget to put the dogs to bed before you come out," she shouted as she opened the car door and slung her armload of gear onto the passenger's seat.

Pippa

Pippa had picked the boys up from the school bus on her way home from the hall and they were happily playing out in the yard with their rather big pet lamb called Gussy. They loved Gussy and she loved them, but the poor thing was smothered in kisses and commanded to stay and walk as required. She bleated after them as they ran down the grassy lawn to the tyre swing, her little legs trotting along.

This was paradise to Pippa, and she was excessively happy. She felt blessed. Grateful for her loving husband and family and the life they had carved out for themselves on the farm. She loved the country, the horses and other animals, the changing seasons and the freedom.

She could walk for miles or find a sunny place to read, fish in the creeks with the boys or bake up a storm. She had her parents nearby and her in-laws adored her. She was everyone's perfect example of what a mother and wife should be and admired from afar by many a farmer who couldn't believe Duncan's luck.

Leaving the kitchen window for a moment, Pippa took out a batch of brownies she had whipped up to give the boys for dessert after their favourite lasagne. Her parents, Cath and Jacob, were coming to babysit, and she liked to spoil them with nice food and a good wine. They would stay the night and make the short trip home in the morning after a family breakfast.

Jacob had been a farmer like his own father and Cath had taught for a time before she became a mother and took to farm work. Jacob was a kind man with a handsome face and Cath had fantastic posture and high cheek bones with slightly olive skin.

Since retiring, they had downsized from their farm, leaving their son Michael to take it over and they had built a new home on some land about 10 kilometres down the valley. It was a great spot with its own swimming hole and plenty of places for little boys to explore.

Jacob had made a beautiful job of the garden, landscaping with rocks from the area and planting traditional plants and a mix of the more exotic that he sourced from further afield. Cath enjoyed the garden too but also liked to paint and she was a patient teacher to each of her seven grandchildren.

Pippa heard her parents' truck pull up and she flicked the kettle on in case they wanted a cup of tea before their dinner. She knew the boys would be in quickly, having also heard the truck and knowing that Poppa and Nan would likely have some kind of game with them to play later or some sweeties from town.

Archer came in just ahead of Hunter, puffing from the run up the yard and sporting muddy knees. Hunter was red-faced and blew out a big lungful of air in exhaustion as he launched himself at the big farm kitchen table and splayed his little body onto the cool wood.

"Hunter," said Pippa with a smile, "go and wash up and then you can come and talk to Poppa and Nan all about your day and the visit to the bread factory with school. You too, Archer, please. I have made some brownies for later and there's lasagne for dinner."

The boys disappeared to the bathroom full of leaps of delight and whoop-whoop noises about their dinner. Duncan arrived and dropped a kiss on the cheek of his mother-in-law and shook his father-in-law's hand before giving Pippa a firm squeeze and kiss on the lips.

"How is everyone then?" He asked, sweeping the curls from his green eyes. "Garden's looking good, Jacob. How's the vegie patch, hope you have plenty of new potatoes for Christmas Day. They are my favourite, aye Pip," he said.

Pippa smiled and looked up at him lovingly. "You and your potatoes, Duncan, it is a wonder you don't look like one. The boys have even started calling him Mr Potato Head, like the toy!"

"Cheeky buggers," Duncan said to the twins as they came back to the table and sat down, snuggling up to their nan and giggling softly.

"Ooh Mum," said Pippa. "I called in to see Mrs Andrews today, just to check on her after that terrible fall she had in her back yard. I took her some cheese scones and a pot of jam to cheer her up. She was black and blue, Mum, poor thing, I just felt so bad for her. We had a nice cuppa and a quick natter and I hope she felt better for it. Can't be easy living alone up at that old place, with no children to call on her and not a neighbour close by. Poor love."

"Right, Mr McKenzie," Pippa said to Duncan, "to the shower with you please and I have an elf to prepare. Once I am changed, I will get the dinner out. Mum, if you could help the boys set the table, please. I am sorry you are not going to be there tonight, are you sure about staying here instead, we can cancel."

"Nonsense," said Cath. "Cancel, my foot. No, your father and I are more than happy to relax with the boys, and we will see everyone at carols and the midnight service on Christmas Eve, so it's no problem at all. Anyway, who wouldn't want to be with these two little cherubs, and if they are good, I bought the old battleship set to play with later."

"Lucky boys. I love that game! Can't wait to hear who wins," she cried as she walked towards the bedroom in time to hear Duncan shut off the water in the shower.

She opened the bathroom door to a steamy room and stepped in for a kiss against his nakedness. She loved Duncan so much, at times, it felt scary. He was a fantastic dad and husband, and she was happy just to be with him for a few minutes before she had to leave.

"That was nice," he said, leaning into her and she pretended to bat him away.

"You're wet, and I am going to be late if we keep getting distracted. I have to be there soon and then you can follow once you are ready. No rush, have a sit with Mum and Dad for a while if you want to. I know they love hearing about the farm. I am sure Lucy will have Jack all lined up to welcome everyone and do the small talk," Pippa said.

Duncan grinned. They both knew that Lucy would have Jack organised to an inch of his life and that the poor sod had absolutely no chance of five minutes to breathe before the next order came from his beloved. Lucy just couldn't help herself, never taking a breath long enough to gauge the room or the feelings of the people around her, just diving in and taking charge.

Sure, she got a lot done and she was a great community support, but her way wasn't necessarily agreeable to everyone and sometimes, she was just downright bossy and over the top. Not that Pippa would ever say.

Pippa wasn't one to talk about others behind their backs and certainly not about those who gave so much as Lucy to those around her. No, Pippa didn't mind taking a back seat to Lucy and providing the quiet efforts behind the scenes that weren't always obvious.

"Ok love," said Duncan with kind eyes as he admired Pippa putting on her elf tights and adjusting her pixie ears. "Anyway, I think I need to save my energy looking at you in that get-up. Sexiest elf I ever saw. Hopefully, you will have some Christmas cheer for me later." He grinned.

Pippa felt the blood rise in her cheeks, silly because she wasn't shy of Duncan but just of the thought that he considered her sexy, especially with her parents so close by and their sons made her feel self-conscious.

Jade

Jade had gotten home and poured herself a large gin. Poppet was cuddled into her fluffy pink basket and some light jazz was playing softly on the stereo. Jade was thinking about Lucy. She could be such a cow in a backward kind of way and yet, at the same time, she made herself look so bloody saintly.

Jade knew that secretly, Lucy thought she didn't belong in Stoney Hollow and that she was some kind of gold-digger. Of course, Lucy had never bothered to ask Jade about her own family, and it hadn't occurred to her that Jade had plenty of money of her own.

Jade's parents, Lord and Lady Ian Derbyshire III were fifth-generation jewellers in London and had supplied pieces to prime ministers, the A-list and of course, the queen and her family and now the king. She had been at school with the queen's granddaughter and went to the same fitness centre as half the BBC and ITV.

Lucy, with her judgemental bones, had no clue and Jade hadn't helped with the way she kept her backstory on the down low. It was only Nelson that knew she was loaded and from good stock as they called it. Lucy, somehow, had it in her head that she was more an East Enders or Coronation Street kind of girl and Jade was never sure if she was completely offended or if it was the funniest thing she had ever heard.

"That you, love?" Jade called out at the sound of the back door closing.

"Yes, my darling," called Nelson back to her. "Just in from the woolshed, think we should be wrapped up by tomorrow night. Have you had a good day?"

"Oh Nels," said Jade, "well, if you can call hanging around bossy Lucy a good day, then yes. But honestly, the way she looked at me when I was late, if looks could kill. You know, she does a lot, a real lot for the place but she is hard work. I always think she is looking down her nose at me. Standing there with that fringe all wild and those ridiculous sensible shoes. Talk about dowdy!"

Nelson was laughing. "Come on now, old chum, don't let Lucy get you all worked up; you know she is oblivious, wouldn't think for a moment that she was insulting or mean. I think she just thinks it's her job to keep us all in line. Good little soldiers and all that, you know."

"Garr, I know, Nels but for the love of God, could she get some decent shoes!" And with that, they both dissolved into fits of laughter and Poppet started to bark at them both.

"Ooh Nels," said Jade, "come with me. You will never guess what I have to wear tonight—a bloody elf costume with pixie ears and everything. The tights are so bloody small, I think we might have to spray paint them on. But I had an idea, this will upset things, I am going to wear my black garter over my thigh, just to stir things up a bit. After all, doesn't Santa usually have a naughty elf?"

Nelson belly-laughed at Jade's revelation. "Ha Jade, that will sure set the cat amongst the pigeons. Better watch out that you don't get banned from church or book club for disobedience. Mind you, I will have my eye on you, you know how those other farmers get their tongues stuck when you come around them. Poor Leo Foster will spit his false teeth out." He smiled.

Nelson was exceptionally proud of his wife, and her resilience when it came to the life they had made together in Stoney Hollow. She had taken his heart completely when he had seen her in the Shepard's Arms and that had been it. He would have followed her back to London if that was what it took. She was beautiful and natural too and he loved her more than life itself.

Jade was equally besotted with Nelson. His strong muscular body and his positive outlook. She liked the way his brown eyes turned hazel in the sun, the small of his back when she hugged him and his rugged looks with their hint of country class.

But he was more than looks to her and when she was distressed or scared or even just homesick, he was the best antidote. His big arms were strong around her, his kisses soft and long and his warmth a source of comfort. He asked nothing much of her and took her just as she was.

He never complained about her little indulgences, and he was always the proudest man in the room when they were out together. Jade knew she was lucky.

"Nels," said Jade, "Lucy says I need to stay late and help her pack up the hall for Sunday school in the morning. Do you want to wait for me, or would you rather take two vehicles so that you can come home earlier? I know you have the last of the lambs to finish tomorrow, so if you would rather travel separately, it's no biggie. I will never hear the end of it if I don't stay, so I don't expect to get out of it. Old Lucy Bossy Pants has my number and that's that."

Nelson crossed the room and took Jade in his arms. "Ok, I will follow you in my truck when we leave here and then, if I decide to come home earlier than you, I can. Let's see what happens and decide later. Now, shall I feed Poppet? Is she having steak or chicken tonight?" Nelson asked as he kissed the tip of Jade's ski ramp nose.

"Steak tonight, babe," yelled Jade, "watch her though because she has been eating really fast and nearly choking the last couple of days."

"OK love," she heard Nelson say as she pulled on the green and red elf top and reached for her red lipstick to give herself a cherry mouth.

Jade and Nelson lived on a farm that had been part of a large station owned by Nelson's grandfather. He had four sons and so divided the station between them, with Nelson's father getting the largest worker's cottage and the woolshed. The land was lush and green most of the year and if Nelson was careful with his stock numbers, he could get through the summer with supplementary feed.

Jade and Nelson had built themselves a new house on the property, close to a gentle stream and tucked into some low-lying curves in the landscape. It was all glass and black panels, long and sleek with a flat roof and clever outdoor spaces that were accessible from several rooms.

It wasn't a huge house, with two bedrooms and a third that was used as a study, but it was stunning with exposed concrete floors and a large copper framed fireplace in the living room.

As Jade came into the kitchen, Nelson whistled in appreciation of her outfit and the way it hugged her. "Wow Mrs Stewart, you are a stunner!" He exclaimed. "I am sure going to have to keep my eye on those dirty old farmers tonight, with you looking so great. I am one lucky man, Jady, so very lucky."

Jade crossed the room and embraced him, locking her mouth on his. "Just wait till I get home, Mr Stewart," she whispered, "then you will know what lucky is."

The Christmas Party

The fairy lights glowed, and the Christmas trees twinkled, there was mistletoe to hang and the drinks to pop into icy buckets and barrels to keep them cool. Lucy had arrived early to find herself alone, aside from the caterers who were having their evening meal.

She had set to putting up the mistletoe and was about to put on her elf shoes when Pippa and Claire came through the door, laughing at themselves in their costumes and the way Claire looked in her elf hat. Lucy could see the funny side of it, Claire's homemade haircut did look funny, the way the hat came down over it and flattened it down.

Luckily for Claire, she was always the sweet one, the fusser and charmer and so no one would pay any attention to her hair. She would have old Mr Foster and Father McDonald eating out of her hand in no time, fussing after them with drinks and food and clearing their plates.

"Righto," said Lucy. "Claire, you get on to the rest of the mistletoe and Pippa and I will bring the crates of beer and the wine in from the chiller." With that, Lucy saw Jade in the carpark and yelled, "Jade, come round the back and you can carry the ice in for us."

Jade smiled, thinking, *Lucy Bossy Pants is at it again*, but she didn't complain and did as she was asked, trying her best not to get the wet ice bags and her skin too close together.

Nelson came to her rescue, having followed her to the hall in his own truck as they had arranged. "Jade, give me that, love, you're going to get wet through and I can hold it away from myself as my arms are longer. Now, where does Lucy want me to put this, not in a glass, I am guessing," he joked.

Lucy, by then, had spotted Nelson. "Nelson!" She exclaimed. "Oh wonderful man, thank you for helping with that. Such perfect timing. Now, if you could just grab the other bags from the chiller for me, I will be forever in your debt." Lucy chortled as she threw beer into a large hollow barrel on top of the ice.

Lucy was warm from the physical work, and she could feel her top starting to stick to her back. Not that she stopped to think about it or to give herself any respite. She ploughed on, stopping to greet neighbours and friends who were starting to arrive.

She was the ultimate hostess, flitting here and there, pouring wine and commenting on everything from Charles Alsop's new moustache to the pattern of Maggie Scott's dress and the Christmas reindeer earrings that Julie Roberts had dangling from her ear lobes.

Pippa had finished her tasks and was talking to Julie Roberts when Duncan arrived, looking refreshed and clean in a navy shirt and lighter blue pants. He had his good boots on and his curls were wound tight and springy. Pippa loved the smell of him after a hard day and a good hot shower and she nuzzled into his chest when they met in the hall.

"Mmm," she breathed, "you smell delicious." Duncan laughed and pulled at her elf hat, ringing its tiny bell.

"You not only smell good, darling, but you look amazing too. The cutest elf in the room," Duncan whispered.

Pippa smiled and pinched Duncan's round bottom. "I better be!" She said. "Or you will be in huge trouble."

Claire was talking to a group of older farmers and their wives about the judging she did for the young shearer competition. "Well," she exclaimed, "they were all such strapping lads, muscles everywhere, I could barely focus on the sheep! I bet you were like that Wally when you were young, look at you now, I can still see the muscles bulging. Such a fine specimen you are."

"And you, Malcolm Roberts, district champion I hear, still have the local record for number of sheep in an hour too. What a star you are!" She flirted. Malcolm and Wally were laughing their heads off with Claire and chuffed she had offered such flattering opinions.

"Now, who's for another drink? Julie, shall we go and see what we can find in the silver buckets and be naughty?" Claire suggested.

Jade and Nelson were talking with Mark, Claire's husband. Mark secretly looked up to Nelson, saw him as someone who had taken control of his life and gone after what he wanted with Jade. He was content with Claire, but really married her out of expectation, and he also knew he wasn't a born farmer.

He regretted not having had more gumption when he was younger, so that he could have told his parents that he wanted to join the navy when he was leaving school. But he hadn't and instead did what was expected and stayed on the farm to help his father, later taking it on when his father died in a boating accident.

It had been hard, and he tried but he never did feel comfortable in the role, and Claire often said that made him distant and sometimes lost in his thoughts. In truth, Mark knew that Claire was the better farmer and she certainly was better with people than he was.

"So, Mark, what's the plan for Christmas then, aye?" Nelson said. "Are you having a shindig up at your place with your mum? And how is Mrs Green getting along, is she still keeping that garden looking a picture and making sure your kids don't grow up too wild?"

Mark grinned. "You know Mum, Nelson, she's a bit old school and doesn't always appreciate the kids' modern ways. She still threatens to tan their hides with the jam spoon! Claire has absolute conniptions. But yeah, Mum's coming up to the house for Christmas and Claire's brother hopes to call in too."

"We'd like to get away for a few days over New Year, but I want to wait and see what the weather looks like before we make firm plans. If I can get some marlin fishing in, I will, but the young lad gets seasick, so we can't all go together."

"Flora though, she's a ripper that one, pulled her first kingfish last time we were out, proud as punch she was and so was I, the thing was nearly as big as her!" Mark explained.

"Impressive for such a young lady," said Nelson. "She'll be pulling in the marlin in no time. You better watch out, Mark or she will take the boat without you as soon as she can drive."

"Yeah," agreed Mark, "Nelson, I reckon she would too. Right spirited young thing she is, all action and the faster, the better. Not like Francis, he isn't so keen on the physical side of things, just prefers his computer really. Of course, Mum has plenty to say about that but what can you do, and I don't want him to farm if he doesn't want to."

"Even though I wouldn't mind some help here and there. Kids aye, it's a different world to ours, Nelson that is for sure, what the hell did we know about mobile phones and *Fortnight*. I think you and I were catching frogs and having bonfires at their age."

Lucy was banging a large copper gong to signal it was time for dinner. Jack had been standing a little too close and he wasn't sure that he could hear after the drumming stopped. That was Lucy though, everything with gusto, no halfway.

Lucy was speaking into a microphone from the small low stage on the far side of the hall where the band would play after dinner. "Ladies and gentlemen, dinner is served. Please go to the buffet when I call your table number and charge your glasses."

Over dinner, the drinks flowed, and the glasses clinked, full plates were soon empty and there was a very merry atmosphere in the hall. Lucy and Jack sat with Claire and Mark and Pippa and Duncan, while Nelson and Jade sat behind them at the next table with others from down their road.

Claire nattered on about whether it could possibly be true that Santa was the result of a marketing campaign like Mr Simmons had told her in the shop that morning and she felt sure that a claim of such magnitude must be fake for surely the whole world wouldn't believe an advertisement.

Jack laughed at Claire's muddled attempt at logic and smiled at her warmly. Mark had the face of a man that had heard much of Claire's theorising and didn't buy a word of it and Duncan was far too taken with his wife to hear much of anything.

Lucy, on the other hand, was looking like she was about to blow a gasket. "Claire, seriously, do you believe everything that you hear? Of course, Santa was made up by someone, but not an advertisement, you don't really think he exists, do you?" Lucy said with exasperation.

Claire's face flushed and she looked down. "Well Lucy, I was just saying what Mr Simmons said, it wasn't me thinking it, I was just saying," she desperately tried to explain with composure.

Jack could see Claire's embarrassment and came to her defence. "Lucy, I have heard that very same claim, so it is not beyond the realms of possibility that there is a little truth to it. I think we can all agree that Santa is a concept borne out of historical custom across the world."

Claire looked at Jack in awe. He had put what she wanted to say in really posh words, and she was impressed as she often was with Jack and what he said. She wondered why she struggled so much to make sense of things, and she smiled at Jack, glad of his rescue.

"Well, that was awkward," whispered Pippa to Duncan as she took the last of her dessert off her spoon.

"Yip," said Duncan, "remind me never to repeat something I heard to Lucy until I can prove it. Come on, Mrs, let's dance," and he took Pippa's hand as they walked through the chattering crowd to the dance floor.

"Whoops," said Pippa, laughing as she slipped on the floor with her felt elf shoes. "I nearly came a cropper then, imagine that, going home to Mum and Dad with a broken leg. Wouldn't that be a disaster for Christmas?"

Duncan smiled. "No way would I let you go long enough to fall, my love, this Christmas will be our best yet," he said and then he kissed her firmly on the mouth.

Lucy was getting wound up. After all the bloody work she had done, everyone else seemed to be having a better time than her. And bloody Jack, coming to Claire's rescue. Let her own bloody sop of a husband man up for once, she was muttering to herself in the chiller as she opened a bottle of wine and took a long refreshing drink.

Just typical, Lucy grumbled, Jack always out to defend the weak and the stupid but not her, no, never her. She was poor old Lucy, left to muddle through. Taking the bottle, Lucy went back out to the hall and took up her hosting duties again.

"Oh, come on, Paul, you're a twinkle-toes, get yourself out there for a boogie. That's it, Justine, wake that man of yours up a bit and swing him around the floor," Lucy suggested, taking another long drink from the wine bottle.

Jade was pointing at Lucy and talking loudly to Nelson, so he could hear over the music, "Look at that Lucy Bossy Pants drinking from a bottle. It must be a rough night."

Nelson looked concerned. "It is a bit unlike her, Jady, do you think you might check on her, you know do the girl thing and make sure she is alright?"

"She's just Lucy, love," said Jade, "she's fine but yes, just to put your mind at rest, I will go and have a wee word, make sure that bottle doesn't turn into two and find her a glass."

Pippa had noticed too, and she knew Lucy better than Jade. The bottle swigging was, in large part, a plain-as-day tantrum, defiance in disguise. Pippa knew that Lucy would be smarting from Jack defending Claire and that her attention-seeking was because she was embarrassed and annoyed. Lucy was like that, quite the tantrum thrower when she wanted to be.

"Pippa!" Lucy yelled, draping her arms over Pippa and rocking her. "Did you see that, Pippa, did you see? Bloody Jack defending Claire like that. We all know she's not the sharpest but defending her so strongly like that, bloody Jack."

Pippa half-smiled and half-grimaced back at Lucy. "Come on, Lucy, you can't be drinking like that, you're the hostess, chief of the party, queen of the night. Let's put the bottle down and I will get you a coffee and some Christmas cake to soak things up, aye. You just sit yourself down with Duncan and he will look after you," she said, nodding at Duncan so he would respond appropriately.

Duncan patted the chair at the end of the table next to where he sat. "Come on, Luce, you can tell me all about those shearing champs coming up and who the favourites are for the big prize."

That was enough for Lucy, she was off. "Well Duncan," she said, "the competition is hot this year. There are, of course, the usual suspects, although Darren Scott is out of favour since he stole the boss's wife, and then there are two newbies on the scene who have been generating quite a lot of interest."

"One is as fast as Benny Briggs and the other isn't far behind. So, it could be a big year for the competition, if everyone is at their best."

"Sounds great, Lucy," said Duncan with enthusiasm. "I will have to make sure I have some time free and bring the boys for a look."

Lucy didn't reply because she had her eyes on something else. She was looking at her husband who was hardly what you would call a dancer and did so under duress when she asked him. Jack was dancing with Jade, Claire and Julie Roberts in the middle of the dance floor.

Julie was ringing his little bells on his pocket and Jade had put her elf hat on Jack's head. *Good grief,* she thought, *Jack has no rhythm, and he looks absolutely ridiculous,* and then whether it was the shock or the alcohol, she started to laugh and left Duncan to his cake while she went and joined in.

Lucy

Lucy was up early, preparing the vegetables for Sunday lunch and putting the cream on top of the trifle for dessert. She had been home late after the clean-up the night before and wore a floral apron over her church dress with her signature flat shoes in navy to match.

Her fringe was wild and the rest of her hair had been rather hastily tied back in a ponytail. She had the radio on the news channel and a cup of strong coffee on the bench beside her.

Jack was up and out, feeding the dogs and collecting the eggs. Lucy had been surprised to find him still up when she got home, freshly showered and sipping a large whisky. They had talked, well, she had talked, for a while and then gone to bed, noting that James was still out shooting rabbits.

This morning, Jack had said he enjoyed last night, and Lucy was pleased. She took what he said as a personal compliment to her arrangements and efforts and her heart was full. She thought things had gone pretty well, and that people had seemed happy and to be enjoying themselves.

She had also reminded herself that the food went down well and that she had been right. People wanted hearty simple food and not the city stuff that Pippa had served up the year before.

Mid-thought, Lucy was suddenly not alone, and Jack appeared red-faced and chasing a young dog who had made his way to the kitchen. "Banjo!" Jack yelled. "Wait!" But it was to no effect as the excited young dog saw Lucy and wagging his tail like a helicopter, he crossed the floor towards her.

Lucy bent down and caught the pup in her arms. "Banjo," she said, "have you come in to visit me, boy? Well, that is very nice, but you know there are no dogs allowed in the kitchen. Come on, let's take you outside and you can find some nice sunshine to warm up in, quick sticks."

Banjo looked at Lucy and took on a face of resignation. It was clear that he wanted to be in the comforting smells of the kitchen and not out in the yard with the other dogs. And while Lucy loved the dogs and it was tempting to make him a house dog, she knew that was a slippery slope and she couldn't deal with all five dogs making tracks in and out of the house, especially in winter when they would be muddy and wet.

Jack sat at the kitchen table, having poured a fresh mug of hot coffee from the machine. He was a little tired and chasing around after the bloody dogs hadn't helped. The coffee was welcome, and he drank it as hot as he dared in big swallows.

"Jack," said Lucy, back from taking Banjo out, "now, I think you should have some cereal this morning, get some fibre in for the day and then you can have a good lunch when we get home. I have yoghurt in the fridge and some banana you can put in the cereal for extra bulk, help keep you full while we wait for lunch."

"And don't wear that grey shirt again. It will be four weeks in a row you have worn that shirt and the parishioners will think I can't look after you properly. So, I have put your navy and white checked shirt on the bed, and you should wear that with those navy pants you like and a brown belt."

"Yes, brown will be best and then match your shoes to the belt, so maybe the brown boots I bought you last winter. When your parents come up, I think you should take your dad straight up to the shed to see the tractor that will give me time to finish the gravy and carve the roast."

"Then, we can all sit down to lunch and have a nice meal. But you and your dad will need to wash up first, don't forget."

Jack nodded silently. He was used to being instructed to within an inch of his life, but he would be lying if he didn't admit he sometimes thought it was a bit much. He knew that some of the other men in the district thought he was a hen-pecked farmer and that Lucy had all the say, and for the most part, they were right.

Lucy did have all the say, mostly because Jack struggled to get a word in, and even if Lucy had been listening to him, she might never actually hear him for the constant chatter he was sure went on in her own head. He noted that sometimes, Lucy's brain went faster than her words could cope with and that at times, her sentences appeared even more garbled than usual while she fought her own brain to get the words out.

It was like she started with a thought, said five words, thought something else completely different, and then had to readjust what was coming out of her mouth to fit.

Jack was looking forward to Amanda and Anna being home for Christmas and the distraction they would be for Lucy. If she had others to focus on, Jack got a bit of a break from the constant ordering and judgement Lucy brought forth. He knew the kids loved their mother, and she was a very good one, but they left home quickly and part of him more than understood.

He knew that the orders, judgement and regiment of the household wasn't one that allowed much room for self-expression, creativity or even just finding out what you might think. Yes, it was more than sensible of the kids to leave home and explore the world beyond Lucy's firm grip.

"Come on, Jack, get a move on, we don't want to be late for church, do we?" Lucy was saying. "Can't sit around staring into space all day, we have things to do. Now, mind those elbows while I change the tablecloth, up, up, that's right, there we are."

Jack sighed, *sod breakfast,* he thought, *I will just go and shower and change and wait for the next instruction.*

Pippa

Pippa was warming croissants and flipping pancakes in her large kitchen, with the windows and doors open to the light, but warm breeze and the smell of summer roses and lavender. Her cotton PJ shorts, and t-shirt top were the perfect accompaniment to a relaxed morning and her feet were bare.

The boys were in front of Sunday morning television inside a pillow fort and Duncan was having a small lie-in before breakfast.

Pippa poured fresh orange juice into a large glass jug and sat at the kitchen table for a few seconds while the pancake in the pan started to bubble on top. Her parents were up and just dressing, and she could hear them chatting away to each other, just as they always did.

Pippa was feeling a bit worn out from the day before and had a late night helping Lucy and the others clean up after the last of the locals left the party. When she got home, Pippa's parents were already in bed, no doubt worn out by the twins and their antics over the evening. Duncan had come home just a little ahead of Pippa and was snoozing on the couch when she came in.

She had kissed him gently and he had responded warmly, slowly making love to her on the sofa, peeling off her clothes gently but passionately. It wasn't fast crazy sex but slow longing sex, the kind that made her feel warm and loved, even though she was secretly praying that they didn't wake her parents. Pippa smiled, thinking about it as she got up to flip her pancake.

The boys emerged from their fort, still in PJ's although both had donned superhero capes to add more superpower to their outfits. They were busy telling her that the fort was actually a secret cave where they did superhero business that was top secret. She smiled as they both said secret, as both had missing front teeth, so their little tongues poked through the gap, in both of their smiles.

"Wonderful," said Pippa, "well, I hope my little superheroes are hungry for this very super powered breakfast coming up. How about you wash your hands and pop into Dad and your grandparents and let them know breakfast is ready?"

The boys took off, capes flowing behind them, racing through the house, making flying motions as they went. Pippa's parents were at the table promptly and Duncan emerged a little later, hair tousled and looking sexy in the morning light.

She kissed him good morning and put a fresh mug of coffee into his hand before he sat down. "Hmmm, this looks amazing!" He said as he pulled out his chair and took a seat at the table. "I don't know what to have first, Pip," said Duncan, "and look at those strawberries, they are enormous!"

Pippa smiled. Duncan couldn't resist a strawberry and that was evident from his food habits, he loved strawberry jam, which was on the table for the croissants and strawberry shortcake and even had to have strawberry ice cream and milkshakes.

The flying superheroes could be heard before they were seen and raced to the table, hungry for their breakfast. Pippa sat down and they all dug in. The boys first aiming for pancakes and maple syrup with bacon and some strawberries on top and Pippa selecting a crisp and flaky, warm croissant and some homemade strawberry jam to have with her Earl Grey tea.

Mouth full of pancake, Hunter asked, "Mum, did you see Santa last night at the party? Were there presents or was it just old people and funny hats?"

Pippa laughed. "Actually, we did have a Santa but not presents and there was Christmas cake and even dancing. Lucy hung mistletoe around the place, and do you know what happens when you stand under it?"

"No," said Hunter. "What happens?"

"Well," explained Pippa, smiling at Duncan, "if you stand under the mistletoe, you have to kiss the person next to you and it's bad luck if you don't."

"Yuck!" Archer said. "I am glad I didn't go. I might have had to kiss a girl!" He exclaimed, making a face.

Duncan and Pippa and her parents laughed at the face and the innocence of what would be a completely changed view at some point in the future. "Aww," said Duncan, "kissing girls isn't yuck, especially if you love them. I love kissing your mum."

At that, both boys covered their eyes and said in unison, "Oh Dad, that's gross!"

Pippa looked at her family, grateful for every one of them and the joy they brought her. She was lucky and she knew it. "Who is up for church this morning?" She asked the other three, knowing her parents would be going regardless.

Duncan nodded to signal he was happy to go and the boys both screwed up their faces. "Do we have too?" Archer whined, sticking out his lip.

"It is Christmas time," said Pippa, "and we are so lucky, boys, we should give thanks for that, and who knows what cool stuff might be going on at Sunday school, you might miss out if we don't go."

With that, the boys rethought and suddenly developed some enthusiasm for the idea. "Ok," said Archer, "we'll go, but can we get ice creams on the way home?"

"After six pancakes and lord knows what else," laughed Pippa, "we will see how those tummies are feeling later."

Claire

Claire was still in bed, and it was later than she expected. Mind you, she had been late home, much later than planned. By the time she got in, her mother-in-law had left and the house was quiet, save for Mark's light snoring and the hum of the fridge in the kitchen.

She had wanted to shower when she got back after the party, but didn't want to risk waking everyone and so now, she lay in bed, looking at the clock and knowing that before she did anything else, she needed a shower and a strong coffee.

Mark was not beside her in the bed, and she knew he wouldn't be, and that he would be checking the animals and feeding out before coming back for breakfast. *God breakfast*, she thought, wondering what on earth was in the pantry.

Flora came bounding in with a plate of rice bubbles and milk spilt down her clean t-shirt. She had made an attempt to tie back her hair but the ponytail was crooked on her little head and she had missed half of the hair at the back.

"Francis is being a pain, Mummy," she said. "He won't let me use the tablet and I want to play my game."

"Oh Flora!" Claire exclaimed. "Never mind that, go and tell Francis I said to get some breakfast for himself and to put the jug on when he hears Dad come up the drive, while I have a quick shower and dress for church."

Flora huffed and stomped out of Claire's bedroom, yelling, "Francis, Francis, Mum says get breakfast," as she disappeared down the hallway.

Claire was in and out of the shower in less than five minutes, a habit formed from years of country living where water was scarce, and you didn't want to run the tanks dry. She was, for once, glad of her no-fuss haircut, no matter how 'local' it looked, and she rushed to pull on a fresh floral skirt and a navy t-shirt with leopard print around the neck. A quick dash of lipstick and a smile and she was almost done.

She could hear Mark in the kitchen, telling Francis about the lambs that had escaped the front paddock onto the road and how the old sheep dog, Nelly, had them rounded up and back safe in a jiffy. Francis was grunting like he was listening, but the truth was he was more interested in the new coding tips he had found on the internet.

Mark did try to get Francis enthused about the farm and was very keen that he take it over once he was old enough, but Francis just didn't seem to have the interest, well, not yet anyway.

"Mark," said Claire, puffing from rushing around, "are we going to church?"

Mark looked up from his drink and toast. "I don't know, Claire, don't we normally?"

"Well yes, yes we do," said Claire, "but I just wondered with last night being so late and all, whether you might prefer not to go?"

Mark looked at her, puzzled. "Claire, you know we always go to church, so why suddenly are you asking about going? Mum will be expecting us to go and she is doing lunch, so yes, Claire, we are going to church."

"Right, righto," said Claire, "kids, church clothes, where are they and let's get sorted quickly. We are already late!"

Francis and Flora were used to being late and they were used to chaos. Claire wasn't always great at the domestic side of things, but she worked harder than anyone and Mark was lucky to have her. Francis found his church pants stuffed behind his bedroom door and was spreading out the wrinkles with his hand.

Flora had a fairy dress on and one shoe and was looking for the other. Claire came rushing down the hall with a clean shirt for Francis, a polo, which was lucky because it would do without ironing.

Mark was in the bathroom, splashing his face and brushing his teeth in quick long strokes. Claire yelled, "Mrs Stokes, the dental nurse, says brush in round circles, Mark, so as not to wear down your Emanuel on your teeth."

Mark yelled back, toothbrush in mouth, "It's enamel, Claire, not Emanuel, for God's sake."

"Oh yes, silly me," Claire said as she dragged a brush through Flora's hair and pulled her ponytail tight.

"Mummy," Flora said, "why do you get stuff like that wrong all the time?"

Claire stopped; Flora had noticed her stupidity. "Oh Flora, sometimes, I just hurry too much and mix things up," said Claire. "You and Francis are way cleverer than me, and Daddy just has to help me remember the right words or way sometimes."

"Yeah," said Flora, "like when you mixed up the baking soda and the baking powder and the scones were flat and hard, and Dad said it was basic and you had been making scones for years and should know the difference."

Claire blushed. "Well yes, I guess that is another example, Flora, yes, yes, it is."

Jade

Jade and Nelson were still in bed. They lay intertwined in their nakedness and just a crisp white sheet hung over them with Poppet between their feet. Jade's hair was splayed all over her white pillows and Nelson was nuzzled up to her neck and breathing softly. Jade stirred, reaching out her hand for him and pulling his arm around her.

"Mm, this is nice, darling, just us in the peace of the morning," she murmured as she kissed his hand.

"Jady," said Nelson, "honey, you are the best thing that ever happened to me. Now, come here and help me christen the new dawn." He laughed as he turned her gently towards him.

She responded willingly and pushed herself towards him and feeding the desire that had grown between them. She kissed him deeply and longingly and he grabbed her buttocks and squeezed them softly, their firm flesh yielding in his warm hands.

Jade knew that they were not going to make it to church that morning, as she held onto her husband and whispered how much she loved him. And it was true. Jade loved Nelson with her whole heart. He was her everything and she was happiest when they were together cocooned in their sanctuary.

Jade climbed onto him, her hair sweeping his face and her lips searching for his. Poppet had yelped and jumped off the bed as her spot was disturbed.

Nelson groaned. His breathing quick and urgent.

Sweet sweat starting to form on both of them and the sheet was long discarded.

"Oh Nelson," Jade said in a breathless whisper, and they relaxed in pure afterglow.

Church

The church in Stoney Hollow was more than 200 years old. It was stone, and in the winter, it was freezing. There was a small graveyard in the front of the church and a parking field where the large farmers' trucks and SUV's lined up, side by side.

Lucy and Jack were already standing outside the church with his parents, Lucy talking as fast as could be about the Christmas nativity and the choir having been rehearsing Christmas carols.

Claire, Mark, Francis and Flora arrived in Mark's double cab. It was used for farming so was not very clean and the dirt and grass, feed and farming paraphernalia had made for an uncomfortable trip. Claire had lost her keys somewhere between driving home last night and leaving this morning, and hence, the farm vehicle was the only option. Claire knew that Lucy would have something to say.

Shuffling the children off to join the Sunday school, Claire stopped to say hello to Lucy, Jack and his parents. "Oh, nice day, isn't it?" She said to them all. "Just the day for a lovely service before a nice lunch. I bet you will be looking for a nice cuppa afterward too. Thirsty work, all those hymns and Christmas carols. Right then, hurry along, children," Claire motioned to her two, "see you inside, Lucy," she said as she went off, smiling at Jack from under her lopsided fringe.

Lucy was bemused. "Oh Jack, look at the state of those children. Flora looks like she is in fancy dress, and I don't think Francis' pants have seen an iron yet. You would think Claire would take more pride. Mind you as I have said before, she can barely dress herself. Fancy leopard print with floral. Cardinal sin, cardinal sin," tutted Lucy.

Jack had heard enough. "Lucy," he fumed, "if you can't be Christian at church, you shouldn't come. Just listen to yourself. Poor Claire, we all know she holds that farm together; she doesn't have hours in the day to turn out kids pressed to within an inch of their lives. Find some charity in you, girl!"

Lucy glared at Jack. Of all the places to chastise her, and in front of his parents too. She would have her say later, but for now, she wiped her angry fringe from her eyes and strode inside the church to find a pew. Jack could look after his own parents for once because she had just declared herself off duty!

Almost stomping as she made her way down the aisle, one of Pippa's boys caught Lucy's foot and she flew forward and into Duncan. "There, there, Lucy, old girl," he said, "catch your breath and steady yourself before you fall over, love."

Lucy flushed and forced a smile. "I am sorry, Duncan," she said. "Whatever will you think of me, flying at you like that. Oh, and Pippa, you do look like you had a late night, are you feeling well this morning?"

Pippa smiled and thought to herself that it was just like Lucy to deflect onto her with all the suggestion of Pippa doing something untoward. "Really Lucy," said Pippa. "I feel great actually, we have just had a delicious breakfast together and a happy morning. Duncan and I had a lovely time last night," she said, winking at Lucy, "and the boys are enjoying the summer berries and festive fun."

Lucy was seething now. Pippa was just all Miss Perfect with her cherubic children and her dashing husband. She always looked effortlessly put together and had all the right things to say. Her husband wouldn't chip her the way Jack had just done, but then, Pippa would always do and say the perfect thing at the perfect moment. *Well, how boring,* thought Lucy as she continued to stomp her way to the pew where she always sat, second row from the front.

The service was extra-long on account of the carols and Lucy struggled with her sulk all the way through. Instead of the usual pleasure she got from a jolly good hymn, she found the music grating and her tolerance for the various abilities of those around her far from high.

At one point, she was sure that Jack's father had nodded off and she was most unhappy that the sermon was not particularly Christmas themed but more about the Ten Commandments. *The Ten Commandments, yes, well that is all very good but those commandments can be very tested at times, very tested when one's husband talks to one as if one is uncharitable and unchristian. Commandments indeed,* Lucy scoffed to herself.

Claire enjoyed the service and the messages about the Ten Commandments, but she did find that sometimes she struggled to keep up with all of the things that Father McDonald was saying. She didn't really enjoy the symbolism and sometimes wished he had a picture or a chart to help her understand his points. She liked visuals and she felt other people might as well.

Perhaps, she thought, *she would suggest it to the Father, and they could get the old projector out and give it a try*. Anyway, a chart wasn't going to fix the way Lucy looked at her this morning and Claire wasn't sure she could bear it. Lucy had a way of just cutting you down, even when she said nothing. Claire knew she wasn't so good at putting things together or keeping the children up to scratch, but she didn't need Lucy to remind her.

Pippa and Duncan held hands during the service, and she rested her head on his shoulder for a few moments when the sermon got a little long. She liked the Father though. He was younger than most and not too bad on the eye. He had a nice way with his words, and he made his messages relevant to the community and easy to understand.

Pippa had helped him a few times with jobs that a pastor's wife might normally do, like the morning tea for when the church committee met and the flowers for the Easter service. He was a nice man and she thought he might be a bit lonely but so far, there was no sign of a Mrs McDonald. *Maybe he liked his own company good enough,* Pippa thought.

At the end of the service, the children came in from Sunday school, all in crooked rows and various states of dishevelment after whatever their activities had been. The church children's choir set to singing a lovely arrangement of Christmas carols that the other children were able to sing along too. It prolonged things a little but was a special touch to welcome in the Christmas spirit and bring the congregation together in celebration.

Right in the middle of *Oh Holy Night*, Detective Sergeant Sam Dorsett had come in and spoken quietly to the pastor, who then located Lucy and Jack. The pastor asked Lucy and Jack, in barely a whisper, to walk down the aisle and meet the detective sergeant outside the church doors.

The final strains of the carol faded slightly as all in the church focused on Lucy and Jack and the gusto went from their voices. Pippa whispered to Duncan, "That doesn't look good," and he nodded in agreement.

"It's never good news when a policeman can't wait to speak to you," he said.

Lucy was agitated still and when the policeman arrived and got the pastor to make a spectacle out of her and Jack by dragging them out of church, her blood pressure skyrocketed. *What on earth could warrant that behaviour?* She thought.

She was about to give the officer a piece of her mind when something in his face suggested she might want to take a breath. He certainly did not look like he had good news to share.

Lucy was nervous now. "Lucy, Jack," said Sam, the detective sergeant, "I hope it's alright to call you by first names, but I have some very sad news I am afraid that couldn't wait." Lucy drew breath after realising she was holding it.

"Unfortunately, just a few minutes ago, we located your son, James, and I am very sorry, but he is deceased," said the officer.

Lucy needed to check she was hearing correctly. "Officer, are you saying that our son, James, is dead?" She blurted out.

The poor man looked at Lucy earnestly. "Yes, Lucy and I am sorry but yes, James is dead; oh and please called me Sam. My name is Sam, Sam Dorsett."

Jack was holding onto Lucy for dear life. She could feel the pinch of her skin as his fingers dug into her arm. She wasn't sure in the moment who was holding who up. She wanted to fall but her legs held firm. Jack wasn't speaking and she turned and saw that he was white, pure white like he had died too.

Lucy couldn't think, she just didn't know in the moment how to think, but she forced herself to speak. "Oh," she said softly, "can I see him?"

Sam patiently explained that James had been found on the side of the main road not far from town. It appeared he may have been hit by a car and in falling, he had hit his head on an old concrete trough hidden in the grass. It wasn't possible to see him now, because he was being taken into the city and the cause of death would need to be established.

Jack found his voice. "Thank you, Sam, for letting us know. I realise it's not an easy thing to do. I think if it's alright with you, we might get off home and wait to hear about when we can see our son," he said with a shaking voice.

Sam replied, "That is fine, Jack but I think it's best someone drives you given the shock. I can ask someone to do that and then I will follow as I need to ask you some questions, but they can wait until you're at home. Does that sound alright?"

"Yes lad that will be good," said Jack, looking to Lucy.

Lucy, who was always the boss but who had no words, no sensible remark and just a blank stare, and then, as the service completed and the doors opened, Lucy began to scream.

Lucy

The ride home had been excruciating and all Lucy wanted was to get there. The car had been silent and the drive just seemed as if it would never end. Sam had asked a young and pretty female constable to drive them and it was clear she was lost for words, just as they were.

They passed the site where James was found, taped off with police all over the place in white coveralls. The road was down to one lane, orange road cones marking out the spot where cars could not travel. Lucy wasn't even sure if James was still there, lying there, cold with strangers all around or if he was already gone, cold in a plastic body bag, to the morgue. She felt numb and like she might throw up at any moment.

Jack had let out a gasp and Lucy had seen a single tear run from the corner of his eye down his cheek and drop onto his shirt. The one she had gone on about that morning, as if that mattered a jot. She suddenly looked at Jack, really looked at him and she saw the signs of age and heartbreak that she didn't notice on normal days. Not that she expected a 'normal' day ever again. James was gone.

As they came into the kitchen, what was to have been the welcoming smell of the Sunday lamb roast slowly baking, made Lucy's stomach churn. She ran to the bathroom, hand over her mouth, trying to hold in the vomit that was rising in her throat.

Her eyes watered, not of tears for her boy but because of the dry retching. As she reached the bathroom, she could hold out no more and she vomited violently into the toilet bowl, gasping for air between each retched heave. And then she clung there, unable to get up. She didn't know what to do. She had no answer and no thought. Her mind would not work and neither her legs.

Lucy wondered what people did do in moments like this. Was there a list for this sort of thing, some kind of internet blog or did people just know what to do? Lucy had no idea and for once, the only thing she was confident of was that she might never be able to know what to do again.

Jack came and found her moments later and he picked her up from the floor, helped her get her toothbrush and washed her face. It helped, for a moment. "Lucy," Jack said carefully, "the police need to talk to us; they say it would be best now but if you can't manage it, they can wait. What do you think? Do you feel you can speak with them now?"

Lucy couldn't think. "The police? What do they want to talk to us for, what can we possibly tell them, oh Jack, I don't know," she wailed.

Jack managed to convince Lucy that it was best for James if they talked to the police now and that seemed to make up Lucy's mind. She had changed and run a brush through her hair and with Jack's steadying arm, made her way back to the kitchen.

She startled at the number of people around the table, especially having forgotten that Jack's parents were joining them for lunch. Her mother-in-law was busy wrapping food and putting it into the fridge and there was a fresh pot of tea on the table, a jug of milk, the good sugar bowl and some homemade baking from Lucy's tins.

As she came into the room, everyone stood up. Jack's mother came to Lucy and hugged her tight. "We will take ourselves off, love and leave you to it. We are here when you need us," she said with tears in her eyes.

Jack's father, stooped and calloused with age, touched her arm and looked into her eyes, his stoic and strong. He said nothing as he followed his wife out. The two police officers had mugs of tea they were clinging too, either for comfort or courage, or both.

The one with the dark hair spoke first. "Mr and Mrs Smart, we are so sorry for your loss. We appreciate you taking some time to speak with us and hope not to take too long. My name is Sam Dorsett, and this is my colleague, Joanna Craig," said Sam, gesturing across the table to the young woman who had driven Jack and Lucy home.

Lucy and Jack nodded hello and Lucy poured her and Jack some tea, not because she thought for one moment she might drink it, but because she suddenly needed to do something with her hands.

"Now," said Sam gently, "Jo will take some notes while we talk if that is okay. It really is just procedure and nothing to worry about. That way, we won't have to be asking you the same thing over and over. Let's start with what James was doing last night, shall we?"

Lucy felt as if she was watching a movie of her life, she was above her body watching this scene, not connected to it like the reality of the moment. "Well," she started timidly, "James is home from university and when it is the summer break, he shoots rabbits for local farmers."

"He left yesterday evening and we just assumed, well, I did anyway, that this morning he was in bed. I didn't even check to see, and my boy, oh God, Jack, our boy," Lucy wailed desperately, wishing the truth away and discovering the horror in each moment as she started to understand that James was gone.

Jo and Sam were kind, and they gave Lucy some time to calm down with Jack. Jack had started talking then and explained James' usual habits and where he was shooting. He explained that James was a competent shot and often stayed out very late to make the most of the night.

He had stopped going to church with his parents when he was away at boarding school and so, they had no expectation of his attending this morning, hence they left him to sleep, or so they thought.

"And what about yourselves last night?" Sam asked. "Were you home or were you out?"

Again, Jack took the lead, and he explained about the party in the township and how it was for Christmas, and that they had travelled separately because Lucy was on the organising committee. Neither was exactly sure about the time that they left town, but Jack knew he had left earlier than Lucy.

Lucy felt it was close to midnight when she left town, and she remembered she had been the last to leave after Pippa had driven off ahead of her. Jack explained that after he left, he had gone to check on some stock and load up for feeding out the next morning.

Jack was home ahead of Lucy, having showered before she returned. Neither Jack nor Lucy could remember seeing James' car when they returned home from the party and neither noticed it was not at home this morning before church.

Both felt terribly guilty about having missed that detail, but it was explained because James was often not living with them, and they got out of the habit of looking for his car.

Lucy was tired and she had answered enough questions. "Sam," she said, "when can we see James?"

Sam looked at Lucy and Jack sincerely. "At this stage, I don't know," he explained. "We need to move him today from the scene and there will be an autopsy. This may be a crime and so, it is important we look after anything that might tell us what happened, and unfortunately, at the moment that includes James. I understand how hard this is and I promise that I will find out when you might see him just as soon as I can."

Lucy flared then, and she began to rant, "Sam, that is simply not good enough. James is our son, and we insist on seeing him right away. Take me to the roadside please. I need to see him. It cannot wait. Jack, make them take us."

Jack was calm and resigned to what he had heard. He understood that James was not theirs to have at this time and that they needed to wait. He also understood how hard that would be for his wife.

"Lucy," he said kindly, "I want to see him too, but we must do what Sam says now. It is best for James this way. It isn't just about what we want, it is about finding out what happened to James, our dear boy. We need to be patient."

Lucy looked at Jack with hard eyes. "I should have known you wouldn't stick up for me," she sneered.

Sam stood up, looking uncomfortable, and so did Jo, and Jack got up also. "I'll see you out, officers," said Jack quietly. The two men walked together out of the back door and into the driveway, and Jo followed respectfully behind them.

Neither Sam nor Jack spoke. They shook hands, like you did in the country, and Sam and Jo left slowly, Sam steering his vehicle back to the road. Jack breathed in deeply and sighed. His boy was gone and he had absolutely no idea how to cope with it, let alone with Lucy, who was barely holding on. *Life is cruel*, thought Jack as he reluctantly made his way back into the house.

News Travels Fast

The thing about living in a small district where Stoney Hollow is the centre, was that any kind of news, good or bad, travelled fast. In the old days, it would have been via the party lines or the telephone exchange operator, but these days with the internet and text messaging, it was instantly quick.

Jack and Lucy had been shuffled into the police car as the church congregation flowed out of the doors and so, there had been no time for speaking with either. Claire had been on the drive home when she first heard the news. Mark was just as shocked as she was and the children solemn in the back seat.

Claire was surprised when Mark had said that everyone would be under suspicion now, especially anyone who was out last night, and to watch out for anyone washing their car today. Claire hadn't understood what he meant but she guessed Mark knew something about these things and was probably right.

"Mark," said Claire tentatively, "what do you mean everyone will be under suspicion?"

Mark looked over at her, a little perplexed. "Well Claire, what I mean is if it's true that James may have been hit by a car, the police will want to know which cars went past that location around the time they think he died. So, I guess that means they will want to speak to those who drove that road last night at the right kind of time. And if that is true, then they will probably want to speak with us."

Claire grew a little panicked then. "Really, because we were out last night?" She asked.

"Yes," said Mark, "it stands to reason they would, unless of course, they have other evidence that discounts us straight away."

"Other evidence?" Claire questioned. "What kind of other evidence might that be?"

Mark looked back at her. "Not being an expert, Claire, I can't be sure, but perhaps if there is paint from the car or something that is identifying at the scene that would narrow down the suspects, I suppose."

"Oooh, it just doesn't bear thinking about. Poor James. How could someone just leave him like that and not get him help?" Claire said, dabbing at her eyes.

"Yes," said Mark, "it is very upsetting and to think, it could be someone local responsible."

Claire dabbed at her eyes again as they had quickly filled with more tears, and she was trying to hide her distress from the children. Digging in her handbag, she found some barley sugars from a recent bus trip and handed them back to Francis and Flora.

"Sweeties always make life better," she said as the children eagerly unwrapped the sugary candy.

Pippa and Duncan had stayed after church, partly to help with tidying up and because both boys had misplaced belongings over the morning and needed to find them before they went home. The police visit had been the talk of the congregation after the service and then came the news. James was dead.

Pippa couldn't stop shaking. Duncan was concerned and in his usual kind way, was trying to provide comfort. "It's ok, my love," he said softly, "a nasty shock, I know. Let's get the boys home and later, you can go up to Lucy if you like. I am sure she would like some company. You always know the right things to say and do in those situations. Lucy will need your help, love."

Pippa knew Duncan was right. She did need to get herself together and go and see what she might do to help Lucy. Even if she just held her hand or made a cup of tea that would be something, she thought. Poor Lucy, Pippa's thoughts swirled, how, why, she has people coming for Christmas, what will she do now?

The more Pippa thought, the more certain she was that she needed to go to Lucy and give her some help. There would be a lot to think about, practical things like what to dress James in and who to call and then the other things, the necessary but hard things like keeping up the farm, laundry and even showering and eating. The things that paled in comparison to the thunderous life changing event that had happened to Lucy and Jack.

Pippa couldn't imagine the loss of either one of her sons. The idea that they would not laugh again, or need her again, or cry for her again. The thought that they would never grow old, have children of their own or fall in love. Poor James, all that ahead of him and it's finished, Pippa agonised.

Gone in the blink of an eye. Pippa felt the sobs coming and it took all of her strength to hold them back, and she pushed them back down into the depths of her stomach. She couldn't sob, it would scare the boys and they were too little to understand the enormity of what had happened to James.

No, instead, Pippa painted on a smile, flicked her hair and clapped her hands. "Chop chop, munchkins, time to go home."

Jade

Nelson and Jade were enjoying the Sunday papers after their late start and Poppet was nibbling on an organic dog biscuit in the shape of a bone, growling every now and again at the thing as if it were live prey.

Nelson had the car section of the paper spread out across the glass coffee table and Jade was reading the magazine insert that had a story about a famous actress who was taking on a famous director for sexual assault. She was twirling her hair between her fingertips as she read, enthralled.

It was Nelson who looked up first and saw the police car on its way up the drive. In his younger days, he had been a bit of a lad, and this happened a bit when he lived at home. Usually after some stupid prank he had pulled in town somewhere, full of cheap beer and bravado. This time, however, Nelson had no idea what the visit might be about.

Sam Dorsett was accompanied by a younger female officer and they both stepped from the driveway onto the slick front steps of Jade and Nelson's home. Dorsett didn't use the large brass knocker, aware that Nelson had seen him, but just tapped lightly on the door instead.

Nelson appeared, clearly in a lazy Sunday mood and Sam introduced himself and his colleague. "Nelson," he said rather formally, "mind if we come in for chat?"

Nelson was trying to figure out what these two police officers were doing on his front doorstep on a Sunday in a place like Stoney Hollow but he didn't question. "Sure thing, officers, can I get you a cup of tea?"

Nelson showed the officers through to the living room where Jade was on the couch, sitting up and hugging her knees to her chest. "Officers," she nodded politely, "bit of a surprise to see you out here. Can we help with something?"

Sam cleared his throat and started to explain, "Well, Mrs Stewart, I am sorry to tell you both but there was an accident last night. Young James Smart was killed on the main road there just before the turnoff to his parent's farm."

Jade took a big fast breath in and Nelson's eyes got wide. "James? James Smart?" Nelson said in disbelief.

"I'm afraid so," said Sam earnestly. "Very sad, isn't it!" He exclaimed in a deep and sombre tone.

After recovering herself, Jade spoke, "How can we help?"

Sam smiled. "Really, Mrs Stewart, we just need to talk about where you were last night at the time we think James was killed. You see, we are pretty sure it is a hit and run and we need to identify who was driving when he was run down."

"You mean someone did this on purpose?" Jade asked with anger.

"No, no," said Sam, "we don't know but we have some clues about what happened and want to make sure nothing gets past us. So, if you don't mind, can you tell me where you were last night?"

Nelson started first. He explained that himself and Jade had gone to the gathering in town and that they had followed each other on the way into town and then at the end of the night, Nelson had left slightly earlier than Jade, who left in her car to drive home to their farm. Jade was on the road quite quickly after the last guests had left, after a long day and night.

Sam asked, "Approximately what time were you on the main road, Nelson?"

Nelson thought about the question for a moment, rubbing his chin with his thumb. "Well Sam, it was after things had finished up, so it must have been sometime around midnight, give or take."

"And you, Jade?" Sam asked.

Jade was desperately trying to remember the time she left and whether she had looked at any point, either at her phone or in the car. "Sam, I can't be 100% accurate but I think between 12am or just before, is about right. I left before Lucy, Claire and Pippa as they stayed to mop the floors and I had vacuumed before that."

"And I take it you both knew James then?" Sam asked.

"Oh sure," said Nelson, "we knew James, he worked for us on the farm doing pest management last summer. Spent a lot of time here. Good young man and a hard worker."

"And did you see much of him, Jade?" Sam asked.

"I didn't always see him, because he didn't always work on the farm around the house, but yes, I did know him and would bring him a cold drink, or wave when I was out on the horses," said Jade. "It's terribly distressing to hear about what's happened to him. He was a lovely young man."

"Yes," said Sam, "an absolute tragedy to lose a young man like this. We are doing all we can to find some answers for his family. So, if you think of anything, perhaps you saw something, another person or vehicle in the area or if you hear anything, please get in touch."

Nelson and Jade both nodded their heads, agreeing they would, and Nelson showed Sam and Jo to the door. "Very sad business," said Nelson; he shook hands with both Sam and Jo and they left to make more calls.

As Nelson came back into the room where Jade was sitting, she hurriedly wiped tears from her eyes and gave a big sniff. The news had caught her by surprise and as it sunk in, she found herself becoming very distressed at the thought of such a young person being killed.

James had been a lovely young man. Nelson wrapped his big arms around her and kissed her head. "Hey Jady, I know it's a shock, aye, young man like James. Poor bugger probably never even knew what happened. They will catch the person who did this for sure, there can't be that many who drove the road last night. Don't you worry."

Jade looked up at Nelson, new tears pooling in her eyes as she tried to smile. "I know, Nels, but it's awful, isn't it, right before Christmas and with so much to live for," she cried.

Lucy

Pippa had arrived at Lucy's not too long after Sam had left and she was greatly welcome. Lucy was stuck sitting at her kitchen table, still with the tea things from when the police had come, unable to organise her thoughts or to decide what to do next.

She was holding on to a mug of cold tea that didn't appear to have been sipped at all. Ironically, the mug was one that had 'world's best mum' on the side. Lucy was staring into space with a blank look and her eyes were wide in shock.

Pippa had come straight in and wrapped her arms around her. "Oh Lucy, I am so sorry. Poor James. He was a lovely beautiful young man," she said as she held Lucy warmly.

Lucy looked up at Pippa, as if seeing her for the first time, tears flooding her eyes. "Oh Pippa, what am I going to do now?" She said, resigned.

Pippa looked around her in the large, homely kitchen. She knew that this room would have held a lot of special memories of James and that the heart of his family was right there. Pippa sat down at the table then, gently moving the milk jug and sugar bowl slightly more towards the middle, and she took a notebook from her handbag.

"Well, first things first, Lucy, let's make a list and then we can figure out how to get it crossed off, aye," explained Pippa, knowing how Lucy would normally approach making a plan. "Now, have you called the girls?" Pippa asked gently.

Lucy looked at her, startled. "The girls," she gasped. "I hadn't thought, oh God Pippa, how do we tell them? They will be so distressed and then they will want to come, and the drive, how will they drive in a state, oh Pippa, what will we do about the girls?"

"Lucy," said Pippa calmly, "it will be alright. We can ask someone to pick them up if we need to or the police will help and they have their lovely husbands to support them as well. Don't worry, we can make sure they are looked after, ok?"

"Ok," said Lucy tentatively. "Yes, we need to talk to Jack and see what he thinks too."

"Right," said Pippa, "now, who else do you want told, because darling, I know it's hard to think about, but this will be all over the news and at some point, the media will find out James' name, so you need to tell people soon or they will hear it some nasty way and you wouldn't want that, aye love."

Getting organised was good for Lucy. It was her safe space, the place she knew well and where she flourished. "Right, good thinking," said Lucy, and she went to her phone to get the numbers of the people she needed to call.

Pippa was glad to see Lucy move from the kitchen table, even if it was with a heavy heart and reluctant footsteps. She had never seen her friend so broken, and it felt good to be able to help her, even if the help meant hard things, like telling people James was gone.

After listing all the people that would need to be told, Lucy and Pippa moved on to things that needed to be completed to get the house ready for people to arrive. Luckily, Lucy was very organised and so, the girls' rooms were ready and the majority of the supplies for the holidays were already in the pantry or the freezer.

She wanted Jack to check the water but wouldn't worry him about that now, noting that he appeared to have gone out on the farm. That wasn't something that surprised Lucy, Jack always took his emotions to the sheep, rather than work through them with her. He had done it their entire married life.

Pippa put a wash on, and Lucy boiled the jug again, because it was habit rather than because she really wanted another cup of tea. They had discussed what to dress James in, funeral matters and the possible date, where people might stay and what Lucy might do about Christmas Day.

It was tough on Lucy and there were moments where she wobbled dangerously close to the edge of despair, but she got through it and by the end of a couple of hours, there were good plans in place and Pippa had made the necessary arrangements for the girls and others to be told.

Lucy had decided she couldn't wait for Jack to help with those decisions and so, she went ahead with Pippa's guidance. Jack would just have to cope, Lucy reasoned.

Lucy dreaded the girls' arrival. Of course, she loved them so much it hurt, but it was because of that that she was fearful. She knew that she would struggle not to dictate and meddle in their grief, and she was afraid that it would end badly with one or other or both girls retreating to their homes at some point.

Deep down, Lucy knew she was hard work, but even so, she wasn't great at managing her emotions or being kind when all she wanted to do was scream. And frankly, she was more than a little annoyed at Jack for just disappearing again, and not helping out with the difficult tasks that faced them.

Jack

Jack needed the fresh air as if it was his only sustenance, especially in difficult times. The rolling land and the green of the trees and sound of streams bubbling were his comfort. Lucy always said he loved the sheep more than her, but it wasn't about the sheep.

It was often about the relative silence of the countryside, the sounds only of nature and not of Lucy barking orders or displaying her frequent disappointment in him and what he was doing or how he handled things. It was in the open air that Jack could think, deal with his emotions and get the strength to go home to the problems or the drama that waited for him.

Today was different. Not so much a problem or a drama but a thunder bolt, a lightning strike to Jack's complete being, a jab to his heart. Jack felt like he would never properly live again after today. Like a huge piece of him was ripped jaggedly from his flesh, like a massive boulder had landed on his chest and would not be moved.

His son, his wonderful, amazing, beautiful boy was gone. It couldn't be true, shouldn't be true and yet, Jack felt it; it was true, and he was feeling it, stronger than any other kind of pain he had experienced. He was paralysed by pain.

Jack loved the part of the farm where he was, the hills were gentle and the grass was lush. There was a pristine stream flowing over silver rocks that had deep pools and trout that basked in the summer light. He had camped out here many times, first as a young boy and then later as a grown man during musters. He loved the smell of smoke from the campfire and a hot billy boiling over the flame.

Today though, nothing gave him much comfort. It was warm and the sun shone down on his skin, heating him through. But his mind was cold and ravaged by the terrible news of James and he struggled to breathe. Driving further into the back country, Jack knew where he was headed.

The farm boundary that he shared with Claire and Mark. It was there that he felt sure there would be comfort. Claire had made her way towards the boundary that Jack had been aiming for. She was usually out this way on a Sunday, checking on fences and troughs and she hoped she might have seen Jack as she often did.

She was worried. Jack would be devastated about James, and she knew that Lucy wasn't exactly the sort to put his feelings before her own. Not that she intended to be cruel, it was just Lucy, thought Claire.

Sure enough, Jack could see that Claire was up at the boundary, her red gumboots a confirming sign it was her, even if her face couldn't quite be made out. Claire was a robust woman and Jack had long admired her for her work ethic and the support she gave her husband Mark on the farm. She held the place together and saved them several times from near disaster as Mark caved under the pressure and damn near gave it away.

As he got closer, Jack left his vehicle and nearly ran towards her, such was his need for compassion and empathy. Claire climbed the stile and jumped from the wooden step as he got to her. She threw her arms around him, enveloping him in her and stroked his hair.

"Oh Jack, I am so sorry, he was a wonderful lad, truly wonderful. You just hang on, okay, hang on to me, I am here, Jack, here for you," she said with tears in her eyes.

Jack sobbed for what seemed an endless amount of time. Claire, patient and kind, held him close and tried her best to give him some comfort. She had some screwed-up tissues in her pocket and a sweetie at the ready if he wanted it. Jack's breathing became deeper and more controlled, and she gently pulled his face up to look into hers.

"Oh Jack, how can I help?" She asked. "Just tell me, what do you need?"

Jack recovered himself and when he was slightly more composed, he started to speak. "I don't know, Claire; I just don't know what to do. How do I do this, how can I say goodbye to my boy, my precious boy?" He cried. "You know, Claire, Lucy has already put the walls up, it's my fault in her eyes, all my fault." He sniffed.

Claire knew how hard Jack found Lucy to manage at times and this would be the worst of all. If she wasn't blaming him, she was bossing him, and Claire understood how hard it was for Jack. She knew marriages could be difficult, heaven knew her own could be, and she just had so much feeling for this man before her and his situation.

There was something else on Claire's mind as well and she was trying hard to find the words to bring it up. "Jack, have the police found anything out about what happened to James?" She asked gently.

Jack looked at her softly and shook his head. "They really don't know much at all yet," he said quietly. "They need to have a post-mortem to find out how James died first."

"Oh Jack, a post-mortem, how hard that is for you, I am so sorry you have to go through that as well," said Claire.

"Yes," said Jack, "Lucy went mad because we can't see him until after that and well, Claire, you know what she is like, she just hounded and hounded the poor officers but the police just can't allow it, they explained to us."

Claire didn't really understand why that would be, but she didn't want to say that, so she just nodded as if she understood. "How are your girls?" She asked.

Jack was a bit taken aback, in all of his grief, he hadn't thought about the girls and telling them, and he was immediately ashamed by the question. "I don't know if they know. I just couldn't take it with Lucy going mad, so I just came out here. What a terrible parent I am, Claire, imagine forgetting the girls like that, what the hell is wrong with me!" Jack cried as he stifled another sob.

Claire couldn't have him thinking he was a bad parent, because she knew he was far from it. "Jack, now you listen to me, you have had the worst shock anyone can have, none of us would cope any better. You need to be kind to yourself and taking care of yourself first is a good thing."

"The girls will be looked after, I am sure. They both have their husbands to turn to. The police will know what to do."

Jack knew that Claire was talking sense, but it wasn't easy for him and he felt awful about not thinking of the girls before himself. Seeing Jack's guilt about the girls meant Claire couldn't ask him what she wanted to. It would seem selfish and shallow, and she wouldn't do that.

Instead, she sat on the grass and patted it for Jack to sit with her. They sat together, his head on her shoulder, for the longest time.

Lucy

Pippa had done a wonderful job of helping with things and she and Lucy were sitting at the kitchen table, having a breather while the police were back to ask more questions and look at James' room. Jack was still out on the farm and Lucy refused to worry or try to call him. She was back in control and Pippa had been just the tonic for her.

Sam had come back with the young police officer called Jo, and they had asked to see James' room. Lucy wasn't all that keen on the idea, but she understood that it was important they find out anything that might lead them to whoever may have hurt James. So, it was with a sigh that she had agreed to let them go into James' room and look at his things, even if it was painful for her.

Sam tried to be as kind as he could in the circumstances and had reassured Lucy that they would leave James' things as they found them, and only take anything that might be needed for the investigation. The young officer had nodded and looked as dazed as Lucy felt in this situation.

She led them to James' room in the second wing of the house and left them there to get on with their business. It wasn't something she was ready to cope with, seeing strangers pick over her boy's things. Lucy felt it was a complete invasion of James' privacy and she struggled to allow the police to search at all.

Pippa had poured cool drinks for them both and they sat in the kitchen, trying to be as normal as possible while the police searched James' room. Lucy had the police go and see the girls and arrange for one of their husbands to drive them up and they would be there in the morning.

The girls had been teary and distressed, as completely expected and reasonable in the circumstances, but they were also glad that they were together and able to help each other through until they got to the farm. They didn't really understand what was happening and Lucy thought it best to keep the details as minimal as possible until they were home and safe and calm enough to hear what she had to tell them.

She was dreading it but knew that the girls would want to understand what was happening and what had happened to James. They loved him dearly and all of them would feel the hole forever present in their family from here on.

Pippa had hung out washing, prepared some food for later and rung a number of neighbours and friends Lucy had listed that she wanted told about James, before the media did the job for her. Lucy had been busy talking with Jack's parents, calling her own extended family and talking to Father McDonald about the funeral and what would be possible over the Christmas break.

Just as Pippa was placing some cheese and crackers on the table, Sam and the young officer appeared from James' room, and Jack walked in at the exact same time. Lucy was quick to explain to Jack what Sam was here for and Jack looked bewildered as he took it all in.

"Lucy, Jack, thank you for letting us look at James' things," said Sam. "We are going to take a couple of things with us for follow-up but nothing to worry about. Just some papers really, and a photograph. It's highly unlikely that they are related to anything, but we will check them out just to be sure."

"Will we get them back?" Lucy asked quietly.

"Sure," said Sam. "I can't say when at this stage but yes, I am sure you will get them back. Now, we are doing the post-mortem in the morning and that will help us understand more about what has happened. Lucy, I know you want to see James as soon as you can, understandably, and as soon as that is possible, we will be in touch. In the meantime, I hope your daughters arrive safe and sound, and we will be on our way."

"Thank you, Sam," said Lucy. "We appreciate it, don't we Jack?"

Jack nodded and shook Sam's hand and then Constable Jo's as well. "Yes, thanks, we do appreciate it," he said almost robotically.

"Right," said Pippa, "let's get you a drink, Jack, you must be thirsty after being out on the farm."

"Thanks Pippa," said Jack. "That would be lovely. So, the girls are coming then, Lucy? When is that?"

"In the morning, Jack, one of the boys will bring them, so they don't have to drive and for now, they are staying the night together. They are very upset as you would expect but I haven't told them too much, I thought it better they have more detail once they arrive."

"Thanks Lucy, thanks for doing that, I am sorry for darting off, I just couldn't deal with it, and I feel ashamed I didn't even think of the girls," Jack said regretfully.

"Oh well, it's done now," said Lucy in her usual matter-of-fact reply.

Pippa set down a cool drink in front of Jack and picked up her bag and keys. "Lucy, I'll pop off, love. I will come back up in the morning and give you a hand, wait for the girls if you need to go out. Take care, both of you and we are terribly sorry about James, really," said Pippa, backing out of the kitchen.

Alone, Lucy and Jack stared at their drinks and neglected the cheese and crackers. The words unsaid between them just wouldn't come and time almost stood still. Jack stood up sometime later and took Lucy's hand, guiding her to him in an embrace.

She knew she should have yielded and that they needed comfort from each other, but she couldn't do it. After a brief hug, she stepped away, eyes teared up. "I think I will shower and go to bed," she said quietly as she left the room.

Sam

Sam was intrigued. The search of James' room had turned up a couple of things that needed looking at further. For now, though, the post-mortem was the priority and he was on his way to get started. Post-mortems were never easy, and Sam didn't particularly enjoy them.

He was concerned, however, that his victims were respected, at all times, and that they were treated with dignity and compassion. He particularly liked working with Dr Carter, who was excellent at that side of her job.

"Morning Doc," said Sam as he strode into the mortuary. The Doc or Jazmin (Jazz) Carter, as was her proper name, was dressing in her customary white scrubs and gumboots ready for the procedure she would perform on James.

"Morning yourself, Sam," she replied, smiling. "I hope you have had a good start to the day."

"Yes Doc, I am all set and I see that James is first up. Anything new since yesterday?" Sam queried.

The doctor looked over at Sam with empathy clear on her face. "No Sam, nothing of note yet, terrible business this one, such a shame for a young person with so much to look forward to."

"Yeah," said Sam, "bloody awful when it's someone so young but also so hardworking and naturally driven. His family are devastated and if we can, I would love to get him ready for them to see him after the PM if that is okay. Mum's a bit frantic and Dad is taking some time to process, so I think seeing James is very important."

"Understood Sam," said the Doc. "I think we will be in a position for the parents to see him in the later part of this morning and to release the body by about 5pm. You can let the family know if you like."

Sam smiled back at her, appreciating her clarity and willingness to work with him. "Thanks Doc, I know that will mean a lot to them."

"Right," said the Doc, walking into the area where James' body had been rested on the table, removed from the body bag after careful forensic examination and covered in a white sheet. "Let's see what James can tell us, aye."

Looking at James' body was confronting. He didn't have many outward or obvious injuries and even the places where he probably was hit by the car didn't have severe bruising or lacerations. There were some marks but nothing like you might expect had a car been travelling at speed when it hit him. The Doc then felt for any particular injuries on James' head and found the injury at the front where she assumed he hit the trough, close to where he had fallen.

"Judging from this injury, Sam, I think this will be what killed James," explained the Doc, pointing to James' head, rather than the contact he had with the car. "We will have to scan him and investigate the wound further, but my gut tells me that's what we are looking at in this instance."

"Ok," said Sam. "Pretty unfortunate then, Doc, isn't it? If the trough wasn't in the way, he might have lived?"

"Looks that way, Sam. What a terrible shame!" The Doc reflected.

"That is overall consistent with the scene, Doc. No sign of speed, no skid marks, nothing to suggest it was a high-speed contact, like him being knocked out of his shoes even. Having said that, that in itself is a little strange, being a main road with a 100-kilometre per hour speed-limit, cars often speed down that way."

"That is odd, Sam," said the Doc, puzzled. "I am glad that is your department, I am just happy to deal in the facts that the body gives me."

"Hmm," huffed Sam, "well, it is an odd one. I just wonder if the vehicle had stopped, perhaps even to talk to James before it hit him, like perhaps it was someone he knew, and they had a conversation. Or it stopped a little before him and didn't see him as they were pulling away again. Either way, at this stage, it's a bit of a mystery."

The Doc took blood samples and swabbed the body for DNA or other matter that might hold some clues. The blood would help with understanding if James had alcohol or other drugs in his system or if there was some physical or biological contributor to his death.

The swabs would also identify other DNA on James' body, say from the driver or any other person James had contact with over the evening, like a lover. It was also possible that whoever did hit James, might have tried to save him immediately afterward and so checking for DNA might explain whether he had been resuscitated, for example.

Sam thought, having been at the scene that it was highly unlikely that help was rendered; however, it was important not to overlook those kinds of possibilities. Sam also expected gunshot residue to be present on James' body, to reflect the rabbit shooting he had been doing over the course of the night.

Sam would be interested in the toxicology results, especially as he had found weed in James' room that suggested he was at the least a recreational user. There was also some evidence that James was interested or was engaged in some kind of relationship and Sam was hoping to put that possibility to the other party immediately following the post-mortem.

The Doc was packing up, having taken all the necessary samples and sown the incisions back together, leaving James with a highly visible Y-incision between his shoulder blades and down to his genitals. Sam readied to leave and confirmed with the Doc that results would take between hours and days, and she would be in touch with any relevant news as soon as they came in.

"Thanks Doc," said Sam. "Appreciate your help on this one. Not a particularly pleasant situation right before Christmas, so hopefully, we can wrap it up quickly for the family."

"For sure, Sam," said the Doc. "It is so horrible for them, so hopefully, we can give them their boy back today so they can at the least start the grieving process."

"Speaking of family," said Sam, "they will be here shortly, so I will go and clean myself up and be ready for them. Will you bring James to the viewing room?"

"Absolutely, Sam," said the Doc, "that is the least we can do for James and his family!"

Lucy

Lucy hadn't slept and her eyes were red and puffy from the tears and the fatigue. Her wild fringe was at its worst and there was nothing she tried that could make it settle. Jack had gone out early to feed the dogs and check on the animals and Lucy knew that in part, it was to get away from her. Truth was, she just didn't care about what Jack was doing at that moment, even though she knew she should.

After dressing in a black top with black pants and flat shoes, and taking a call from Sam who had said they could go in and see James later in the morning, Lucy went to the kitchen and turned on the jug. Just as she went to sit at the table, the back door flung open and both of her daughters exclaimed, "Oh Mum!"

As they collapsed into her arms, a mess of tears and snotty noses, Anna's husband, Pete, stood in the doorway, looking afraid to come in, awkwardly leaning against the frame and watching the emotional scene before him.

Anna was the elder of the two girls and at 24, was a couple of years out of university after studying environmental science and law. She worked as a lawyer for a company in the city and had met Pete through work, as the company he was a lawyer for, was a key client.

She was taller than Lucy and slim with long rich brown hair that was halfway down her back with just a hint of natural wave. Her eyes were green like Jack's but framed with long lashes and a smattering of freckles across her cheeks. As a keen netball player, Anna's nose was crooked from a break in her boarding school days, but this was a redeeming feature and not an exaggerated misfortune.

Amanda was different to Anna and more like James. Her hair was curlier and lighter and her eyes more like Lucy's than Jack's. She wasn't quite as tall and at 22, was just a little younger. Amanda was in her first year out of university after having studied teaching and was enjoying her job at the boarding school that she and Anna had attended. It was the same school Lucy had gone to when she was young.

Her husband, Todd, that she married that past spring, was coming up tomorrow as planned and was a police officer in the city. They had met in a bar two years ago and hit it off straight away. Todd was athletic and tall, he ran marathons and enjoyed multi-sport events.

Amanda did her first event a year ago and was getting the knack quickly after having been a champion swimmer during her school days. They both loved the farm and running the tracks and hills as training.

Lucy held onto her girls for the longest time, taking in the scent of their shampoo and the softness of their hair. It felt good to have them with her and she was immediately relieved that they had arrived safely.

"Okay girls, and of course, you, Pete," she said, "let's have some tea aye and what about breakfast, did you have any earlier or shall I make some now?"

"Don't fuss, Mum; we can make our own if we want it, but to be honest, it isn't a priority right now, we want to just sit with you and understand what happened to James a bit more. You know it's hard to take in, Mum, almost unbelievable," Anna said as she started to cry softly.

Lucy welled up too and Amanda was already crying and had been since she came in the door. "I know," Lucy said softly. "I can't believe it myself, but I guess we are just going to have to support each other through, right girls, just be there for each other."

"Where's Dad?" Amanda asked. "We thought he would be here too."

"Oh yes," said Lucy, "well, Dad is just doing some chores and when he comes back, we will all go in and see James. They will have finished with the post-mortem by mid-morning and Sam, the officer in charge of James' case, said he will meet us at the mortuary. I think that will help us all. To see James and to be with him."

Amanda was sobbing now. "Mum," she cried, "I don't know if I can do that, you know, see James. I just don't know."

Lucy looked at her middle child and her desperate face as she cried for her brother. Her heart broke as it would many times over the coming days, and it took all her strength to steady herself.

"Amanda, it's ok," she said quietly, "there is no pressure. You don't have to come if you don't want to. You can wait and see him in the funeral home or if it is best for you, you can just remember James from your last memory and not see him at all. Please don't worry, no one will make you do anything. Okay?"

Amanda, relieved, started to calm down. "Thanks, Mum," she smiled through her tears, "I just need to think about what to do."

Jack arrived at that moment and the girls ran to him and the tears flowed again. He wasn't doing so well at holding it together and seeing his girls sobbing made it harder than ever. He clung to them for comfort, and they rocked together in their grief.

"Jack," said Lucy, "we can go and see James mid-morning. Sam is meeting us at the mortuary, are you coming?"

Jack was surprised he wasn't being ordered to go but in fact, he was being asked for once. "Yes, Lucy. I will come, I need to see our boy," he said plainly.

Jade

The late morning sun was hot on her back as she rode her horse across the hills, galloping and then slowing to a walk on the steeper parts. The tracks were worn and the pasture green, not yet brown from the summer sunshine. The horse was blowing heavily, and Jade was glad for the solitude and to be alone with her thoughts.

She couldn't get James out of her head. He had been such a sweet young man, hardworking and strong. Nelson liked his work and had been keen to have him back over the summer, but it wouldn't be possible now. Jade was sorry.

In the distance, she could see the house nestled in the hills and the driveway where a cloud of dust was rising, indicating that a vehicle was on the move. She wasn't expecting anyone but that didn't mean much out here with the comings and goings of stock agents, vets, feed deliveries and the rural postman. Given Nelson wasn't at home, she gave her horse a firm kick and set off for the house at a gallop.

As she drew closer, she could see the visitor was Sam, the police officer looking into James' accident. She found that a little odd, as both she and Nelson had given their information about that night and Sam had seemed satisfied. Perhaps there was something new he wanted to ask them about, she thought, though she couldn't imagine what that might be.

Tying up the horse and making sure it had some water, Jade stood in the driveway, waiting for Sam to get out of the car. "Hello Sam," she said, "wasn't expecting you back today."

Sam was interested in this woman and her smile. He found her attractive, of course but it wasn't her looks that piqued his interest. "Jade," he smiled back, "nice to see you again. I wondered if we might have a private word. Just you and I please."

"Of course," said Jade, "come on into the cool in the house, we can talk in there. Would you like a cool drink? I have some orange juice or sparkling water if you would like some."

Sam was hot and bothered from a busy morning and the juice sounded appealing. "Juice would be great, thanks," he said to Jade as he took a seat at the kitchen counter. Jade, in tight jodhpurs and boots, moved easily across the kitchen, filling two large glasses with the cool juice and some lumps of ice from the dispenser built into the fridge.

"Mmm that's so good after a dusty ride," she said to Sam as he took a drink.

Sam nodded in agreement and then got straight to the point. "Jade look, this is a bit awkward, so I won't beat around the bush. Yesterday, after we found James, we took a look in his room, protocol in these situations, I am sure you understand. Thing is, we found a photo of you in his beside draw and well, it's a bit compromising and I need you to explain it for me," explained Sam, taking the photo from his pocket and slapping it down on the counter.

Jade blushed. It was compromising. She was in the stables, blue jeans undone and her arm across her naked chest, and she was laughing. If you looked closely, you could see a man's shirt and boots in the background. Then, the emotions hit her, smack, hard in the stomach.

The guilt, the passion, the rush of excitement, the regret. And then to her horror, she was sobbing. Big ugly sorrowful sobs between big sucks of air, air that was never enough.

Sam was patient. He was surprised but he was patient. There was a story here and he needed to know it, but he also could see that Jade was distressed and needed to compose herself before she would make any sense. He scanned the room for tissues and having found them close by, passed them across to her.

Jade took the tissues and blew her nose. She gulped in several deep breaths and tried to form her words. "It was only once," she explained. "James worked for us last summer and when he was around the house, I would make sure he had cool drinks and food, as I would do for anyone else working here, and we became friends."

"Nelson was often here and so, it wasn't a secret that we got along. Perhaps it is because we were closer in age than I am to Nelson or perhaps it was just because we had things in common, like the farm and my friendship with Lucy, his mum."

"Maybe at times, I flirted. I don't know. Maybe I didn't appreciate his feelings. He was certainly a lovely young man," she said, her eyes flooding with tears, "and I liked him a lot. One day, Nelson was in the city doing some business and I had been doing some work in the tack room in the stables."

"James had come into the stables from the opposite end and didn't realise I was there. He was hot and he took off his shirt and washed his face with cold water from the tap. When I heard him, I came out of the tack room. Maybe it was the light, the golden colour of his tanned skin against the drops of water running down his chest, I don't know. Anyway, next thing I know, we are kissing and well, like I said, it only happened once," she said, blushing and feeling stupid.

"James took that photo of me afterward. I begged him to delete it and he told me that he had. He finished up for the summer a week later and I hadn't seen him again. And now, he's dead and I won't—" she sobbed. "Please, I know you will think I am a horrible person. You can't know how guilty I have felt and how hard I have tried to make it up to Nelson. He doesn't know, of course. You won't tell him, will you?"

Sam smiled softly at Jade. This was a story as old as time and one he had heard in various versions more than a few times in his career. They were never simple situations, and he knew that had James not died, probably everything Jade was saying was true.

It was a one-off and wouldn't happen again. Trouble was these things had a habit of finding their way out and it might be best if she did tell Nelson to avoid that possibility. Better that than an enraged Lucy telling him, thought Sam.

"Jade," Sam said kindly, "I am not here to cause you trouble. But these things, these secrets often mean something when an accident like this happens. James obviously thought a lot of you, or he wouldn't have kept the photograph close. Are you sure you didn't see him after he came home this year?"

"He didn't try to convince you to perhaps have a relationship with him, to rekindle your feelings for him from the previous summer? Perhaps he was more forceful, and you didn't know how to make him stop? Was that it, was he blackmailing you or suggesting he would tell Nelson?"

"Sam, let me stop you right there. That is all ridiculous. I never ever saw James again. We didn't talk, there was no communication while he was away, I didn't see him when he got home this summer, full stop. I didn't know he had the photo, like I said, I thought it was deleted."

"As far as I am concerned, we had a one-off thing, never to be repeated and I am committed to Nelson and always will be," she said firmly.

Sam drained the last of his juice from the tall glass and stood up. "Ok Jade, thanks for the drink and for your time. I would strongly urge you to think about telling Nelson what happened. There may be other copies of the photo and it would be far better him hearing it from you than someone else. But that is your business, of course. I will be in touch if anything else comes up that I need to ask you about," he said as he walked to the door.

"Thank you," said Jade softly. "I am sorry about James, you know, he was a good kid," as she let Sam out.

Once Sam was gone, Jade collapsed onto the soft couch in the living room and sobbed and sobbed. She cried for James, of course, but mostly, she cried for herself. She didn't want to tell Nelson and now James was gone, it seemed crazy to do so. James couldn't tell him.

She did understand that the photo was a problem, but maybe it didn't need to be. If there was only one and Sam had it, then who else would ever know? She was sure the risk was low and there was no way she wanted to compromise what she had with Nelson. She loved him deeply and she knew she had been stupid. James was lovely but it was never going to be more. Nelson was her forever man.

Being so guilty, Jade had put that summer day to the back of her mind. Talking to Sam had bought it all back. It had been exciting, passionate and spontaneous but also dangerous and stupid. James had an amazing body, toned and sculpted from his physical work and his skin was soft and smooth. Apart from the hair trailing from his navel down, he was hairless, and the sweat was slick on his skin.

She had felt his hardness as they kissed, and his tongue searched for hers. His kisses were sweet at first and then urgent. She was surprised that he was not more nervous, but instead, he was confident and skilled, and her body responded. She knew she wasn't going to be able to stop herself after they first kissed, and he wasn't about to ask.

She had taken her own shirt off first and moved to unbutton his jeans. He had kicked off his boots and untied the shirt from his waist, all the while kissing her and moving his hands over her tenderly. They had fallen together into a hay-filled stall and he had unbuttoned her jeans. Reaching into the front of them and down to her, making her draw her breath sharply.

She was so taken with his body. His firmness and muscular tone. The way his arms felt around her and the softness of his lips. She savoured the moment, tracing his lines to his hardness and taking him in her hand. He responded, moaning and kissing her harder. She opened herself to him and he took her, thrusting strong, meeting her rhythm and sustaining her.

Jade shuddered even now at the pleasure he had given her and of the memory of her sin. She knew everything about it was wrong and yet, the intensity of the moment was one of the best experiences she had ever had with a man. Even now, she longed for something that came close to it.

Pippa

Pippa had been out to Lucy's and taken a fresh batch of scones and some of her blackberry jam from last summer. She knew that the last thing Lucy would have on her mind was feeding people, but they all had to eat sometime. She had stayed and talked with Anna and Amanda, who had shared stories of James as a little brother and the messes he got himself into.

They had laughed so hard when they talked about him putting baby chickens in his bed or trying to shower with his pet lamb. They cried when they remembered how sweet he had been as a little one, when he was learning to talk and used to call Amanda, Nah mana. It was a bittersweet conversation, but heartwarming and Pippa had been glad to be a part of it.

When the family left for the mortuary, Pippa had finished drying the dishes and let herself out. She was sad for them all and for all the Christmas' to come when James would not be home with them. It was a terrible loss, and she knew that had it been one of her boys, she simply would not recover.

She also knew Lucy was strong and that she would continue to be a community champion with her clipboard and sensible shoes. Pippa then went and visited a little with Jack's parents who, of course, were just as upset about James' passing as anyone else in the family.

June, Jack's mother, seemed glad of the intrusion and happy to have something useful to do as she busied herself making tea and cutting fruit loaf. William was sitting quietly in an easy chair, doing a crossword puzzle.

"Ah Pippa," he said, trying hard to smile, "a lovely surprise to see you here. Now, what do you think? This is five letters, last letter is an r and the clue is—"

June interrupted him, "Will, Pippa hasn't come to solve that crossword, now let's all have a cuppa and a chat."

They chatted solidly while drinking their tea and June and William shared some lovely stories about James and what a kind grandson he had been, chopping wood and driving them to town when he was around.

"James was a wonderful young man," said William quietly. "Just a great person and would have made a fantastic husband for some lucky woman one day. It's just such a shame we won't see that. Such a shame."

June touched her eyes in the hope of warning her tears away. "Oh yes," she agreed "James had the makings of a lovely father too. Just so kind and warm. Nothing was too much bother." She smiled. "Now Pippa, how are things at the house? We saw the girls arrive and they are coming over later when they get home, but what about Lucy and Jack?"

Pippa was caught a little off guard at the question, and she realised that perhaps June was subtly asking her if they were arguing or uniting. "Well June," said Pippa carefully, "I think everyone has had a moment to recover from the initial shock and they have come together in James' memory and are working through things from what I can tell."

"You know Lucy, she is so strong and while she had some difficulty at first, she has been able to kick her natural organiser gene into action and she is getting things arranged and looking after everyone. I think Jack is okay too. He spent some time on the farm yesterday and this morning, but since then has been with Lucy and the girls and they have all gone together to see James."

"Yes," said June, "Lucy phoned to say they were doing that earlier. Good thing, I think, helpful, you know, makes it real, I suppose but might be a comfort too in a strange way."

"You know," said William, "Jack was very much like James when he was young, before he was with Lucy. He was driven, kind and family-oriented. He loved the outdoors and did plenty of fun things with friends. He was wonderful with his siblings, very caring and playful."

"Now though, I worry he spends far too much time on his own, off across the farm. Never known a man to be out in the hills as much. I worry about him and now with what has happened to James, I just don't know how Jack will cope with such a blow."

Pippa could understand his concern. Lucy was a lot to deal with, for all of her good traits. She was dramatic and she did go off or have the sulks at times, but Pippa was sure they were strong. *Maybe losing James will bring them closer,* she thought.

"Well William, I think that it will take a long time to heal from this, of course, but they both know how much James loved his family and I am sure they will both want to stay tight and keep the girls close and yourselves to help them recover." She smiled gently.

June smiled. "Pippa, somehow you have managed to make us feel a little better. Before you came, I thought that wouldn't be possible today and yet, it is true. Thank you," she said.

Pippa smiled back and got up to put her cup in the kitchen. June wouldn't have it, taking from her and saying, "Now love, I won't have anything to do if you take your cup away, will I? Give me a job today, it will keep my mind off things."

Pippa agreed and passed her cup over. "Thank you for having me," she said to them both, "please let me know if you need anything, won't you, it is easy for me to pop back anytime," as she made her way out to her car.

Driving past where James was found was heart-wrenching and Pippa noted that people had started to leave cards and small trinkets to mark the spot. Someone had made a small wooden cross with James written simply on it in black paint.

The grass was bent over where people had come to leave flowers and to pay their respects. Someone had put a Christmas wreath in a nearby tree and some Christmas angels amongst its branches.

Pippa had known James most of his life and she couldn't imagine not seeing him again, joking with his sisters or having a beer in the local pub with his mates. He had been a great role model and her own sons had looked up to him. She wiped a tear away and continued driving down the familiar road, so sad for the loss of such a bright young man.

Town was busy as she pulled into a park and went to buy the last of her Christmas supplies. Standing in the queue for the cashier at the supermarket, several people could be heard talking about James and what might have happened to him.

Most of it was genuine concern but in one case, there was some nasty speculation about whether he was drunk or had taken something. Pippa was cross. Lucy and her family had enough upset without having untrue rumours spread around about James and what happened.

Unable to hold her tongue, she took her opportunity, "You know, Bobby Wilson, you would do well to keep your thoughts to yourself, it isn't kind to speculate and imagine if Lucy or Jack were to hear of what you are saying, it wouldn't sit right, would it?"

Bobby Wilson took on a reddened glow and mumbled his apologies. He knew better and Pippa had rightly called him on it. Pippa had no time for rumours, and she was distressed for Lucy, but she didn't comment further. It wasn't worth it to make a scene and she wanted to be a support, not part of the story. She paid for her groceries and went back to her car. As she was about to unlock it, Sam called to her from across the street.

"Pippa," he called, "can I have a moment?"

She was a little startled but seeing Sam was not entirely unexpected and she was aware that he was asking questions of those who had been out the night James was killed.

"Sam," she smiled, "what can I do for you?"

Sam knew Pippa was a great person and she regularly stood out as a pillar of the community who was first to volunteer or cook a meal for someone in need. He also knew Duncan and that neither of them was a drinker or likely to take risks when driving.

"Look Pippa," he said, "the thing is I need to talk to you about the other night, when James was killed. I know you left a little before Lucy to go home from the party and that you hadn't been drinking at all. Is that right?"

Pippa smiled at Sam. "That is right, Sam, absolutely, I was just a little ahead of Lucy and pulled out of the parking lot as she was locking the doors and putting the rubbish into the skip. I didn't drink that night and I looked after Lucy when she got a bit upset and decided to drown her sorrows."

"That's great, Pippa," said Sam. "Now, just wondering, did you see James on your way home at all? Did you see his vehicle, him perhaps walking or anything?"

Pippa thought about the question for a moment, making sure she considered every possibility. "Sam honestly, I didn't see a thing. It was dark, as you know it is on our roads and I didn't see anyone else on the road either walking or driving. I just drove to our road and turned off. It was all normal and uneventful."

"OK," said Sam, "and you didn't notice James at all. Didn't see a muzzle flash from someone shooting or hear any gunshots for instance?"

"No, sorry, I didn't, Sam," explained Pippa. "I just drove home and didn't see anything out of the ordinary at all. Oh Sam, I understand you are doing your job, but this is just terrible. Do you have any idea at all about who might be responsible?"

Sam raised a weary hand to his brow and wiped the small droplets of sweat away. "It's still an ongoing investigation, Pippa and at this stage, we know very little about what happened except to say that James was extremely unlucky to have been killed like he was. Very unlucky indeed."

"Actually, Pippa, you said just then that Lucy was drowning her sorrows?"

Pippa froze, aware for the first time what she may have implied. "Oh Sam, it was just a turn of phrase. Her and Jack had a little bit of a moment, and she took a couple of swigs from a bottle, that was all. She stopped right away and had food in her too, so I am sure she wasn't even the slightest bit tiddly," Pippa explained.

"And the moment between her and Jack, what was that about, Pippa, do you know?" Sam asked.

"Sure, yes I do," said Pippa. "Lucy was just being Lucy and saying something a little unkind and Jack chipped her for it. It wasn't a big deal, but well, Lucy just reacted badly to it. It was all forgotten in the blink of an eye."

"I see," said Sam. "Well Pippa, I think that is all for now. I better let you get going and get that shopping out of the heat." He smiled.

Claire

Claire was hot. She was standing in her kitchen with her morning's work fresh from the oven. The shearers were in, and she needed to feed them, as was tradition the week before Christmas on the farm. She had done a lot of the work ahead of today but the fresh baking like the scones and Victoria sponge cakes had to be on the day, so she had been up early.

Claire's children were on a camp overnight; she was glad of the space, so she could bake, but also think. She just could not get Jack and Lucy and James out of her head. James had been such a sweetie and she had really liked him. He had been great with her kids and worked hard.

Claire and Mark had him doing some work on the farm the summer before last and he had outstripped Mark's efforts well and truly. His fencing was excellent, and he handled the sheep like a master.

Claire was worried. Lucy wasn't an easy woman and Jack was distraught. Claire didn't have time to dwell on that however, and she started to pack for the trip to the woolshed when she noticed a vehicle coming to the house. She recognised Sam, the police officer, when he stepped out and she quickly wiped her face of flour and sweat and brushed down her front.

"Yoo hoo," she called to Sam, "I'm in the kitchen, just come on in."

Sam was hot too and hardly feeling the Christmas spirit. He had had a long 24 hours and he was making very slow progress. "Claire," said Sam, "nice to see you again. It has been a while, hasn't it? We've not really seen each other since that business over the sheep last year, if I remember rightly."

Claire smiled. "Oh yes," she said, remembering the sheep incident that resulted in a good stern talking to for some of the local kids who let a mob out on to the road.

"Look Claire," said Sam, "I can see you are busy, and I don't want to keep you, but I just have a few questions about the other night when James was killed, if that is alright."

Claire frowned, confused. "Right but what would I know that might help, I wasn't with James that night."

Sam tried to look reassuring, and he knew from past dealings with Claire that she was kind and gentle but also a little challenged when it came to some parts of life. "It's okay, Claire; it's not about being with James, just about whether you might have seen him or anyone else on your way home."

"Now Claire, can you tell me when you left the party and approximately when you got home here?"

"So, you want the times, Sam, is that right?" Claire asked.

"Times are great if you have them but just the roundabout times are ok too if that is all you can remember," Sam explained.

Claire didn't reply straight away, and it was clear she was stepping through things in her head before answering. "Right, okay then," she said. "I left just after Jade and I could see her taillights all the way to our road, or what I mean is they were in the distance when I drove along. I think it was just before midnight but perhaps a little earlier. I didn't look at the time when I got home, so I can't say when I got there."

Sam calmly carried on, "Claire, it is okay if you don't know the time, but can you tell me if you went straight home?"

Claire looked up at him for moment. "Straight home?" She queried. "Did I go straight home?" She stated, almost to herself as if she was thinking. "Well, when I got home, Mark was already in bed and I thought about a shower but then decided not to do that as the pump is sometimes a bit groany and it can wake you up, so I thought, no Claire, just get into bed and have a good wash in the morning."

"So, you did go straight home then?" Sam said, feeling a little unsure of what Claire was actually trying to tell him.

Claire was blushing now and more than a little flustered. She wasn't sure how to answer Sam's question. "Oh, Sam, you must think me so silly," she said in an unusual, almost giggly way. "I left the party and could see Jade in the distance before I turned off onto our road because, well, Jade doesn't live in our road."

"I didn't see James anywhere, mind you, I wasn't really looking for him or anybody. I was just driving normally in my Christmas outfit, and I remember around then there was a really good song on the radio. Ooh, I do love a great ballad, don't you, Sam?"

Sam was getting a little annoyed now. "Well yes, Claire, but I am not here to talk music with you. I need to know what you did after the party and whether you went straight home. Claire, it's not a difficult question," he said with irritation.

Claire looked down at the floor of her old farmhouse and started to cry. She had been spoken to in that irritated way her entire life. *Stupid, silly Claire, always getting on everyone's nerves,* she said to herself.

Claire sniffed and wiped her nose on a handkerchief that she took from her bra. Sighing, she looked back at Sam. "I was with Jack," she said. "I was with Jack after the party, so no, I did not go straight home."

Sam looked at Claire in astonishment. This was Claire, salt of the earth, farmer's wife, Claire. Claire, who wasn't regarded as particularly bright but who was lovely and cheerful and worked her fingers to the bone on the farm and on the books. He was struggling to put it together.

Claire kept talking, "You see, when I turned into our road, I turned again at the gate that leads to the old worker's cottage on Jack and Lucy's farm. The driveway isn't very easy to spot and once you enter it, you cannot be seen as the trees are thick on either side. It also means you can't see who is coming either on the road. Jack and I meet there when we can."

"So, Jack was waiting for you when you got there then?" Sam asked.

"Oh yes," said Claire, "he left the party a good half hour before I did, and he was at the cottage when I arrived."

"Did he mention anything to you at all about his drive to the cottage?" Sam asked. "Did he see James on the road, or did he see anyone else?"

"He didn't say he did," explained Claire. "He just said that it was so dark, he almost missed the turnoff to the cottage, but nothing else."

"And Jack was completely as you would have expected him to be?" Sam asked.

"Yes," said Claire, "absolutely as expected. Happy as a clam."

Remembering the scrap of paper in James' room Sam suddenly understood what it meant. James must have known about Jack and Claire. Why else would he write Dad and Claire with a question mark like he had?

"Claire," asked Sam, "did anyone else, anyone at all know about your meeting place and relationship with Jack?"

Claire looked concerned. "Anyone else?" She questioned. "No, not that I am aware of, not at all, Sam."

"You see, Claire, I think James might have known," he explained.

Claire was scared then. She had no idea that anyone might have known, let alone James and even if he did find out somehow, how had that come to Sam? Claire was panicked and her thoughts started to scramble, too much for her brain to cope with.

Sam noted Claire's distress and he wondered what the hell else was going on in Stoney Hollow after Jade's revelation and now this. It seemed like everyone had a secret and a reason to hide and he wondered just how much that was clouding what really happened to James.

He had word from forensics and the preliminary assessments turned up nothing that pointed to a particular vehicle hitting him, there was no paint transfer or broken pieces from any vehicle on the scene. This, Sam considered, was consistent with a low-speed collision, given that it was the blow to the head that killed James and not the collision itself.

Sam told Claire what he told Jade that morning. These things have a way of coming out, regardless of how much he might want to promise Claire confidentiality about what she had told him. He counselled her on how much better it would be to consider telling Mark and for Jack to consider telling Lucy before that happened.

Claire had actually laughed then, telling Sam that Mark was so half asleep that he probably wouldn't hear what he was told anyway. He had stopped noticing anything she did a lifetime ago, she had explained.

Lucy

The visit to the mortuary had been difficult. Lucy had been so desperate to see James. What she hadn't quite expected was how it would feel. So final, so cold. Seeing him lying there had been the most confronting moment of her life. Her baby, who should have outlasted her, gone.

Worse than anything was how he looked, almost perfect. His head wound was visible, of course, but other than that, he looked exactly as if he was sleeping. Peaceful but cold.

Lucy had worried that she might scream or collapse. She didn't. None of them did. They all coped in dignified silence, silent tears running down cheeks. No one spoke. All wrapped up in their grief. Lucy had struggled with watching her girls and their reactions.

Seeing their pain on their faces pulled at Lucy right from her core and she was amazed at their dignity and the way they harnessed their feelings to maintain a calm presence with their brother.

Jack was ashen. He appeared like stone at the side of the mortuary trolley, a stiff hand outstretched to hold onto James'. Jack was holding his tears in, eyes brimming but not spilling, as he rubbed his thumb back and forth over James' hand.

Lucy thought the grief on Jack accentuated every line, every spot and every grey in his hair. It was as if they were magnified and had come into focus like never before. Jack was aging before her eyes, rapidly.

It had been hard to come away and leave James again. It had felt like betrayal for Lucy, and she wrestled with it. Lucy felt her heart physically pull towards James with each step she took away from him. Step, step, step and her heart stretched, tugging and straining as the distance grew. The physicality of her emotion was overwhelming, making her breath ragged, and her head spin.

They drove home in silence, each locked in the thoughts in their heads. Each breath Lucy took felt exaggerated and loud against the silence and she almost stopped breathing as a result. Anna and Amanda had ear buds in their ears, and each disappeared into their grief with the music playing through them.

Anna enjoying the strains of *Hallelujah* and Amanda listening to some country crooner. Jack concentrated on the drive, eyes looking straight ahead, his body rigid and stiff as he guided the car. Every muscle felt the strain and Jack was glad of the pain, a distraction from how he felt in his heart.

Once home, the girls went straight to see their grandparents to explain about James and that they had seen him. June and William were waiting patiently for news and maintained a respectful support but also a distance to allow the four remaining members of the five, to manage their feelings and challenges without unwanted or unhelpful interference.

They knew the family dynamic well and didn't expect Lucy would be terribly comfortable with them being too close or intrusive. They showed enormous restraint and respect, especially for people with their own genuine heart-breaking grief.

Home was comforting for Lucy. The dogs, the garden and the familiar domain where Lucy felt in control. She was relieved to be back in her sanctuary. The place where she felt order and clarity. Walking into the kitchen, she flicked on the kettle and hovered over the drawer where she kept her tea assortment, unable to decide what she would like.

A normal task that now felt overwhelming, she was stuck. Jack came in and muttered something vague about the sheep and back of the farm. While Lucy had solved the dilemma of the tea and set to making it, he had emerged from their bedroom, changed from his good clothes into his farm clothes and ready to leave.

"So, I guess we are not going to talk about James," Lucy had said to him. Her speech laced with the boarding school annunciation that gave her the sound of a plum in her mouth. "Jack, our son is dead. I would have thought we might have something to talk about. Can't the bloody sheep wait?"

Jack spun round on his heels then. "Wait Lucy!" He exclaimed. "Wait for what? James is gone, so what the bloody hell do they need to wait for? There is nothing. James is—" Before Jack could finish, they were interrupted by a knock at the door.

It was Sam. He had left them at the mortuary with James and said he would be coming to the farm later. No one had remembered. Jack let him in while Lucy boiled in her emotions. It took all she had to speak and ask Sam if he would like a cup of tea.

"Thanks Lucy," said Sam, "that would be lovely. Mind if I take a seat, I would like to talk with you both about James if now is a convenient time."

Jack pulled out a chair for Sam. It was of quality timber with a fabric of bright yellow lemons on the seat cushions. "Of course, Sam, here take a seat," he said.

Lucy came over with the tea and some shortbread from one of her baking tins. "Right Sam," she said in a serious and demanding tone, "what can you tell us about our boy?"

Sam smiled gently, knowing that what he had to say would be hard to hear. As much as he had done this job many times, talking to families about how their loved one died was never easy and he didn't enjoy it. He did make it as compassionate as possible and he was kind, choosing his words as carefully as possible so as not to hurt unnecessarily or offend.

"Lucy, Jack, what I can say now with certainty is that James did not suffer. It would seem that he was hit on the side of the road at very low speed but that was enough to push him forward and in doing so, he hit his head on the water trough and would have died almost instantly," he explained.

Sam waited for the information to connect with Lucy and Jack before he spoke further. Jack looked at Sam. "Instantly you say, that is something then that he wouldn't have really known what had happened."

Sam continued on explaining that there was no evidence from the vehicle either on James or at the scene, which contributed to the theory of a low-speed impact. He explained that he had spoken to people across the district who had been out driving that night but that he had nothing particular to go on in terms of determining who might have hit James. He said it was possible but unlikely that whoever it was may have not known what they hit.

Lucy flared up at that view. "Not known, not known what they hit, seriously, how is that possible, Sam? How could you hit James and not know?" She cried indignantly.

Sam was patient. He explained that in the dark, as James walked in the long grass on the side of the road, there may have been another reason why the vehicle that hit him was moving so slowly. Perhaps that reason distracted the driver, and they didn't realise they had hit James.

Jack understood. "I see," he said to Sam. "That is plausible."

Lucy was less charitable. "Plausible, Jack, plausible? For God's sake, they hit someone, surely, they would know. It is not as if they hit a rabbit!" She exclaimed.

Sam could see the grief playing out for Lucy and the desperate need she had for this to be a clear and rationale matter that could quickly be cleared up. Unfortunately, he didn't think it was going to be an easy one to solve. No evidence, multiple vehicle movements over the evening and timing a little unclear.

In Sam's mind, it all made for a great mystery. Of course, he also knew that getting to the truth might take time or it might not happen at all. "I am so sorry to you both for your loss," said Sam gently. "I understand that this news isn't easy to take and that you are yet to say goodbye to James. Please know that I will do all I can to help you, but please, I also need you to understand that sometimes these things are difficult, and this investigation may not result in any further information."

Jade

Jade was still reeling from Sam having discovered her secret about James. She was wracked with guilt all over again and desperate to find a way to keep her marriage to Nelson without the truth breaking it apart.

In her panic, she decided to get away from the farm and took her car for a good blowout before deciding to visit Pippa and the boys. She loved the boys and their little faces, the dirt on their knees and the way they loved the outdoors, and all of the hiding places their farm had on offer. They were spirited and healthy and just as she had once imagined children of hers might be.

All that had changed, of course, when she married Nelson. He had decided against children years before, and had a vasectomy and even when they tried and he had the procedure reversed, they hadn't been lucky enough to get pregnant.

Now, Jade and Nelson had grown used to their life and decided to choose contentment together rather than the ongoing agony of disappointment each month. It was bittersweet for Jade, but she wouldn't trade Nelson for anything and over time, the heartache did ease.

Poppet loved the twins as much as Jade did, and she was vocal as they pulled into the familiar driveway, whining and yelping in excitement. The boys were on the front lawn and had a net between two chairs that they were on either side of with old tennis rackets and a shuttlecock.

They missed more than they hit but they made huge efforts, swinging their rackets with gusto and spinning around after them. "Jade, Jade," they called to her.

"We are making up a game, look how far we can hit the shuffle lock," said Hunter.

Jade laughed and yelled back, "You are so strong; those muscles are doing a great job." The boys smiled wide grins with gaps where they awaited their adult teeth, and went back to hitting the shuttlecock with all their might.

Pippa appeared, wiping her hands on a towel and smiled at Jade. "Hello," she said warmly, "shall I put a coffee on?"

Jade was so glad to have found her at home and shouted over, "Yes please," as she walked across the lawn and up the steps of the expansive deck. Pippa's kitchen smelled divine. It was warm and Christmassy with fresh gingerbread cooling on the rack that Pippa was covering with a Christmas themed tea towel fresh from the laundry.

"Ooh," said Jade, "treats for Christmas. You are such an amazing baker and cook. I bet your guests will be looking forward to Christmas Day that is for sure."

Pippa blushed gently. Cooking was her thing, and she took pleasure from it and making others happy, but she was never good at taking praise without feeling very self-conscious. "Thanks Jade. I love doing it and it's so much more fun with the boys now," she explained.

Jade smiled. "The boys are having a great time out there. They will be knackered by the time they finish, I would think. They have so much energy. It's lovely that they have each other to play with," she said.

Pippa nodded in agreement. "It certainly makes it easier, now that they are older, to have the two. They can entertain each other and there isn't so much pressure on me for attention or to be the opposite in games that need two. Are you ready for Christmas, Jade?" Pippa asked.

"Well," said Jade, "it's only me and Nelson and we are easy pleased, so it's not the effort that it is for families. We just buy each other something extravagant and then pop open the champagne to start the day. We will likely graze on cheese and nibbles mostly and then have something simple to eat if we want to in the late afternoon."

"Sounds like bliss," said Pippa. "We will be like grand central, and the food will keep coming here with a big lunch at about 1 in the afternoon and ham sandwiches for supper."

Jade liked the sound of that and said so. Perhaps having a lot of people around would be fun, she thought. While the boys were out of ear shot, Jade bought up James.

"Oh Pippa," she said quietly. "I can't stop thinking about James and Lucy. Isn't it just awful? He was so full of life and just starting out. Lucy must be a wreck. Have you seen her or Jack?"

Pippa explained that she had been out to Lucy's a couple of times and seen them all. She told Jade about her conversation with Sam as well and that the family had been to see James at the mortuary. Jade's eyes filled with tears at the thought. "How sad, how truly awful for them," she cried.

Pippa was aware that James had spent the summer last year working with Nelson, so she wasn't surprised that Jade was feeling a bit upset. No one liked to see a young person lost in their prime.

"Did Sam visit you also?" She asked Jade.

"Yes, he did, a couple of times actually," Jade explained. "He saw Nelson and I the day they found James, and he came back and spoke to me when Nelson was out."

Pippa thought going back to see Jade on her own was a little odd. "Was he looking for Nelson when he came back, or did he want to talk with both of you?" She asked.

Jade really started to cry then. Big wet tears fell from her cheeks onto the tablecloth, and she looked distraught. "Good God, Jade," said Pippa, "are you alright? I know it's a big shock. Do you need a drink? We have some whiskey in the cabinet."

Jade put her hand up to wave away the offer of whiskey, but the tears continued to flow. Pippa offered tissues and Jade took them gratefully, wiping away her tears and blowing her nose loudly.

Finally, after what seemed a very long time, Jade spoke, "Sam came to see me because he found something out. He found a photo of me in James' room and came to ask me about it. I didn't know that the photo existed. I mean, I knew he took it, but I had asked him to delete it. Obviously, he didn't and when the police went looking for any hint of what might have happened to James, they found the photo."

Pippa looked at Jade, a little confused. "Ok, so he took a photo of you and didn't delete it. Was this when he worked at your place last summer?" She asked.

"Yes," said Jade, looking Pippa in the eye, "it was last summer, and he took it when we were in the stables together."

"Right," said Pippa, listening carefully to Jade, "in the stables together."

"Yes," said Jade, "in the stables TOGETHER."

Pippa suddenly realised the problem and why Jade was so upset. "Oh Jade," she said with pity. Clearly, Jade had feelings for James and until now, no one to talk to about what had happened. Pippa's heart went out to her. She knew Jade wouldn't have set out to hurt Nelson and while she worried about that, she also felt for her friend. Life wasn't always black and white.

Jade sobbed. "It was just the once," she cried. "I, we, it wasn't planned or anything like that. I had been riding and it was just the hottest day, and he was in the stables when I got back and he was cooling off with his shirt around his waist and well, he made the first move, and I just got caught up in the moment and oh Pippa, it was wonderful, but I felt, feel so guilty." She sniffed.

Pippa's mind was racing a little. Jade was in a right state, and this wasn't a simple situation. For one thing, Nelson would be heartbroken if he knew and for another, Lucy would damn near kill Jade. There was no way Lucy would see what happened as anything other than Jade's fault and influence.

"What are you going to do, Jade?" Pippa asked.

That started her off again, sobbing, she said in a strained voice, "I don't know, Pippa, what should I do? Sam said he couldn't promise this wouldn't leak or be mentioned in the investigation and I should be prepared. So, I can't be sure it will be confidential, and it is a risk if I keep quiet. But, oh God, I can't tell Nelson. He would be so upset, and I love him, I love him so much. Why was I so stupid?"

Pippa wondered that herself, but she also knew that these matters were never simple, and judgment wouldn't help at all. Jade was beating herself up big time and that was enough.

"Ok," said Pippa, "well, I think you have two choices, pull yourself together and go on as normal or tell Nelson exactly what happened and hope that he will forgive you. As for Lucy, say nothing and just hope she never finds out."

"Oh, Lucy will hate me," said Jade. "It already took her ages to welcome me into the community without thinking I was some kind of gold-digger and now, I have gone and proven her right, I am not good enough for Nelson."

Pippa thought about what Jade was saying. She was less concerned about Lucy's distress for Nelson and more because what Jade had just told her gave her motive if you wanted to look at it that way, for James, for his death. That was the thing she was worried about, that Lucy would seek justice from Jade, without the evidence. *Surely that is why Sam spoke with Jade also,* she thought.

Pippa took a gentle tone. "Jade, did you see James this summer? Did you see him that night he was killed?" She asked.

Jade looked up at Pippa with a gaze like steel. "Did I kill him, you mean? Fair question, I guess but honestly, no. I hadn't seen James this summer and I never saw him on the road that night, but I know it looks bad."

Pippa believed her. Nothing she knew about Jade until now had ever suggested she wasn't honest. "So, about Nelson then?" Pippa asked.

"I don't know, I really don't know what to do," Jade said in anguish. "I can't lose him, Pippa; he is the love of my life."

Pippa understood. It was an awful predicament and what could possibly come of it now that James was gone. It wasn't as if they were carrying on behind Nelson's back in a relationship and it most definitely wouldn't happen again. On the other hand, if she were in Nelson's shoes, she would want to know, wouldn't she?

Pippa couldn't believe she was going to say this. "Don't tell him," she told Jade. "Just hope it doesn't come out. But don't tell him if you don't have to. It will destroy him."

Jade looked at her, wide-eyed. This was Pippa, solid as a rock, honest as the day was long, Pippa the one with the most perfect life. Pippa was telling her to lie. As if reading her mind, Pippa said, "Jade, it isn't lying if he doesn't know, it's only lying if he asks you and you say no."

Jade got the nuance even if she wasn't sure she agreed. It would be easy not to tell Nelson. She had done it for a year after all, before James was killed. Nothing would be different. She just had to hope that the photo didn't leak and the detail she gave Sam would stay with him. She knew that was a lot to rely on but somehow, it was better than the alternative. Pippa was right.

Lucy

Lucy couldn't wait for Sam to leave. She was full of grief and anger and Sam's words somehow made her feel worse. Her darling James, his death so unnecessary and premature and worse still, probably wouldn't have happened if the trough hadn't been in the grass.

She knew that asking why was not going to help, but she also knew that she needed logic and a rational explanation to help make it through. Jack left straight away to go out and work the farm and she was glad. She couldn't bear the pain in his face or the way he could barely speak to her. She also knew that part of that was out of fear of what she might respond with. Her tongue was toxic when she was stressed, she had little self-control. Even the girls seemed happy to be out of her reach, off to the grandparents as soon as they could go.

She pictured the loving scene that would be playing out. William doted on the girls and June would fuss with Christmas baking and lots of tea. She was glad that they were there for the girls and that they would find some comfort in their home.

Lucy was always one for keeping busy, particularly when she wanted to ignore her feelings or was stressed. It didn't matter what the task was, just that she was moving and being productive. She set about mopping the kitchen floor and moved on to wiping down the cupboards.

She was starting to sweat in the heat of the day and stopped briefly for some cold water, the condensation running down the glass and mixing with the perspiration on her hands.

Deciding to sit down briefly, she took a chair from the table-top, where she stood them to do the floor and sat heavily upon it with a sigh. Her wild fringe was damp and sticking out and she wiped her arm against her forehead roughly. As she had worked, she dwelt on what Sam had said.

James was hit by a slow-moving vehicle, not a fast-moving vehicle as she would have expected. She thought that was such a strange thing, unsure about what that meant.

Claire

Jack had gone to the cottage after arranging to meet Claire. He was distraught and needed her comfort and warmth. Claire had been at the shearing shed and was in a flap after her conversation with Sam, that she was yet to explain to Jack. She was dreading it, knowing it would make his tragic situation feel even worse. And God help them both, if Lucy found out.

Claire bustled into the cottage, trying to be bright and breezy for Jack's sake. He was looking older and grey, and her heart went out to him. "Come on then," she said, smiling, "bring it in." She hugged him tight and kissed him tenderly. He was receptive and she was aware that he was crying gently.

"It was so awful," he said to Claire. "James lying there, cold. He had a big bump on his head, and it just felt so final. Like he wasn't there at all. Lucy seemed to do quite well and the girls, but I just couldn't wrap my head around it. It was James but I just couldn't relate. What the hell is wrong with me, Claire? He's my son." He sobbed.

Claire straightened them both up. Looking into his eyes, she was kind but firm. "Jack, it's normal. Don't beat yourself up. You have had a big shock. I wouldn't know how to handle it. God Jack, I cry when a lamb dies. So, come on, let's get a cup of tea on and I bought you some Christmas cake. I bet you haven't had much to eat, have you?"

Jack sniffed and took out a perfectly ironed handkerchief to blow his nose. Claire wasn't at all surprised to see the ironed corners so perfect and stiff. She could barely do the washing, let alone iron it, but not Lucy, oh no, for Lucy, it was nothing. She couldn't help but feel a little smug, here was Lucy, so bloody perfect and yet, she couldn't even look after her own husband when it mattered.

Jack sat down at the little table, it had been his parents when they first married and was still a nice piece of furniture, if not a little worn. Claire made the tea and dished out some cake on paper towels. Theirs was a relationship of mutual respect and kindness, with passion, of course, but not at the expense of the foundations of friendship.

Claire never could feel guilty about it. She didn't really see it as betrayal even. They were just two people who found each other in the chaos of their lives really. Nothing planned about it, just fate. Simple as that for her.

They had things in common that made for good foundations, particularly their farms, and as Claire did a lot of the work, she was as familiar with farming as Jack in lots of ways. Mark would probably argue about that but nearly the whole village knew Claire was more of a farmer than he was.

Lucy, on the other hand, had always been ready to pitch in, plant a tree or feed a lamb but she wasn't heavily relied on like Claire was relied on by Mark. Lucy ran a spick and span house with military precision, and everything was pressed and cleaned to within an inch of its existence.

For all that though, Lucy could be desperately unkind, and her tantrums were famous in Stoney Hollow. When she wasn't spewing forth with vitriol, she could stomp and sulk with the best of them. Her cruel tongue often betrayed her desperate attempts to appear good and charitable.

Lucy was in the habit of engaging her brain more slowly than her mouth and so, there were a lot of half-finished sentences and rapid scrambles of thought. Jack learnt early in their marriage that it was useless to take Lucy on unless absolutely necessary.

The days of silent treatment or sulking were not worth it. He couldn't count the number of times his dinner was nearly thrown on the table and the doors had been slammed. Even when the children were little, Lucy didn't curb her behaviour and for some blessed reason, Jack was fortunate that the children didn't repeat those habits.

Instead, they had his calmer disposition, tolerance and goodness, which helped calm the house and keep Lucy from blowing her gasket too often. Their rolled eyes, however, did not escape him, and he was at times pleased that they had not fully given in to their mother's military ways.

He looked across at Claire lovingly and was grateful that she was with him in that moment. Claire was the salt of the earth. A genuine person who wasn't anything other than what she seemed. She wasn't complicated but had a big heart and appreciated simple things.

Jack didn't feel he had to live up to anything with Claire and he hoped she felt the same with him. Claire smiled back at Jack as she sipped her tea. She would never have imagined herself with him like this but somehow, they had found each other, and she loved his hardworking honest ways and his kindness.

Claire felt so valued with Jack. He didn't make fun of her when she got words wrong or made silly comments. He didn't pick on her dress sense or tell her off. He liked to discuss the farm and the sheep with her, and they both enjoyed talking about their children.

They didn't often talk about their spouses though. In some ways, they felt irrelevant in their relationship, but also, they both respected the boundaries of those partnerships and of their own.

Claire packed away the tea things and came back to Jack, putting her arms around his neck and kissing him gently. Jack stood up and embraced her fully. He found her neck and covered her in feathery kisses and then found her mouth and opened his to her with warmth.

Claire felt the passion in her build, and she pulled at the buttons on Jack's shirt, running her hands over his chest. His breathing changed and he pulled her closer, holding her buttocks in his cupped hands.

Jack grabbed Claire's hand and gently led her to the bedroom. He lay her delicately over the bed and moved to undress her, caressing her in careful strokes. Claire felt for him, feeling the small of his back and the muscles that held him strong in her hands.

His kisses were deeper now and more urgent and she responded, arching herself towards him and wrapping her legs around his waist. He whispered her name as he found her softness and they joined together in a knowing rhythm. Claire felt the deepness of his touch and he stiffened. Waves crashed over them both and brought them together a sense of pleasure and peace.

For a short time, they slept. It was the first proper rest Jack had been able to get since James was found and he needed it. Claire woke first and gently woke Jack. It was late in the afternoon, and she needed to be getting home to organise dinner for the children and Mark and to prepare food for the next day when family would visit.

Jack was startled when he first woke and then his face flashed with recognition and then pain as he remembered his reality. "I can't do it, Claire," he said. "I can't go home and face Lucy."

Claire understood but she also knew it was what must be done. Lucy would wonder where he was and the last thing they needed was any trouble. And then, Claire remembered she hadn't told Jack about her conversation with Sam.

"Jack," she started, "it is important that you go home to Lucy and the family. Not just for them but for us as well. I forgot to say that Sam came to ask me questions today. He pushed me about the time that I got home, and I got all flustered."

"You know how I can't think straight under pressure. I told him the truth, Jack; he knows I was with you."

Jack was wide awake now and surprised. "What do you mean you told him, Claire? Did you tell him everything?"

Jack's head was spinning. What on earth would happen now with Sam in the picture? Did he plan on telling Lucy? Should he tell Lucy instead? What about Mark? Claire was afraid of him finding out.

"I'm so sorry, Jack, I didn't give him details but I did say we were here together. I just didn't know how else to answer his questions and he pushed me for an answer and well, fiddlesticks, I just folded," she cried.

Jack didn't really mind. His world was so far from okay that another complication didn't seem to make any odds. "It's ok, darling," he said sweetly, "don't worry about it. If it helps find out what happened to James, it's the right thing to do."

Claire was relieved. She had expected what always happened with Mark, that he would scold her and say she was stupid and that he was a fool to have married her. Jack, on the other, did none of those things. He pulled her to him and hugged her tightly, giving her all the reassurance she could possibly need.

Claire remembered the other thing about the morning then. She looked up at Jack and said, "I forgot to say, Sam thinks James knew about us."

Lucy

The next day, after spending the morning going through photos with Amanda and Anna, Lucy had busied herself over the afternoon with all manner of Christmas preparations and funeral arrangements. She didn't, for the life of her, know where Jack was, and truth be told, she didn't much care for all the use he was to her.

She had never been able to reconcile how emotional he was with his background or her expectations of a man. In her mind, men should keep a stiff upper lip and be the backbone of the family in a crisis, not the limp soggy mess Jack seemed to become every single time things went pear-shaped.

Oh well, Lucy sighed, as she tucked the last of the Christmas presents under the tree. At least she was organised and didn't need to worry about last-minute rushing about for Christmas Day. She had presents for everyone, some extras in the cupboard for surprises if needed, the baking tins were nearly full and all of the groceries for the meals over the Christmas period were in the pantry.

To Lucy, this was a satisfying achievement. Others might see it more as a coping strategy, avoidance of the real challenge of the moment, a way of managing what could only be the deepest of grief.

Tomorrow was Christmas Eve. James' funeral was at 11am, dinner with the family and Jack's parents was at 6pm and the family, or those who would go with Lucy, would go to midnight mass. It was tradition for Lucy, and she had been to mass since childhood, always enjoying the excitement of it all and then coming home to tuck up in bed and wait for a visit from Santa.

Lucy had a childhood of privilege and she never had to doubt that the jolly fat man would make his way down the chimney and bring her exactly what she had wanted and then some. It was a magical time and she loved it, even though her personality didn't necessarily always manage to replicate that magic for her own family in the way she imagined it might.

Over the course of the afternoon, the girls and both husbands had gone to the swimming hole on the farm for some sunshine and respite before James' funeral tomorrow. Lucy had encouraged it, mostly because she wanted to be on her own while she wrapped presents and got prepared for what was to come.

She also had hoped to catch Jack to discuss how they might get through the next few days and what his plans were so that she was not surprised by his presence or in fact, more likely his absence.

When Jack didn't arrive back at the house until after the girls were home, that opportunity was lost. Lucy was pretty sure Jack had avoided being home on purpose. She was wise to what she called his lack of addressing matters face on and she wasn't surprised.

Not the kind of behaviour she expected of the men in her family, but that was Jack, never quite measuring up to the family patriarch that she had expected of a husband.

Lucy was in her comfort zone when he did arrive, standing at the sink, scrubbing new potatoes from the garden that she planned to boil and serve with a large Caesar salad and the two roast chickens she had in the oven. The kitchen was large but warm in the late afternoon and her wild fringe was sticking to her forehead, damp with sweat.

"Oh, so you decided to come home, did you?" Lucy said sarcastically as Jack came in the back door. "Nice of you to grace us with your presence, Jack. It isn't as if we might need you around here with everything that is going on, but at least the sheep are well looked after," she sneered.

Jack was not surprised to find her in this kind of mood. He was thankful the girls and their husbands were out of ear shot, for that would have been embarrassing, but with just Lucy and him in the kitchen, it was just typical.

"Lucy, if you need me to be somewhere, just tell me, I am not a bloody mind reader!" He exclaimed.

"Mind reader," snapped Lucy, "well, perhaps if you just stopped to think for a moment, you wouldn't need to be because it would be obvious that you should be here with me discussing tomorrow and making sure everything is organised."

Jack sighed. "I am sorry, Lucy that I was working on the farm, but I am here now, so please, what do you want me to do?"

Lucy didn't relent. "Well, it's all done now, isn't it Jack? I have done everything. The presents, the food, the funeral arrangements. Don't you even care about your own son's funeral? Do you even know what is arranged or does that not matter to you?"

"Alright Lucy," sighed Jack, "please can you tell me about the arrangements you have so kindly made for our son."

"Yes Jack, our son, your son," Lucy jabbed back. "Right, well, your suit is all ready, and I have ironed your white shirt to go under it with the blue tie that has tiny bees on it. You are a pallbearer with the girls, James' school friends, Lachie and Daniel, and Duncan."

"Pippa is going to do a reading, I chose one about everlasting life and freedom in the fields, and I am going to do James' eulogy. You can read it if you want to, but I am not changing it now, it's in my head, so there is no time for changes."

"James is going to be buried in our family plot, as you should have expected, so after the church, we will move to the cemetery for the internment. I have arranged the headstone and it will be ready the week after Christmas. Pippa and Claire will hand out service sheets at the church and make sure people sign the remembrance book."

"Some video people are coming from town, and they are going to live stream the service, so those who can't travel can still be with us. I have asked Mrs Hart on the church committee to do the flowers, I know James loved ferns and greenery, but I think some flowers amongst that is nice too."

"Pippa has done the catering for the spread afterwards and we will go to the hall for that. I asked for nothing Christmassy, just sausage rolls, mini pies, club sandwiches and sponge cakes because it will be after lunchtime by then and being country folk, people will need something substantial in their bellies."

Jack was embarrassed now but also hurt. Lucy had done an excellent job of all the planning, as per, but he had no part in it and it seemed now it was too late to add to what she might say about James or ensure that what was said was reflective of the warm and loving person he was.

In part, Jack knew this was his own fault, but also, he was angry that his wife didn't expect that he might have had things he wanted for James. Like most things with Lucy, Jack sighed in resignation, too late for a fight and not one he would win, so that was it. They would say goodbye to James tomorrow, Lucy's way.

"Thank you, Lucy. You have thought of everything just as you always do. Thank you," Jack said again and then he walked out to shower before dinner.

Lucy wasn't sure what she expected Jack to say but thank you wasn't at the top of her list. She was surprised he didn't push back on anything or ask to see the service sheet or the photo she had used or to hear the eulogy. She was pleased though that there wasn't any resistance to what she had prepared and reassured that she was organised and well planned.

By now, the potatoes had started to boil and the chickens were ready to come out of the oven and rest before being broken up into pieces for serving. Lucy had decided it would be nice to eat outside and she loaded up plates and cutlery to set the table on the back veranda where the evening sun's warmth was present in the shady wisteria leaves that hung over the lattice work.

The table was large and long and there was an assortment of chairs down one side and a long bench down the other. Lucy had put a red gingham tablecloth on that had little weights in the corners to avoid it blowing up in the wind. There were three small pots of lavender on the table also and two citronella candles to keep the bugs away.

The girls and their partners found their way to the table, and all praised Lucy for the setting and the garden before them. The roses were in their second bloom for the season and the scent was fantastic. Jack arrived, fresh from his shower, in t-shirt and denim shorts and he looked more lined than Lucy had seen him in a long while.

Losing James had aged him almost overnight and she was sorry. Of course, losing James was evident at the table too and his seat, well, the seat that he would have been in, was sadly vacant for all to see. Lucy brushed aside a tear at that thought and went back inside for the potatoes.

Jack knew he needed to try for the sake of his daughters. "Righto girls," he said cheerfully, "who wants a drink?" Both girls were enthusiastic in their response, suggesting white wine for dinner or maybe some bubbles and so Jack went off to find what they had and get the glasses.

The boys were happy with beer and so would Jack be, so he was glad they were easily pleased. "Just off to get the drinks," he said to Lucy as she passed him coming from the kitchen with a huge bowl of steaming potatoes, buttery with mint sprigs on the top, and his parents trailing behind.

"Make mine a G and T, thanks," she said as she passed, and Jack nodded in acknowledgement.

He would need to watch Lucy if she was on the top shelf stuff, the last thing anyone needed was Lucy full of gin and nursing a hangover in the morning. Too much to drink and her loud and difficult personality would be magnified and that was a recipe for disaster in Jack's mind. He certainly didn't want to see his daughters have to manage that. They had enough to deal with in losing their brother.

Dinner was a reasonably comfortable occasion and Jack and Lucy were both pleased to have the company of the four young ones to lighten the mood and keep the conversation flowing with Jack's parents. Both Anna and Amanda recounted stories of James, of how he could be the annoying little brother who put frogs in their beds but also of how he was great fun and always up for a laugh.

They talked of their adventures at the swimming hole, of watching James learn to drive the tractor and the Ute, and of the times when they camped out in hay barns and pretended to tap dance in the woolshed. Jack and Lucy were warmed by the memories and the bitterness of their conversation earlier seemed to melt away a little.

Pippa

Pippa was feeling a little up against it and had rung Jade for extra help. She was preparing the food for the spread after James' funeral, but she had been later starting as Duncan had taken her to the city for a surprise purchase that morning.

For ages, Pippa had talked about replacing her vehicle. She had wanted a slightly larger one with the idea of starting the boys at pony club and being able to tow a horse float. Her smaller SUV wasn't quite of the grunt required for the job and so, she had been discussing with Duncan when they might replace it.

As a Christmas surprise, spur of the moment thing, Duncan had announced that morning that they were going to the city in her vehicle and that she should take everything out of it because they were going to get it groomed.

Pippa did think the grooming idea a little odd, but she went along with it. Of course, when they got to the dealers, it wasn't for grooming at all. Duncan had bought her the large SUV she had wanted, brand-new and sparkling red with leather seats and a sunroof.

She was beyond thrilled and excited. The new car smell, the grunt of the engine and the fun of finding out about all of the features on board had made for a brilliant morning and Pippa had loved the surprise element also. Duncan had laughed at the look on her face when it finally registered that the shiny red machine was hers. He had said it was priceless and the look alone was worth the extravagance.

Pippa had to put all that to one side, however, and focus because she was under the pump to have the food organised for the funeral tomorrow. What Lucy had requested was not especially difficult but did take some time to put together and so, she needed to work into the night to get the early preparations done and then be up and onto it again in the morning to make the sandwiches and fill the sponges.

Jade was a godsend. She arrived within half an hour of Pippa phoning her and played a great role of part-time nanny to the boys and part-time chefs assistant to Pippa, chopping and mixing and setting timers. Pippa made the sausage rolls from scratch, adding in extra filling like grated apple and carrot and herbs to make the meat more flavourful and exciting.

Jade wrapped the meat in pastry and placed them on baking trays ready for baking lightly, so that they would be warmed and finish baking through in the morning.

Pippa had relayed to Jade the excitement of her morning and the new car. "It's the best present I have ever had," she explained as she gushed over the details.

Jade was excited for her. "That's so cool, Pippa. I love a new car, the smell of the leather and the feeling like you are the only person to drive it. So wonderful," she said.

Pippa showed Jade how to take the apple and carrot and extract any juice to avoid the sausage meat getting too wet for the sausage rolls. Wringing it out through a towel, Jade was surprised at how much liquid there was. She was also thinking about James and the tragic nature of tomorrow's service and the loss of a life so young.

"Are you nervous about doing the reading?" She asked Pippa.

Pippa looked up, flour across her check, and smiled. "Yes, of course," she confirmed, "but I know that the nerves will go once I get up there. Well, I hope so. I just want to do a nice job for James but for Lucy and Jack and the family too. It is such a privilege to be asked really. Quite unexpected."

"Do you know if they will do that thing that is sometimes done where others can speak if they want to?" Jade asked.

"No," said Pippa, "I am unsure about that. Why, did you think you might speak?"

"Oh God, no," said Jade. "I am hopeless at doing that, I will struggle not to sob from the moment the coffin comes in, let alone speak at all. No, I just wondered who else might want to talk, you know, it's always quite interesting to see who comes forward. Maybe the person responsible could confess."

Pippa hadn't thought of that possibility, and she wasn't sure it was possible at all really. "That's an interesting thought, Jade! Do you think someone might get really emotional and be coerced into a confession?"

"I don't know," said Jade, "but I guess we will find out tomorrow."

"Have you said anything to Nelson about James?" Pippa asked.

Jade knew she meant about that day in the stables, and she hadn't. "No," said Jade, "I am just going to wait and see what happens. He might never need to know, and I would prefer it that way."

Pippa wondered if that was a big risk, even though she thought it best, but she didn't say. She nodded and went back to mixing her sponge. She felt sorry for Jade in a way, having made such a mistake, and Pippa did think that she loved Nelson genuinely and didn't want to lose him.

"Mum, Mum," the boys yelled as they came in the house with dirty knees and cupped hands. "Look what Dad found us," they said with delight as they showed Pippa and Jade their handfuls of tadpoles.

"Dad says if we look after these guys really good and feed them and everything, they will turn into frogs," said Archer.

"Can we, Mum, can we look after them and see them get to be frogs?" They pleaded.

Pippa laughed. "Well, so long as you do look after them. When I was young, I forgot about mine and one day, Nana came down to the laundry and there were six frogs jumping all around, she got the fright of her life!" The boys and Jade laughed, and Pippa found them an ice cream container each for making their tadpoles homes in.

Jade was great with the boys and Pippa often wondered why she didn't seem to want babies of her own. Watching her, down on the floor, fingers in the tadpole homes, talking about what to feed them and googling how long they would be tadpoles before frogs, she was in her element.

Pippa didn't raise babies with Jade though, because she knew that behind her childlike engagement with the boys, there may be something deep that she didn't want to discuss. Fertility wasn't straightforward these days and Pippa was well aware that Jade may well be hiding a desire for children as a protective coating against what she could not have.

Jade was laughing at the boys as they rolled on the floor, pretending to be tadpoles. They had pushed their legs together almost mermaid style and were crawling on their bellies with stiff arms by their sides. It took a lot of effort, but their strong wiry little bodies held together well, and they looked so funny, it was hard not to laugh as well as to admire them.

"Come on, boys," called Duncan from the front deck, "time to go and feed the dogs."

The boys leapt from their tadpole state and bounded to the door. "Can I drive?" Hunter shouted as he raced to be first to the quad bike that would take them up to the dog kennels.

Pippa laughed. Her boys loved the farm and the simple things that they did each day as much as any fancy computer game or Lego. She was glad that they enjoyed the environment and that it gave them lessons in life as well as pleasure.

"God Pippa," said Jade, "it won't be long, and you will have to lock the keys to the bikes and the vehicles away for fear of them racing off across the farm together." She laughed.

Pippa smiled. "My thoughts exactly, Jade, and I wouldn't put it past those two. One gets an idea and no matter how silly, off they go! Lead on, brother!"

Jade had gone back to chopping fillings for sandwiches which they would construct tomorrow. She thinly sliced cucumber and tomato, mashed egg and mayonnaise to go with washed and chopped cress and cried her way through countless onions for cheese and onion.

Now, she was chopping through chives for the egg and the cheese, holding the green grass like herb in thick bunches and dragging her knife satisfyingly through its end.

"Thanks for including me today, Pippa," said Jade. "I appreciate being able to do something to help, and its way better than sitting in the house thinking about how awful this whole situation is. I just keep going over in my mind what must have happened and why no one has come forward."

"I mean seriously, how can you hit a person on the road and not stop, not get help for them. I just can't imagine doing that."

Pippa looked up from her sponge tin. "I know, Jade, I am as perplexed as you. Surely, it can't be someone local. Someone local would have stopped. Wouldn't they? Poor James, such a waste of a young life. God knows how Lucy and Jack will get through tomorrow. We all know Lucy isn't the easiest at times and he must be distraught."

"You know Lucy is doing James' eulogy? She has written it herself and insists that she is going to do it. I don't even know if Jack has looked at it."

"Wow," said Jade, "that's brave of her. I don't know if I could be that brave."

"No," said Pippa, "Duncan and I were talking about doing it last night. You know, just thinking about what we would do, in their situation. I am certain I couldn't do it but then I guess if Duncan didn't, and I didn't, who would do it? It's very hard to know what you would do, I suppose."

"I keep thinking what if the person responsible is present, at the funeral?" Jade explained. "Like they feel really bad and turn up to show support but all the while, they are the person who knocked James down. That would be creepy, wouldn't it?"

Pippa hadn't really thought about that possibility at all but now that Jade had mentioned it, she did think it could happen. "I wonder if the police will go, to watch out for anything or anyone that seems suspicious," said Pippa.

"Awful that they would need to though, isn't it?" Jade said, tearing up.

"Oh Jade," said Pippa kindly, "you really do feel bad, don't you? It's ok. We all really liked James and we all deal with things differently, so don't worry. I am sure I will be tearful tomorrow too. I always am at a funeral, no matter the circumstances. I hate seeing others upset."

"Now, shall we get these next sponges in the oven; you can slice through the sausage rolls into bite-sized pieces and I will hull the strawberries for putting in the sponges tomorrow. And let's have a glass of wine, shall we; a reward for all of this hard work." Pippa smiled.

Claire

After seeing Jack that morning at the back of their farms, Claire had made her way home with the last of her Christmas shopping and a thumping headache. In her dreams, she imagined walking into her home, spick and span, ready and waiting for her to whip up a magical dinner and finish her Christmas preparations. Her reality was not quite the same.

As she came in the door, Mark was in the sitting room with his farm clothes on, drinking his third beer and reading the newspaper. Francis was playing video games in his room and Flora had watercolours all over the kitchen table where she was making 'Christmas paintings' for everyone.

The kitchen bench was crowded with the morning's cereal dishes, including flies floating in milk puddles between the leftover cereal grains, empty yoghurt pots and the remnants of toast and whatever noodles had been lunch. The wet washing was in the machine still and the dry was in an ever-increasing mountain on the side of the couch, waiting for folding and putting away or ironing.

It was clear that the farm dogs had been in the house, with paw prints all over the floor and big tail swipes up the walls. A chewed sandal was on the deck and an empty dog biscuit packet in the middle of the kitchen floor.

In her head, Claire was screaming, screaming at all of her useless family to help, clean up, keep the dogs out and have some bloody pride in where they lived, but outwardly, she said nothing. She knew that the screaming didn't work. Nothing did. No one else in her house saw the mess the way she did, and no one ever helped her clean it up, well not really.

She knew her mother-in-law thought her a hopeless farmer's wife, never having the place in order for a visit or an afternoon tea and Claire herself hated that her house was always a hovel of mess and chaos just as much.

Exhausted, Claire started her nightly routine of clearing up and cleaning before beginning to get some kind of meal on the table. Flora protested at her request to clean up the kitchen table and Claire struggled to contain her frustration as she noticed that the wrapping paper she had brought for presents two days ago now had soggy paint-smeared edges.

Tempted to bin it completely, she lifted it gently out of the puddle it sat in and popped it upright into a tall vase on the lounge room floor that would let it stand and dry.

"Francis, please finish up your game and take your things off the kitchen table if you have any."

"Not my things," muttered Francis, not even looking up from the screen.

"Alright then, finish up and come and help me load the dishwasher please," asked Claire.

"Not my dishes," said Francis.

"Mark," said Claire, "can you please make a start on the washing for me, there is wet to peg out or dry to fold, whichever you want to start with is fine."

"In a minute, love," said Mark. "I am just finishing the rural section." He grunted as he straightened out his newspaper, again without looking at her.

Claire could cry. It was hot and the house was like an oven, the flies were rampant from all of the food left about and the rubbish was overflowing from the bin. *What the hell is wrong with her,* she thought. *Bloody Lucy can keep her house and her son has just died. Why is she so capable and I am so bloody disorganised?*

Claire wiped away hot tears with an angry swipe. Sighing deeply to calm herself, she boxed on, loaded the dishwasher, cleared the bench, got rid of the rubbish and wiped up the puddles on the table. Oven on, she popped in chicken nuggets and oven fries for the children and prepared to make a steak sandwich for herself and Mark, using up leftover bread and the steak from the beast they had killed for Christmas.

As she stood in her hot, cluttered kitchen, Claire thought about Jack and the fantasy she had of one day being with him, even if it was in the tiny cottage on the farm. Of course, she knew that this was just idle thought, as the reality was she was a mother of young children and even if she wasn't with Mark, she would still have the responsibility of her kids to think about. And she did love them.

As hard as her life could be, Claire was certain of that. Her kids were her everything. Nothing would come between them. Although she did wonder how hard Mark would fight her to keep them if they did split up; most often, she decided he wouldn't fight at all. He was too lazy to be bothered.

Flora's reluctance to clear the paintings she had done from the table was outweighed by her desire for chicken nuggets and so finally, Claire could set the table for dinner. She sighed cynically when no one seemed to struggle to get up and come to the table, despite their inability to help her when she asked. But she did like coming together at the end of the day as a family and sharing a meal, and it calmed her.

"Mark," said Claire tentatively, "are you coming to James' funeral tomorrow?"

Mark looked up from his sandwich, a little perplexed. "What a strange question, Claire?" He said, looking at her with a furrowed brow. "Of course I am. Jack and Lucy are our neighbours, it's the right thing to do, isn't it?"

"Oh yes, it is," said Claire. "I agree, but I just wasn't sure you were thinking of it. Now that I know, I will iron you a shirt and make sure your church pants are clean."

"Thanks," grunted Mark. "I won't need a tie though, right; it is too bloody hot for that, Claire,"

"Alright," said Claire, "no tie. Did you hear that Lucy is doing the eulogy herself?"

"Figures," he huffed. "Lucy would have to because no one could possibly do it better in her eyes, I guess."

"I suppose," said Claire, "but all the same, won't it be very hard for her? I know it would be for me."

"Mummy," said Flora, "what's a loggie?"

Claire smiled. "Well Flora, it's a funny name for a kind of speech that you make about someone who has died. At least I think that is what it means."

"So, when I die, Mummy, will you do a speech about me?" Flora asked.

Claire smiled. "All going well, darling, we will never need to worry about that, well, not until you are very old at least."

"Good," said Flora. "I want you to have plenty of time to practice."

Mark bristled then. "Let's not talk nonsense like this," he barked, "no one is dying around here and after tomorrow, there will be no more talk of dying. James' death is very unfortunate, but it is what it is. The funeral will be the end of it—okay?"

Claire thought it was a strange thing to say but then, Mark had no patience for trivia or for ifs and maybes so; perhaps it wasn't such an out of place comment. She did think a little more compassion was warranted but then Mark wasn't big on compassion either, so she said nothing.

Dishes done and table cleared, Claire played a quick game of *Guess Who?* with the children and then folded the laundry and put the bulk of it away and the ironing in the basket for another time. Mark was on his computer in the study on the pretence of doing farm work, but Claire was pretty sure he was avoiding helping her more than anything else.

It wasn't unusual for him to exit when there were chores to be done. He was happy to mind the children, now they were somewhat self-sufficient, but that didn't come with any extras, so she always knew the children were safe in his care but that the house would be a bombsite on her return.

With the children asleep, Claire pulled out the last of their Christmas gifts for wrapping. Financially, they didn't have any particular worries, and so providing for the children with gifts and all of the other things they needed to support them was not an issue.

Engagement from their father on the other hand was problematic and while he didn't offer much input on presents or what they should have, he was generous and that was something Claire was grateful for. She didn't ever want her children to think they were hard done by or that their parents were mean with money. She wanted them to have the magic of childhood without those worries for as long as possible.

Her thoughts turned back to James. His childhood had been good from what she could see and had observed, even under Lucy's regimented mothering style. James had excelled at sports and wasn't too shabby academically as well. Claire imagined that came from Jack.

Jack seemed to be very positive about what life had in store for James and Claire was sick about how things had ended up. She couldn't believe she would be at his funeral tomorrow. It was like walking through a dream and she almost wanted to pinch herself to wake up.

Claire was dreading the stark reality of the funeral in the morning. She didn't know how to act, to ensure she was supportive of Jack but didn't overstep the bounds of their public relationship. How could she give him the love in her heart at the same time as he bore the worst a parent can imagine? Would he even see her and if he did, would he know how much she bore his pain?

Sighing, Claire packed up her wrapping things and took the gifts back to her hiding place. Her last job for the night was to decide on what to wear and to iron the things her and Mark would need in the morning. She picked out a plain navy shirt for Mark and navy pants and for herself, a black dress with zebras on the collar and cuffs and white sandals with hot pink studs along the straps. She chose a red wrap in case of a chill in the air.

    A week ago, Claire would not have imagined this situation. James dead. Jack distraught and Lucy battling on through with enormous levels of determination and perhaps pig headedness. Claire did understand though where Lucy's energy came from, that guttural desire to do what was best and right for your child. Claire felt it too. She would do anything to protect her own children, anything.

The Funeral

Jade and Nelson arrived early along with Pippa and Duncan, so that the two women could make the sandwiches and fill the sponges for the morning tea and pre-heat ovens to warm the sausage rolls. Lucy had asked for mini pies as well but Pippa just couldn't manage any more baking and so the sausage rolls were extra plentiful to compensate. Nelson and Duncan were great friends and so, they easily found a spot in the sun with steaming mugs of coffee while they waited.

The church was quiet, save for last-minute rustling of flowers and the gentle strains of organ music wafting from the sound system. Later, as people started to arrive, there would be a slide show that James' sisters had lovingly put together that walked through his life, the early years, the funny bits, his sporting efforts and family time. His consistently cheeky smile, that mop of hair and a look of health and wellness that comes from growing up in the outdoors.

The coffin would sit on a wheeled trolley and there was a large spray of wildflowers to go on its top together with James' rugby shirt and photo. Lucy had quite a job getting the stains out of the jersey, but she had pressed it well and it would sit perfectly on the shiny wooden box that she had chosen for James.

Jade worked hard alongside Pippa in the kitchen, filling sandwiches, which Pippa was then cutting and placing in layers of damp kitchen paper to keep them fresh. Jade wore a black sun dress with sheared bust and tied straps on the shoulders.

She had patent leather black sandals on her feet and her finger and toe nails were painted with a shimmery rose gold glitter. Her hair was pulled back from her face and she wore discrete makeup and a shimmery gloss across her lips.

"Nelson was feeling very sad this morning," Jade said to Pippa. "He was saying what a great help James was to him last year and how he was a credit to Lucy and Jack. Said it was such a waste to see a young man taken like that and whoever is responsible should go away for a very long time."

"Oh Pippa, I just felt so much worse when he was saying those things, you know, because of what we did, but I am also glad because he is right, James was a good person, and he did work hard."

Pippa smiled back at her friend and touched her hand warmly. "Don't upset yourself, Jade," she said, "you are right, James was absolutely a wonderful young man, and you made one mistake. Just breathe through today and respect his memory and then move on with Nelson and your life. This isn't something that deserves a life sentence, it was a mistake that is all."

Jade sniffed and nodded. Pippa was right, her stupidity should not cloud the memory of James for others. He was good, all good and she knew that. Duncan and Nelson came in then, bringing their empty cups and sniffing around teasingly for any available morsels before they went to the church.

Pippa and Jade laughed and made half-hearted attempts to bat away their advances before folding and giving them a sandwich each. "Oh aye, Nelson, don't these two make a great sarnie. Best ever, I reckon," Duncan teased with a wink.

Nelson nodded in agreement and pinched Jade's bottom as he walked behind her. "Bloody brilliant and just about as good looking as the cooks too," said Nelson cheekily.

The fun was interrupted when Anna and Amanda appeared in the doorway, both in black dresses, Anna with a capped sleeve and Amanda with no sleeves. Pippa and Jade crossed the room to embrace each of them with warm hugs and watery eyes. They looked so tiny and childlike in their grief.

"Mum wanted us to remind you about the dicky oven," said Anna quietly. *Trust Lucy*, thought Pippa, *of all the things to be thinking about, she is worried about the oven.*

"Thanks, loves," said Pippa gently, "that's really good of her to let me know."

"How is Mum doing today?" Jade asked carefully.

"She's okay," smiled Amanda, "well, you know Mum, organising us all and barking instructions but then that's normal, so I suppose it's a good thing."

They all laughed then, Duncan and Nelson included, who had been hiding somewhat sheepishly in the back of the room. "Good to hear she is in fine form," said Duncan in acknowledgement.

Pippa and Jade checked that the young women had all they needed, and they spent some time chatting about James and what fun he was. Anna was struggling visibly, and Pippa worried she would find the service very difficult. Amanda seemed more at peace but then perhaps, the reality of what had happened was yet to hit her properly and Pippa was worried about that.

"How long are you home for?" Jade asked, trying to keep the conversation flowing.

"We will be here until after New Year's," explained Amanda. "It was all planned before, well, before James, so we haven't changed anything. Our partners are here too, and we will stay unless Mum and Dad would prefer that we didn't."

"Oh lovely," said Pippa. "I am sure your Mum and Dad will be so happy you are here with them; it will comfort them to have you close."

"Yeah," said Jade. "I bet having you two around is the most precious thing for them right now. So, don't go rushing off, alright, and you can always come over and visit Nelson and I if you need a break."

Anna and Amanda smiled through watery eyes and were grateful. "Thanks so much all of you for helping and supporting us," Amanda said. "We know how lucky we are to live in this community and James did too. He always said coming home was like walking back into another world where there were so many open arms you could never escape. He meant it in a good way."

"Well," said Jade, "James was much loved and very popular. I know Nelson and I were really impressed when he worked for us last summer and he was a great sport and hard worker. The community has lost someone very special that is for sure." She smiled.

Amanda and Anna smiled back gratefully. "Thank you for being so kind," said Amanda, just like James.

"Mum won't really talk about what happened, at the moment," said Anna. "You know how she is, keeping busy with arrangements and cooking and avoiding the heart of things. Do you have any idea who might have hurt James? We just can't understand how this happened in our community and why no one has come forward. Dad isn't really talking about it either. He has been out on the farm most of the time, but then he can barely get a word in at home anyway."

Pippa's heart felt for both girls, and their situation. Having parents who were not able to talk with each other, let alone engage in difficult family discussion, was hard and she could imagine the tension in the house.

"I know it must be really hard for you all right now," Pippa empathised, "you know we all manage these things in different ways. I am sure that the police are doing all they can, but I know that doesn't really help, does it? It won't bring James back. I am sorry."

Jade, eyes filled with tears, stuttered her own apology. "I am sorry too," she cried. "I really liked James and he was good and kind. He didn't deserve this."

With that, the peace in the kitchen was lost and Lucy came marching in with purpose. "Righto girls," she shouted, completely oblivious to the conversation she was interrupting or the comfort that her children were so clearly needing in that moment.

"Come on now, your father's waiting," she barked as she herded her daughters like sheep to the door of the kitchen. "Chop chop," said Lucy, almost pushing Anna as she shuffled her through the tight doorway.

Jack was indeed waiting but not particularly for anything other than the day to be over. He couldn't face the reality of what the funeral meant, and he didn't want to say goodbye to his son, his dear son that he loved beyond words. He wanted to just melt away into the ground and hide for a good long rest, but he knew that was not possible and that Lucy expected him to put on a display of strength and unity for appearances sake if nothing else.

Thankfully, right in the moment where his flight instinct was about to take over, Jack spotted Claire in the arriving throng, and he relaxed in the knowledge she was close. Claire was such a comfort to him, and he so valued their relationship.

If it wasn't for Claire's understanding and quiet patience with him, he wasn't sure he would have survived the past few days and he knew he would need her over the coming weeks too.

Jack forced a smile at several neighbours and friends as they made their way into the church. The Patterson's, Manderson's and the Dixons had all arrived and were long established local farming families. Jack shook the hand of Mr Patel from the petrol station in town and thanked him for coming.

He looked up to see Mark standing there, hand outstretched. Jack took Mark's hand, and they shook firmly, saying nothing but acknowledging the circumstances. Claire stood behind Mark and once Mark's hand dropped from Jack's, she swooped in for a firm hug and kiss on the check.

"Oh Jack," she whispered, "I am so sorry."

Jack knew that Claire needed to be careful, for appearances sake, and it was all he could do to stop himself from grabbing hold of her and not letting her go.

She was, in his mind, the only person in his world that truly cared about his feelings and understood his grief.

She was good and kind and comforting which was just what he needed in the desperate emptiness his loss had landed him in. He smiled briefly and met Claire's eyes. "Thank you, Claire," he said earnestly, "your words mean a lot."

"Come on, Claire," said Mark, "let's go inside and get a seat." He put his hand on her shoulder to guide her away from Jack. "Don't fuss over him, girl, it's the last thing he needs, you getting all emotional before he has to face everyone."

"Yes, yes Mark," said Claire. "You are right, I suppose. I just feel so sad for him and Lucy, so sad, Mark, my heart breaks. Don't you think it's sad?"

"Of course, I do," said Mark sharply, "what a stupid question, of course it is sad."

Claire and Mark made their way into the church, and she waved at various neighbours and friends as they walked down the aisle. Duncan and Nelson were handing out service sheets to help Jade and Pippa and Claire was startled by the photo of James on the front of the sheet and how much he looked like Jack in his younger days.

Claire had never quite realised the resemblance before. Taking their seats in a pew midway down the aisle, Claire rummaged in her handbag for a sweetie and offered one to Mark. She wasn't really needing one, but she figured something in her mouth would help to avoid her saying anything stupid, and she knew Mark would appreciate it if she did manage to keep any silly thoughts to herself.

Gosh, thought Claire as Jade and Pippa came in, showing some family to their seats, they both look very sophisticated in their black. Jade had pulled her hair off her face and her dress was stunning but not inappropriate. It reached to just below her knee and she had simple gold chains at her neck.

Pippa had a more conservative look but nonetheless chic. Her hair was down and straight, with pearl drop earrings in each ear and a single strand of pearls at her neck. Suddenly, Claire felt very dowdy indeed. Her face went red, and she wished with all her might that the floor could open and swallow her up.

People had largely filled the pews and Claire was distracting herself with one of the kids' tiny toys that she had found in her handbag as she searched for sweeties. She could barely breathe at the thought of poor Jack and what he would be going through, having to say goodbye to his boy and make things work with

Lucy and her dominant ways. *How lucky*, Claire thought, *that he has his lovely daughters with him, and his parents, of course.*

Music began to play louder than the background hum had been, and the family came in down the aisle. Lucy and Jack were first, followed by their daughters and Jack's parents. Lucy's had long since passed on. Lucy wore a very sensible looking black dress that was A-line and ironed to an inch of its life.

She wore little makeup, her wedding ring and no other jewellery and shiny black flat lace-up shoes. She looked calm but older and her wild fringe was sticking out in the front like she had been resting her hand in a way that pushed it from her head.

Lucy and Jack did not touch. They did not look united. They did not look at each other. They walked, sombre, with eyes straight ahead to the pews at the front of the church, reserved for close family. They did not wave or acknowledge those in the pews as they walked. It was agonising for everyone in the room, the pain visceral and the atmosphere thick with grief.

Father McDonald stood at the front of the church and a slide show of James illustrating his life began to play on the screen behind him. He reminded the congregation of the tragedy of a life lost so young, the time of the year and what it meant to Christians and the blessing of eternal life for those who believed.

Father McDonald spoke of the grief of family and James's friends, of the suddenness of events and of how support would be needed for Lucy and Jack and their family over the time to come. There was barely a dry eye in the church, and Claire was struggling not to sob out loud.

Pippa balled up the tissue in her hand, and looked over at Jade who smiled at her through teary eyes. In the back were three police officers, including Sam and Jo, the female uniformed constable that had been with Sam when he attended Lucy and Jack's and searched James' room, and another female detective.

They had waited in the carpark until the family had made their way inside, so as not to make a spectacle of their presence and to be at least somewhat discrete. Attending the funeral of a victim like James was standard in the circumstances, out of respect for the family but also in case further information could be gleaned from the conduct of those present and the things that were said.

Sam felt particularly sorry on this occasion, for everything he knew about James so far told him he was a great lad with a great future ahead of him. The tragedy of what had happened had not escaped the investigative team and he wasn't surprised to see his colleagues wipe away a tear or two.

After readings, Lucy made her way to the front to give her eulogy. The eulogy Jack had no part in. Even in grief, taking the limelight was typical of Lucy. *God forbid she share it,* Jack thought more meanly than he intended. He knew Lucy loved James, but he knew Lucy, and having this moment was important to her. Possibly more important that the son she had lost, Jack thought with a big dose of cynicism.

Lucy made a good start, with only some minor stumbles as her mouth worked faster than her brain. She spoke about James' birth, his love of the farm from an early age, his relationship with family and his work ethic. Jack was almost relaxing, she had done so well and had been so appropriate for their son.

She went on to talk of his summer jobs, his love of coming home and his plans, for the future. And as you might expect, as she talked about those plans, her voice gave her away a little and she stammered over the words while she regained her composure.

"James just wanted to work with animals and to do something meaningful. He loved all animals, and could not stand it if one were ill-treated or hurt."

Just as it appeared that Lucy might be looking to complete her eulogy, she took an enormous breath. Her face changed to a harder version, eyes pinched and narrowed and mouth thinned. She rubbed her hand through her hair and shifted her feet.

Jack, had been listening intently but not watching Lucy, but the pause in her words made him lift his head. He knew in that moment that something was coming from Lucy that wasn't supposed to be part of the script and he braced for impact.

"So, there you have it. That is James. My boy, my precious son. Take a good look. Because someone here knows what happened to him. Who is shifting in their seat, looking nervous and uncomfortable? Can you see them? Can you see the coward? The coward who killed my son and can't bring themselves to tell me. The coward who drove away and didn't get help. The scum who thought it was ok to leave James alone and pretend nothing happened."

"Well, we are here, in God's house now. Find your courage! I want the person responsible to stand up right now, here in front of us, in front of James. Go on, do it!" Lucy frothed now as she spat out her words and aimed her fury at the congregation.

"Come on, coward, where are you? Everyone is here right now, so show yourself! Beg our forgiveness. Tell us what happened. Do it, do it, now!" Lucy yelled through angrily gritted teeth.

For a moment, no one knew quite what to do. Father McDonald was completely surprised and was trying to use telepathy to work on Jack and get him to intervene. Anna and Amanda were crying, for their brother and in embarrassment at their mother.

Pippa and Jade swallowed hard and looked at each other, questioning whether it might be them who needed to react. Claire literally trembled in shock, half-peeking out from her handkerchief at the scene playing out in front of her.

Suddenly, a large figure moved quickly from the back of the room and scooped Lucy up in his arms, leading her away. It was Sam, the detective sergeant. Jack was soon by his side and the two of them exited to a side room with Lucy, who at this point was sobbing hysterically.

"Jack, Jack," she cried. "I have to know what happened, please, make them tell us, make them confess, please." She sobbed.

Jack was overwhelmed and didn't really know how best to manage Lucy in the moment. He rubbed her back and said, "Come on Luce, it's okay now, we will find out, won't we Sam? For now, though, we need to say goodbye to James, don't we love? He deserves that right, not all this, just a nice goodbye from those who love him."

Lucy looked up at Jack. "That's right," she spat, "just smooth it over and get on with things, Lucy, because that's how Jack likes it, no fuss or bother. You never care enough, Jack, for fuss, do you? You just like things to be smooth, right Jack?"

Jack didn't argue. He stayed calm and just repeated that it was important to finish the service for James. Sam agreed and asked Lucy if she felt she could go back into the church while Father McDonald finished things for James.

Jack could see the inevitable change in Lucy immediately. She had retreated to sulk mode now. The fight was gone and in its place was a look of disdain for Jack and something that was at best reluctant compliance. Lucy looked hard and cold in that moment, and had it not been such a warm room, Jack might have shuddered.

After a quick drink of water and some kind but stern words from Sam about leaving the investigation to him, they made their way back into the church. As the door opened, the congregation stopped talking and came quickly to a hush.

People rustled in their seats and phones were pushed into handbags and pockets. All eyes were on Lucy, and many wondered what on earth was coming next.

The ever-reliable Father McDonald had spoken with Sam outside the church before Lucy and Jack came back in, and was aware that he was to wrap things up in a respectful, but reasonably quick way to ensure no further outbursts. He looked kindly on Lucy and Jack, as they took their seats, and started to talk through the committal.

Anna and Amanda cried softly, looking tiny in the pew between their larger husbands, and then with extreme effort they joined the other pallbearers as they made their preparations, taking their places at the casket.

Anna went to take her mother's hand as she had passed her. While she wasn't much feeling like caring for her mother, she did appreciate the moment and her grief and so wanted to provide some comfort.

Lucy, however, was not in the mood for receiving comfort, and she snatched her hand away from Anna with disgust. Pippa saw it happen and was sure she had never quite seen something so harsh in such a sad circumstance as Lucy's reaction to her daughter.

A sole piper played as the casket was walked down the aisle of the church and out to the waiting gravesite, where generations of Jack's family had been laid to rest. Anna and Amanda placed a small posey of forget-me-nots, the last in the garden, on the casket and held each other, weeping silently as others came to pay their respects.

Some of James' university friends broke into impromptu song, singing their university song with pride. The young men holding stiff upper lips and shaking hands, while the young women sniffed and wiped away big teardrops. There was a lot of smudged mascara and blowing of noses.

After what seemed a very long time, Father McDonald blessed James one last time and the coffin was lowered into its earthy resting place. Lucy and Jack stood forward then and took the first of many roses Lucy had cut from the garden, throwing them down into the grave onto James' coffin.

They stood close as others did the same and were last to walk away from the gravesite and their son for the last time. Lucy was dry-eyed. Jack was not. He felt like his heart might stop pumping at any moment, and that if it did, he wouldn't even mind. Lucy felt angry. Someone did this to her boy and she would not stop until she knew who, and why and how they would pay.

Claire was gasping for a cup of tea, and she had happily volunteered to get cups for some of the mourners who were less able to manage on their own. She poured tea for the retired school principal and his wife, for the great-aunts on Jack's side of the family who were in their late 80s now and were spinsters who never married, for old Mr Thomas and his son Nigel from the local hardware store and for Evelyn Print who had been the dental nurse in the district for fifty years before her retirement.

"Gosh that is hot work," Claire said, as she spoke with Jade in the kitchen. "Lovely service, wasn't it Jade, well, apart from, well, you know, but lovely all the same. James was such a nice boy, great with those animals."

Jade was busy getting sausage rolls from the oven and trying not to burn herself. The delay in the service meant they were extra hot, and she wasn't that keen on blistered fingers.

"Take some of these rolls, will you Claire and pass them around. Lucy will go spare if she thinks there isn't enough food, so make sure you put them in front of her as well. Who knows, she might even be hungry," said Jade.

In truth, Jade was struggling with the whole funeral thing and the sadness she was feeling over James. She wasn't in love with him, of course, but she did really like the young man and she felt something for him and the way his life was so cruelly cut short.

Also, she found Claire going on about trivia just a bit grating while she was feeling emotional, so she was glad to give her something else to do that got her out of her hair.

"Jade," said Pippa as she unwrapped more sandwiches, "you doing ok, love?"

Jade smiled and thought how typical of Pippa it was for her to think of others when she might just as well have been feeling for herself, flat out in the heat of the kitchen with very little in the way of fresh air.

"Oh Pippa, I am fine thanks," said Jade, "just trying to avoid burnt fingers and thinking about James really. Such a sad thing to have happened to such a great young man."

"I know," said Pippa. "I just keep thinking how awful it is and of how I would feel if it were either of the boys. Lucy must be really struggling."

"And did you see Jack?" Jade asked. "He looked so broken and so lost when Lucy went all crazy on him. Like he wasn't quite sure what to do with her and like he wasn't sure he wanted to do anything at all."

"Yes, completely lost, isn't he?" Pippa said. "Poor man just lost his son, and he can't even grieve without his wife going off the deep end at the funeral. How unfair! Hopefully, Lucy's outburst won't be all he remembers of this moment, because there were some lovely things that were said and the photos of James were wonderful."

"And you did a great job with the reading," said Jade, smiling at Pippa.

Claire was back then with an empty platter. "Sausage rolls are going down a treat. I think Lucy is feeling a bit better, she is talking with the police and Jack and Anna said that she had a little something to eat, which is a good sign, isn't it?"

Pippa smiled. "That is great to hear, Claire, Lucy certainly was a little wound up, so good to hear she is getting some food in and talking to people who can help," she commented.

"Yes," said Claire, "I was so worried for Jack when she got off track at the front of the church, I was thinking, well, here she goes and what will Jack do? I mean, who can do anything when Lucy gets upset like that. Poor man. The things he must have to cope with."

"Claire," said Jade, "I reckon Jack is pretty used to Lucy by now. It must have been hard to cope with because of the circumstance and losing James, but I am sure he knows how to help her."

"Oh, of course he does," said Claire, feeling a little foolish that she had perhaps suggested more than she should have about Jack and Lucy. "Of course, he does, he is her husband, of course he does."

Because it was Christmas Eve, the funeral completely finished up at the church. There was no following on to the farm for further sharing of memories of James. Lucy had been deliberate about that, as she planned to attend midnight mass later and she didn't want people drinking at her home and then on the road.

Christmas was a time for families, and she wanted people to be with theirs rather than grieving with hers. This meant that she and Jack had stayed until the last of the mourners had left before heading on their way back to the farm.

Pippa and Jade did the same and helped clean up the kitchen and load food and other bits and bobs into Lucy's car. Duncan and Nelson had kept Jack company and they were doing well at keeping his mind off James with chat of livestock prices and other farming business. Claire and Mark had gone on home just a little before the last of the crowd and she was also planning to attend mass at midnight.

Pippa gathered up her things, and Jade helped with a large load of platters that came from Pippa's kitchen and had helped plate up the sandwiches and other food. They both stopped to talk to Lucy, who was standing with Duncan, Nelson and Jack as they discussed plans for Christmas Day.

"Lucy," said Pippa and Jade in unison.

"Lovely words you said about James," said Pippa. "You really captured him and his big loves, special memories for sure."

"Thanks," said Lucy, subdued.

Pippa and Jade carried on to the rear of Pippa's new car. She was still getting used to the modern gadgets and the way she could wave her foot under the bumper and make the boot open. Jade was laughing at her as she did it, teasing. Neither saw Lucy moving at a pace from her previous position until she was upon them.

Getting up into Pippa's face, she spat, "Where is your car?"

Pippa was surprised and didn't really understand the question. She stammered, "This is my new car," to Lucy who was looking like a woman possessed.

"Why did you get a new car?" Lucy screamed, which made the men look in her direction to see what was going on.

"What do you mean, Lucy?" Pippa said. "I got it this week."

"This week!" Lucy spat. "This week! Well, that is a hell of a coincidence, isn't it? You get a new car this week, just after my son is killed by a car just up the road from your place. What do you say about that then?" Lucy sneered.

Pippa realised what Lucy's problem was now and she was horrified. "Oh no, oh my gosh, no, Lucy, my new car has nothing to do with James, I promise."

"Oh really," said Lucy in disbelief, "nothing to do with James, you say. Then, why did you buy a new car this week, of all weeks Pippa? Just felt like it did you, or did something happen in the old one, something terrible that you are trying to hide."

Pippa felt sick, mortified and almost unable to respond. "Lucy, it's not, it's not—"

"It's nothing to do with James, Lucy," said Duncan's voice from behind them as he walked to Pippa. "I ordered the car for Pippa in October, and it arrived this week. She knew nothing about it. It was a surprise. It is nothing to do with James, Lucy, I am sorry, but you are barking up the wrong tree here."

Lucy looked at Duncan, wide-eyed. "You would say that, wouldn't you Duncan, anything to save your Pippa," she hissed.

"No Lucy, that isn't it," said Duncan, again in a very calm and non-confrontational manner. "I bought the car in October, Lucy, you can check, it has nothing to do with what happened to James, I assure you. I understand how it might look to you, but Pippa is your friend, Lucy, you know her, she is honest and kind, the car has nothing to do with James."

With that, Lucy gave up. She slumped down into a sitting position on the grass and put her head in her hands, pushing her wild fringe upward. Lucy sighed. "Okay," she whispered. "The car is nothing to do with James. Jack, I want to go home."

Pippa

Pippa was shaken and embarrassed by what had happened with Lucy. Duncan drove them home and they would pick up his vehicle at midnight mass that night. Pippa hated the thoughts that Lucy had put into her mind, but she needed to check that Duncan was telling the truth about ordering the car in October. The thing was, if he wasn't, she was worried he thought she had killed James too.

Trying to pick her moment, she asked quietly, "Duncan, you know you told Lucy you ordered the car in October, did you?"

He smiled at her and explained, "Why, Pippa, what if it wasn't?"

"What do you mean, what if it wasn't?" Pippa said. "Don't do that, just tell me. If you told a lie about it, then tell me because I think that means you think I might have killed James, and that makes me scared."

Duncan pulled the car to a stop. "Pippa, I am sorry," he said. "I didn't connect those dots at all. I was just teasing you. Of course, I ordered the car in October. You can't just buy a new car these days without ordering one in advance, it doesn't work like it used to. I ordered the car in October, and it just happened to arrive this week."

"That is all there is too it. As for the crazy notion that I might think that you hurt James, that is ridiculous. I know you didn't hurt James; you couldn't live with yourself if you had, and I know you would tell me something like that straight away. So, we're good, right?"

Pippa was relieved. She hated the thought that Duncan might doubt her in some way. "Yes, so good," she said, exhaling. "We are really good. Poor Lucy though. She really is looking for the person responsible for killing James in every possible place. It is like it's driving her mad. She will be a handful until she gets the truth that is for sure. I hope that happens soon."

"Yes, the sooner, the better, aye," said Duncan. "Poor old Jack can't put up with that kind of behaviour for very long without it having some serious impact on his well-being. She needs to get some help."

"Do you think we should tell the police?" Pippa said. "You know about what happened and about why we got the car this week? I just think I might feel better, Duncan, if we did that."

Duncan scratched his chin while he thought. "Well, we have nothing to hide, so, of course, if that is what you would like to do, we can, Pippa, no problem. Of course, Lucy might have already given them cause to seek us out anyway, but sure, let's front foot it with them after Christmas."

Pippa felt relieved, and then, she felt wrung out. She was definitely going to have a bit of a rest if she was going to make midnight mass. She slunk back in the seat of her new car and enjoyed the ride while Duncan steered them ably home.

Jack

Jack couldn't wait to get home to the farm and away from Lucy. It had been a humiliating day. First, her stunt with the eulogy and then that business over Pippa's new car. He just couldn't take it. Yes, Lucy was grieving, yes, James was killed, and it was the worst thing ever, but for God's sake, it was not an excuse to destroy every relationship with every person they had ever known.
Why the hell was she always so extreme, putting her big foot in her mouth and pushing people so hard? It was enough, he had had enough, she couldn't go on doing this.

It took Jack all his time to even look at Lucy. She sulked as he drove, and he was grateful she didn't even try to apologise or reason about her behaviour. He couldn't have handled that. As they came in the gate, Lucy picked up her things and it was clear she was going straight inside. Jack knew there was food to be taken in, so he had no choice but to do that, so that it didn't spoil.

Lucy had slammed the door to the bedroom, and Jack knew that meant he wasn't welcome. After putting the food away and seeing no one else was around, he changed into some work clothes from the laundry and filled a water bottle. There was only one place he wanted to be and that was out on the farm, away from the house and the drama of the day. He whistled to his dogs and they jumped into the truck, and he set off.

His favourite place was the back of the farm, and it shared a boundary with Claire and Mark's place. Sometimes, she would be there, tending to troughs or feeding out and they would meet and talk. He hoped she might be around this afternoon, but he was also content with closing his eyes for an hour or so and just being at one with the land.

He and James had been the same in that way and so, he felt close to James when he was out there without anyone else but the dogs for company. The dogs that James had also loved and dotted on.

James had been a fantastic son. Exactly the kind of son that a man like Jack was proud of. Great all-rounder, loved his sport, was well-liked, had a career plan and wanted to be on the land. He loved that James understood what the land meant and why the farm was important to the family, he loved that James valued it and that he had a feeling for nature and animals.

When James was small, Jack had spent a lot of time teaching him how to fish, drench a sheep, work in the sheering shed and dock lamb's tails. They went hunting rabbits and possum, shot deer and caught eels and trout. They talked about the environmental projects they wanted to do on the farm, restoring the bush and cleaning up the water in the rivers and streams.

They planned for the seasons, researched new ways of doing things and enjoyed the odd beer together. James wasn't just a son, he was a great friend, and Jack knew his life was forever changed without him. The loss was like his stomach was hollowed out and would never be full again and he physically ached, his pain was that raw.

Jack took his water bottle and hat and found a comfortable spot on the grass beside the boundary of Mark and Claire's and the bubbling stream that was the water source for both farms. He skimmed a pebble across the water and dipped his toes into the chilly depths. A great transition from the warmth of the day that was belting down onto his back from the sun above.

This spot was just to the side of where Jack had taken James for his first camping trip when he was about three years old. They had left Lucy at home with Anna and Amanda and came up to this part of the farm one summer afternoon.

Jack had taught James how to fish that day and they had caught a lovely trout. James was delighted by the rainbow skin of the trout and Jack had used a gas hob to fry the fish so they could eat it, as the conditions were too dry for a fire. James had loved it, even though he cried when he realised the fish could not live if they wanted to eat it.

"Don't like that, don't like dead fish like that, Daddy," he had said with big tears rolling down his cheeks.

Because it was summer, and the night was warm, they had slept outdoors in just their sleeping bags rather than put up the tent. James had been excited about it, until they actually went to bed and the dark got the better of him. He had snuggled into Jack, and scooted down into his sleeping bag at the first sound of an animal walking in the bush behind them and stayed there all night as he slept.

Jack had loved that his son had trusted him in that moment, sought comfort from him and was happy to be in the natural environment. It was the first of many camps and they had both loved those times together.

When James was older, Jack taught him how to shoot and hunt. James loved animals and struggled to begin with at the idea that they were also pests. At first, they spent time getting James' eye in and many a can was blown off the fence at the end of the woolshed by the impact of a shot.

When Jack was satisfied that James was safe with a gun and had enough experience to kill rather than shoot and injure a poor defenceless animal, he took him hunting for real.

They had gone up to some of the blocks of the farm further away from the homestead and firstly shot rabbits and the odd possum. James was an excellent shot even as a young fellow and Jack had been proud of the way he took gun safety and shooting seriously, without being silly or inappropriate.

He respected the kills and learnt how to treat them, skin them and preserve the meat. He even made some early pocket money from his possum skins in those days, and then, as he became old enough and responsible enough, he shot rabbits and other pests for farmers in the district, making enough money for his university study or his rugby trips while he was still in boarding school.

The memories are bittersweet now, thought Jack. *I taught him to hunt and shoot and those were the very things he was doing when he died. Perhaps if he had been a city kid or we let him have more computer games, he would still be here.* He knew it was his grief talking but he smarted just the same and wished with all his heart that James hadn't been out shooting that fateful night.

Jack hadn't really turned his mind to who might be responsible for what happened to James. In some way, it was a defence mechanism and too horrific to contemplate that someone he knew might be the person who killed his precious boy.

He was grateful that it seemed as if James would have known little about it, and he found that fact of comfort. He couldn't bear the thought that James had the horror of seeing his life ripped away from him. That was too painful and too much for Jack. So yes, there was comfort in knowing that what happened had been quick. Brutal, but quick, Jack reasoned.

Jack had never felt the heaviness he did in that moment. The feeling that his very soul was strangled by some kind of huge weight. It was as if he couldn't breathe for the weight, but he knew he was breathing. He felt he couldn't stand for the weight, but yet, he knew he could, and he couldn't think for the weight, but he wished he could, in fact, stop thinking.

Stop his tortured mind from going over and over all the should-haves, would-haves and could-haves that come with such a sudden loss. So, he sat for a long time, crying, his tears like silent pearls dropping from his tired eyes, until the water from the summer stream and the tears felt blurred together and he had nothing left.

Claire

Claire was agitated. She had wanted to try and see Jack that afternoon but Mark was nowhere to be found and the kids were driving her up the wall. She felt tied to the house and wasn't enjoying it at all. It was hot, the flies were annoying, and she was having trouble getting organised for Christmas dinner the next day in between the cluttered bench and the new pile of washing yet to be folded and ironed.

Since coming home from the funeral, the kids had been scratchy with each other after spending the morning with her mother-in-law. Francis was being a right obnoxious pain and teasing Flora with all sorts of ridiculous ideas that caused her to squirm and squeal. The noise was piercing and the more she squealed, the worse Francis got.

Mark had disappeared soon after getting changed out of his funeral clothes and she imagined he was working somewhere on the farm but wasn't sure exactly. He was a terrible communicator, and she never knew where he got to or when he would be back. It made being organised impossible, or at least that was the excuse she made for herself.

Claire had done some bookwork, stuffed the turkey, steamed a pudding and got all of the vegetables ready for tomorrow's dinner. Her brow was wet with perspiration, and she felt like a limp dishcloth, all damp and flat. Secretly, she would have liked a chilled glass of wine, but she boiled the kettle for a nice cuppa and a Christmas mince pie. After that, she planned on trying to find Mark and then getting up the back of the farm to see if Jack was about.

Settling into her cup of tea and her mince pie, Claire felt a bit more relaxed. She liked Christmas time and all of the fun activities, and special treats. She was excited about seeing the kids open their presents and enjoyed sitting down together for a late lunch and all the trimmings.

She was always a little on edge with Mark's mother, but she wasn't going to let her worry her this year, she would just sip away quietly on some specially purchased bubbles and let it all go past her.

Claire fiddled with the little metal pie dish that the Christmas mince pie came in, folding it upon itself as she drank the last of her tea. *Where the heck has Mark got to*, she mused, as she imagined Mark up to his knees in mud, pulling out some old ewe, cast in a hole or behind the tractor playing heavy metal while feeding out.

Getting up from the cluttered table, Claire yelled to the children, "Kids, I am just going to see if I can find out where Dad is," and she popped on her boots caked in dried mud and closed the back door.

The shearers had completed their work and packed up that morning, about to get on the road for the holiday. Usually, Claire would have been there to wave them off, but she wasn't this time, as, of course, she and Mark went into James' funeral. *Best head down and check all is well with the quarters,* she thought, thinking then that she might find Mark nearby, checking over the shed.

The quarters were built in about the 1940s and were very basic. Claire had put new curtains in them three winters ago but apart from that and a new stove and washing machine, they were pretty much as they were back then. The shearers came with their own bedding and towels and there was a large washing machine in the laundry and three washing lines out the back.

A shower block with four toilets was on one end of the building with the shared kitchen living area and several bunk rooms following on. Of course, in the days that they were built, there were only men in the gang but now, there were also women and so, a single toilet and shower had been added to the end of the shower block to accommodate female ablutions.

The concrete outside the quarters was freshly swept and all looked tidy and clean outside. Claire walked into the kitchen and saw that the stove was clean, and the fridge was empty, slightly ajar and left on. The room was tidy and there was firewood in the basket.

Claire was impressed. She hadn't expected the quarters to have been left so clean, and she was pleased. It saved her a job for one thing, although of course, she had better check the bunkrooms and the showers and toilets too.

It was about then that Claire heard a noise, a sort of metal sound. She wondered if perhaps there was still a shearer somewhere in the building and she was going to call out when she heard a man's voice, well, not really a voice but a kind of grunting.

Claire was thinking this was most peculiar and that all the shearers really should have left when, as she came to the second bunk room in the row, she found the source of the noise.

In front of Claire was a bare bottom, blue jeans at the knees and a belt buckle swinging rhythmically to and fro. The blood rose to Claire's cheeks, and they burned red hot even before she could find her words. She knew now what the grunting was all about, and time stood still.

Somehow, the man in the jeans sensed her presence, spinning himself around to face her. It wasn't until then that she got a view of the other bottom in the twosome. She would know it anywhere. It was Mark.

Claire threw her hand over her mouth as her mince pie came to the surface and she raced from the quarters to breathe in fresh air and rid her eyes of the image burnt into them. She retched and retched, in part from shock and in part from the confronting image she had been surprised by.

Her head swam and she thought of Jesus, of Mark's mother and of the kids. She felt the ultimate betrayal, the sting of deceit and the gut-tugging shame. Quickly, Claire pulled herself together somewhat, and tried to make sense of the scramble in her head.

Mark wasn't gay, was he? She thought. Then, she thought something worse, oh dear lord, he was raping Mark, that was it, Mark wasn't enjoying it, he was forced. Then again, she thought, no, he wasn't forced because he would have fought, no, he was enjoying it and she knew it. She knew he was enjoying it because the grunting, that wasn't the man she saw first, it was Mark.

Claire felt ridiculous. All these years of keeping up the farm, washing, cooking, cleaning, helping the kids, putting up with Mark's mother, all of it was a lie. Her husband didn't want her. He never had. He was gay. He loved men. How could she not have known?

Mark appeared outside then, still buckling up his pants. Claire heard a car pull away from the back of the building and she was glad she hadn't seen the man leave. She might have thumped him given half the chance.

"Claire," said Mark, his voice full of reason, "what the hell did you come down here for, aye? If you don't fuss now, we won't have to go over this, will we love? Just forget it, it's nothing, Claire, nothing."

Claire tried to listen to him, but the words wouldn't go into her head. "Nothing," she spat back at him, "nothing! Well, if it's nothing, Mark, let's go now and tell your precious mother all about it, shall we? Nothing, my bum, or sorry that should be your bum! How long, Mark, just how long have you been doing this kind of thing? I deserve to know that at least, don't I? I am your wife, Mark; in case you hadn't noticed!" Claire fumed.

Mark mumbled, "Always, it's always been part of my life, Claire. I am not gay, Claire, but I do like sex with men from time to time. It's really not a big thing. It's not an affair, they aren't boyfriends. It's random. One-offs."

"Oh," said Claire, trying not to yell. "Oh, so that means it's okay, does it? You do that with men from time to time but it's ok because they aren't your boyfriends. Well, how the heavens do you think I process that, Mark? You know I have trouble understanding these things, for heaven's sake, what is wrong with you?"

Mark sat on the grass and even though it was a dramatic moment for Claire, for him, it came with some relief. "I don't know, Claire. Is it wrong? I have wrestled with that question most of my life. I don't feel good about it, you know. Except when it happens. But straight after, I feel shame and I feel guilt and I can't deal with it. It is something in me though, something I seem to need, and I know that is mean, Claire but it's true, I do need it sometimes."

"You need it, do you? Well, have you ever thought about what I might need? Have you ever thought of that, Mark? I need help around the house and the farm, I need a husband that engages with his kids, I need a break sometimes; that's what I bloody need. And yes, Mark, I swore, I know!" She screamed.

Mark looked at Claire for a long time. "I know, Claire. I know you need help, and I am not a good husband to you. I know that. I am stupid, Claire and a while ago, I made a huge mistake and I have been terrified that you would find this out since then. I am so sorry, Claire, truly, but I can't stop, I know I can't because after my big mistake, I really tried. I did, but I couldn't stop even knowing you might find out."

Claire's head was spinning, and Mark wasn't making sense. What mistake? "You are selfish, Mark and you always have been. Why wouldn't you keep a wife who does the lion's share of the work and then go out and do whatever you call that, whenever you like? I am not surprised you made a mistake. You probably got too big for your boots just like you do at home."

"Well, I am telling you this, you are going home to the kids, you will look after them properly, you can tidy the house for tomorrow. I am going for a walk, and I will be back in time for church. If you don't want your mother to know what you have been up to, just do exactly what I have asked. I cannot be around you right now," said Claire with determination and more courage than she felt, and she strode off across the farm.

Jade

The funeral had been incredibly sad, and Jade and Nelson had been glad to get home to their peaceful piece of paradise and just relax with each other. The doors to the house were wide open and there was a gentle breeze, not more than a whisper, cutting the silence.

Nelson was thumbing through his vinyl collection, looking for some suitably moody music to relax to and Jade was curled up on the plush sofa with Poppet, a light cotton summer dress covering her to her ankles. Her eyes were still a little puffy from crying and she looked a little wrung out when compared to her usual perky self.

Nelson was worried about her. She seemed to have really taken James' death to heart and he felt helpless about it. He didn't know what to do to help her feel any better, but he wanted to try and to give her the support she needed. Perhaps it was doubly hard being away from all her family at Christmas, he wondered, and he was sorry about that too.

"Jady," he said gently, "would you like to go home for Christmas next year, love?"

Jade looked up at him with big wide eyes. "Really?" She said. "Is that what you would like to do?"

"I want to do whatever makes you the happiest, my love that is the fact of the matter, so if you wanted to be home with your family next Christmas, then yes, I want that too."

"Oh Nelson," smiled Jade, "you are the best husband ever. Let's see what the year brings, aye, but maybe we could go to my family, it could be fun. We could have a white Christmas, snuggle up by the fire, hit the sales afterwards, maybe take in some skiing somewhere, ooh yes Nelson, it could be great fun babe."

Nelson was pleased his idea had picked her up a bit. He understood it must be hard being so far away from her family and yet, she never once complained about it. Jade had worked really hard to make their little place and the farm her home, and she was doing amazingly at it. He was really proud of his wife, with the way she adapted and fitted in.

"Nelson, what about the funeral today, aye babe?" Jade asked. "It was pretty full on, wasn't it? Lucy is a wreck and having a crack at everyone, and then thinking Pippa had something to do with what happened to James. I am worried Lucy is losing the plot. I mean, how ridiculous, Pippa of all people, she is the most honest person I know. Thank God Duncan was there, so calm with her and just so sensible."

"You're so right, love," said Nelson, "between Jack and Duncan, they had Lucy managed. But yes, she is in a bad way. Understandably with losing James like she has, but to go around accusing everyone, it's not going to help her, not at all."

"People around here will just shut up and then where will the investigation go. She has to get herself together, or else she will damage a lot of friendships if she keeps going. Hard as it is for her, you just can't go accusing people like she is."

"I know you're right, Nels," said Jade, "but I do feel so sorry for her, she doesn't mean to be horrible. She just doesn't have an off switch and so, her feelings come straight out of her mouth and there's no filter to them. Poor Jack must find it so difficult."

"You can see it on his face that he does," said Nelson, "but to his credit, he never says a word about it. I have never heard him complain, just gives her the odd chip here and there as a bit of a correction. Of course, then he gets the sulks from her, and I reckon that is almost worse, the silent treatment that is. Duncan reckons they can go for days without speaking to each other, just the two of them in that big homestead."

"Well, Duncan did a great job with her today," said Jade. "Just gave it to her, nicely but firmly, had all the details, clear as anything. I don't think she seriously thought Pippa was responsible for James, but she did dig in about it. Poor Pippa, I don't think she knew where to look."

"Yes," said Nelson, "it was all pretty embarrassing. Who would ever have imagined old Lucy Bossy Pants would make an appearance at James' funeral? As if whoever is hiding what happened to James is just going to say, oh yeah, over here, Lucy, you got me!"

Nelson laughed but only half-heartedly, because he also felt for Lucy, and especially for Jack. "You know, I have been thinking about it quite a bit and really, there are only two scenarios for what happened to James. Either it is a terribly unfortunate accident, or it was on purpose."

"If it was an accident, the pool of people who could be responsible is endless, but if it wasn't, then it would come down to who perhaps had some kind of axe to grind with James."

Jade looked at him seriously. "Do you think it was on purpose, Nelson? Did James have enemies? I don't know of any but then, I haven't been here long in the scheme of things. What do you think?"

"That's it, Jade. I don't really know that he had any enemies. I have been distracted just thinking about it. He was so well-liked by everyone, so it just doesn't seem as if it could be deliberate. There is only one small thing that I can recall, but even then, I don't have the details."

"Really, you think you remember something?" Jade asked.

"Well," said Nelson, "you remember last summer, and James worked for us."

Jade was nervous now; did Nelson know what happened with her and James, was this it, was he going to tell her? Jade swallowed. "Yes, I remember," she squeaked.

"He told me about a small incident he had with someone local."

Jade swallowed again, thinking whether James might have called her a small incident. "Ah ha," she said quietly.

"Yes, he said that he was with someone married and that they had gone to do a job together, and on the way back, they stopped for a drink which they had down at the river, as it was hot, and they put their feet into the water. Anyway, James was just chatting away to this man."

Jade let out a long slow breath, Nelson was talking about a man, so not about her. She was so relieved that she could feel the burn of tears forming.

"Jady, are you listening?" Nelson had walked over to her and was waving in her face to distract her. "Hello, pretty lady, are you with me?"

"Oh God, sorry babe," said Jade, "you, talking of James, just made me get all emotional again, don't mind me, carry on."

"Ok," said Nelson, "well, he was saying to me that they got a cold drink, they went to the river to drink it and put their feet in the cool water as it was hot. Anyway, they are talking and laughing about stuff, you know, kidding around like friends do, and then this man kind of stopped and looked serious and then he went to kiss James."

"What?" Jade said, surprised. "Someone, this man, I mean, he made a pass at James. Gosh Nelson, what did he do?"

Nelson put some Van Morrison on the stereo quietly and sat down opposite Jade. "He said, he pulled away from the guy, saying whoa man, what are you doing, and the guy realised his mistake and made a joke of it, you know like, ha-ha, just wanted to see what you would do, mate, no harm done kind of thing, and they finished their drinks quietly, and the guy said again that he was sorry for the joke and then dropped him home."

"And you think if James' death wasn't an accident, this guy might be responsible?" Jade asked.

"No, not necessarily," said Nelson, "but I do think if I had to say who might have a reason, it is the only thing I know of that might fit the picture, that's all."

Jade thought about it for a moment. Someone had made a complete misjudgement because James was definitely not gay, or interested in men, from what she understood. He was handsome for sure, and she could understand anyone finding him attractive, but someone's radar was seriously off on this occasion.

Poor James, having such an awkward situation to deal with, she thought. Gay or straight, those situations were always filled with discomfort and she herself had dealt with plenty of unwanted advances. But did that give someone a motive to hurt James, she wasn't sure.

"I totally understand what you're saying, Nels, but it is quite a big jump to make between awkward mistake and murder motive. Except, you say the man was married, right?"

Nelson nodded in agreement. "Well that perhaps complicates things if the guy thought that James might tell his wife maybe or tell someone else who he was or is, for example," Jade considered. "That might be a big enough threat to make someone a little paranoid and feel they need to do something, I guess. And you have no idea who it was with James?"

Nelson shook his head. "Absolutely none, babe, none, at all. James was very fair like that, he didn't tell me who it was, or even hint."

Pippa

Pippa was still smarting from the accusations Lucy had made about her new car. She was so embarrassed and the shine of the experience, having her first ever brand-new car, was lost. She almost wanted to return it now. Lucy had tarnished it with her horrible suggestion.

In her rational heart though, Pippa knew that Lucy was just hurting, and that whatever she said or did at the moment, couldn't be taken as personal. Even if Pippa did feel like giving her a piece of her mind, what Lucy was feeling was the most personal thing of all and Pippa knew that even the thought of losing one of her boys was unbearable.

Losing James must be just the worse pain imaginable and so, she had plenty of empathy and forgiveness for Lucy, when she took that into consideration. That wasn't to say Pippa didn't feel very upset that Lucy had tarnished her happy Christmas present.

Setting the day to one side, Pippa was enjoying getting ready for Christmas Eve, and she had Nelson and Jade coming over and then, they would all go, with the boys and Pippa's parents, to midnight mass before coming home and getting the boys to bed.

Pippa loved this time of the year, she loved the family coming together, sharing food with great friends and just feeling like there was a lot of love around. She was keeping the meal relatively simple tonight. Boiled new potatoes, a big green salad, hot ham, pickled beetroot, fresh minted peas and a decadent cookies and cream cheesecake for dessert with fresh berries and ice cream. It was perfect.

She had made the cheesecake that afternoon, the new potatoes could stay in their skins and the ham was all ready for its glaze, which just needed some warming through and pasting on. She would make the salad while the ham was baking and had given the boys a big enamel bowl, the kind with a blue stripe around the lip, and the peas to shuck at the dining table.

Hunter was laughing at his brother who had managed to get his peas all over the table, as he pushed a pea skin into his mouth with chubby fingers. Archer was scraping up his spilt peas into the bowl and said in a very loud exaggerated voice, "Hunter, I will tell Mum you are eating the peas," in an effort to get Pippa's attention and Hunter into some trouble.

Pippa laughed and didn't bite. She fully expected the boys to indulge, and it was a past time she had enjoyed as a child too. She liked them having these experiences and making these healthy memories. Even if they were a bit short on peas for dinner.

Duncan had been outside doing some farm work after the funeral, and Pippa knew he needed to calm down after Lucy's accusations, so it was the perfect respite for him. She heard him arrive on the quad bike and like a schoolgirl, she still got a little butterfly in her stomach on seeing him.

She loved how he took on the look of a Roman God at this time of year, his skin golden from the gradual tanning of the sun, despite the lashings of sunscreen she insisted he pile on. The tan set against his eyes and hair just made his features even more delicious and she ran to plant a kiss on his cheek.

Duncan smiled and laughed. "Is that it?" He joked. "A kiss on the bloody cheek, come here Mrs and give me a proper one," pulling at the strings of Pippa's striped apron. Pippa blushed and willingly partook of a more intense kiss, even though the boys were around. "That is more like it then," smiled Duncan as he took a handful of her bottom playfully.

"Aww," said the boys in unison. Then, "Dad, Dad, come look at the peas we are chucking," said Hunter, "it's heaps of fun, Dad."

Pippa laughed. "It's shucking, darling, not chucking," she said with a smile.

"Oh yeah, shucking," said Hunter with no less enthusiasm.

Duncan took a seat at the table and asked the boys to show him what to do. Archer was serious as he explained that you had to get all the baby peas out of the shell and into the bowl. "You can't eat them, Dad," he explained, "or there will be none for dinner."

Duncan loved that his son was teaching him and being responsible. His serious tone was betrayed by the evidence of less peas in the bowl than empty shells, but Duncan didn't mind at all.

"So, what is the plan then, Pip? What time are we eating and is everyone going to church or are these devils going to bed?" He teased.

"Daaaad!" Archer said. "You know we go to church with you on Christmas Eve night, we always do."

"Oh yeah," said Duncan. "I remember now, we take you along and one of you gets to be the donkey and one the sheep in the nativity."

"No Dad," said Hunter. "We are not doing the nativity this Christmas, the bigger kids are doing it this year, and we are singing instead."

"Oh, my mistake," said Duncan. "What are you singing?"

Hunter responded first, "We are doing two songs, *Away in a Manger* and *Oh Little Town of Bethlehem*."

"Awesome," said Duncan. "I'll bring my ear plugs."

The boys laughed, knowing he was joking, and Pippa looked on happily at her smiling brood. Leaving the boys to it, Duncan asked Pippa if she had heard from Lucy. He had half expected her to phone and apologise but he also understood that Lucy had other things to worry her and that she probably wasn't in her right mind just now.

"I thought I might call over; you know, take some of the fudge I made a couple of nights ago, but I really haven't found the time today," explained Pippa.

"No, well probably best to leave her alone today, I think," said Duncan. "After her accusations, she is probably feeling a little silly, but at the same time, they are grieving and the funeral was a lot to cope with."

Pippa knew Duncan was right, but she still worried for her friend, despite what had happened. The lines on Lucy's face and the anguish in her actions were plain for all to see.

"Did you see the police at the funeral?" Pippa asked.

"Yes," said Duncan. "I think it is routine in a case like James', but it certainly makes it a pretty sober atmosphere, doesn't it? I wonder if they have any further insight into what happened. Surely, they didn't learn anything at the funeral?"

"Well, it's hard to know," said Pippa. "I have no idea what kind of things they look for."

Duncan agreed, "Blowed if I know either, guilty looks or strange distress maybe?"

"It has to be just an unfortunate accident, doesn't it?" Pippa said quietly, so the boys didn't hear. "I mean, I can't imagine anyone wanting to do that to James on purpose."

Duncan stroked his chin, thinking. "You know, I have been thinking about that a lot. I just can't come up with anyone who would want to hurt James or that would have motive to do that. He just wasn't the kind of person to have enemies."

"I agree," said Pippa. "He was so decent, to everyone, it doesn't make sense. Unfortunately, it seems it is just a terrible accident, and someone is too scared to come forward."

"Too scared or they have something else to hide and James was just in the wrong place at the wrong time," said Duncan.

Pippa looked up at him then. "What do you mean?"

"Well," said Duncan, "why didn't they stop? If they had nothing to hide, surely, they would have stopped, right? That's what I mean, what else were they into or doing that night that meant it was better not to stop, that's really what I am saying."

Pippa had never thought of it like that. Duncan was clever, she knew that he had a brain for this kind of thing. "You're right," she said. "It could be someone who couldn't or wouldn't help for some reason and just left the scene. Why would that be though, were they drunk, drugged, were they doing something illegal at the time? It is all very odd the more you think about it."

"I agree," said Duncan. "Something just doesn't add up."

"Hmm," said Pippa as she pasted sticky gloopy glaze onto the huge ham before putting it into the oven to bake. "I hate the thought that it's someone we all know, hiding from the truth and causing our friends all this pain. It just makes me feel so awful."

Duncan scooped her into his arms then and kissed her forehead. "I know, darling, it's such a terrible time. Let's try and do what we can to make it better for everyone, okay?"

"You bet," said Pippa. "Everyone needs love at this time of year, and we need to spread it around." She smiled.

Duncan laughed. "Well yes, but not the love we have for each other, that is just ours, forever," he said, kissing the tip of her nose. Pippa melted.

"Hello," came a booming voice and everyone knew at once it was Nelson. The boys were up off their chairs fast as anything and running to him with huge bear hugs at the ready. They loved Uncle Nelson and Aunty Jade. Nelson smiled and pretended to be knocked over by the force of impact from the boys. Jade laughed and ran her fingers through their shiny locks.

"What are you two rascals up to then, aye?" She asked.

"Come and look," the twins said together. "We are shucking peas."

Jade and Nelson went to the table and admired their handiwork. "Well done," said Nelson. "I am impressed that there are any in the bowl. Did you eat many?"

Both boys smiled cheekily. "We did," said Hunter, "but not too many, so there is enough for dinner too."

"Yummo then," said Nelson with gusto. "That will be lovely."

"Ok boys," said Pippa, "you know the drill. If you are coming to mass at midnight, then you need to have some rest. Choose some books and go and get on your beds and read quietly until dinner time please. We can't have you conking out halfway through *Away in a Manger*."

The boys protested mildly, but a serious look from Duncan was all it took for them to do as they had been asked. Pippa half expected that she would find them asleep in about ten minutes, given how much they had been doing over the day and the energy they had expended.

Pippa and Jade stayed in the kitchen but in earshot of the dining table as they made the salad. This meant they could drink their wine and add into the men's chatter when they wanted to. Jade was concerned about Pippa.

"You okay after today?" She asked her friend gently while chopping cherry tomatoes and crunchy celery. "Lucy was pretty full on."

"Oh," said Pippa, "yes, I must admit I was a little shaken afterward, and it has taken the shine off the new car, but I do understand, and I feel so sorry for Lucy," spinning the lettuce in the salad spinner.

"You are so kind," said Jade. "I would have wanted to lamp her one." She laughed. Pippa laughed too and it felt good to have fun and humour around the house after the funeral earlier.

"Have you heard anything about the investigation?" Pippa asked.

"Nothing, but we were talking at home, and surely, it has to be an accident, don't you think? We can't really think of anyone who would be out to hurt James," Jade explained, dropping her chopped vegetables into a big white salad bowl.

"Yes that is what we think too," Pippa said, "but then, we can't figure out why the person didn't stop and get help if it was just an accident."

"You are right," said Jade. "We had a similar conversation about why that might be and motive for hurting him, you know, but we can't come up with anything much."

Pippa noted the 'anything much' part of what Jade was saying. "Jade, what do you mean, anything much? Do you have an idea?" Pippa asked with a quizzing look on her face.

"Not exactly," said Jade, "it's more drawing an inference, I suppose. You know, putting two and two together sort of thing."

"Ah ha," said Pippa, "so, spill then."

Jade whispered then, "Ok but I am not sure I am supposed to mention it, Nelson only told me earlier this afternoon."

Jade went on to explain the story that Nelson had told her about the married man that had made a pass at James the summer before. Pippa was very surprised. She had heard nothing about this before and she couldn't imagine who that man might be. She knew for sure it wasn't Duncan, no question in her mind, but who could it be.

"I guess it's dangerous to speculate but who could that be, Jade, do you think it's anyone we might know?" Pippa asked.

Jade shook her head. "No, well, we don't know for certain, but we can't think of anyone we know that might have acted in that way. Not that we have an issue with any kind of sexuality, but we just don't think we know anyone who is male, married and attracted to men."

"Well," said Pippa, "it's a bit of an old-fashioned mystery then."

Claire

Claire was puffing and walking very fast. She couldn't stop and her head was just swimming with what she had seen, and then heard from Mark. She must be incredibly stupid, was all she could think as she strode out over the hills. How could she have been with Mark, all of this time, and not ever once thought that he might have such a secret.

It was ridiculous! Thinking back on it, some of the signs where there, perhaps subtly, but all the same, if she had half a brain, it might have occurred to her. She felt more stupid than ever. Mark had completely duped her!

Of course, in the scramble of her traumatic discovery, Claire was also aware that she had her own secret. Although in thinking about her affair with Jack now, it seemed even more justified than it had before. She was married to a pig, so, of course, she would need comfort and companionship from another man. It was to be expected really, she reasoned.

And then, what about the children? Her kids. The ones she had nurtured, cared for, fed, picked up after, tutored, coached and cheered on. What about Francis? Was his father attracted to him, was he safe? *Oh God,* thought Claire, *he is with them now, is that okay?*

Was being attracted to other men the same as being attracted to male children? She didn't know. *Why am I so dumb?* She thought as she kept walking towards Jack.

Puffing, she reached the boundary fence and the rickety style that she used to climb from her farm to Jack's. Jack was dozing near the water up against a log. He looked peaceful and content and Claire hated to wake him. But as if he had half an ear on the fence, he heard her coming and opened his eyes to squint in the late sun. Sitting up, he groaned a little from being stiff, but he found a warm smile for Claire all the same.

"Hi, you," said Jack sleepily. "I wasn't sure if you would come up today."

Then, he looked at Claire properly and could see that all was not as it should be. She was distressed and he could tell she had been walking hard and she was puffing too. Claire started to cry and then sob. Big raindrop sized tears fell from her cheeks and Jack opened his arms and hugged her tight.

She couldn't catch her breath and he calmly looked into her eyes and sat her so that she could put her head between her knees. "Just breathe in through your nose and out through your mouth, darling," he soothed calmly, slowly getting Claire to calm down enough to recover a normal breathing pace.

"Ok," said Jack when Claire seemed more comfortable, "do you want to tell me about what's happened, or would you rather just cuddle up for a while until you feel ready?"

A big single tear fell from Claire's cheek then, and she muttered quietly, "I want to talk." Jack kissed her gently and gave her some sips of his water before making both of them comfortable, so that Claire could say what was on her mind. He gave her time and space to prepare her words, all the while looking at her with kind eyes and patience.

Claire sighed long and slow. "I went to the shearers' quarters this afternoon. I saw something I wasn't supposed to know about. Mark was there. He was there with another man. They were, you know, doing it," she said in a matter-of-fact statement, not thinking about the startle this might give Jack.

She noted though that Jack drew back, surprised but not shocked, as might have been expected. "Oh Claire," he said kindly. "I am so sorry you have been through that today. Did you talk to Mark about it?"

"I wouldn't say we talked exactly, Jack; it was more that Mark made excuses, tried to brush it under the carpet, and then said it was nothing because these people he does it with aren't boyfriends, just one-offs. I just was so shocked, I never knew, never suspected, nothing. I feel ridiculous and stupid."

"Oh Claire," said Jack tenderly. "I am so sorry. You are not stupid. People work very hard at hiding these things, especially if they think that the people in their lives won't understand or support them if they tell the truth. I think Mark has done that. I am not suggesting he thought that of you either, darling, I think Mark has had his secret most of his life and that he is afraid of his mother's reaction more than anyone else's."

Claire sniffed. She agreed that Mark's mother would not approve. Never. Her son, her wonderful, precious perfect son, no way. Jack was right about her. She would not approve, and she would never forgive him. She wouldn't try to understand or educate herself, she would use emotional blackmail, and her Bible as her defence. Yes, Claire knew Mark would never turn his mother around on this one.

"You're right, Jack, I as much said that when I told Mark, I would tell his mother, because I was so shocked. I won't, of course; that would be spiteful," Claire reasoned.

Claire was running through her conversation at the shearers' quarters with Mark, in her confused head, when she remembered his whittling on about a mistake.

"You know, Jack, something happened, Mark said he made a big mistake and he had been scared it would come out. Obviously, it didn't, because I only found out what I have by accident when I went to the shearers' quarters today," explained Claire.

"Yes Claire, it didn't come out, but I think I might know about his mistake," said Jack quietly.

Claire looked up at him with wide eyes and puzzlement. "What do you mean, Jack, you knew something, and you didn't say?"

"Well, no Claire," said Jack. "I knew nothing for sure, so that is why I didn't say anything. I did suspect though because something that gave me a clue happened with Mark and James. James told me about it straight away. You know we were close, and he confided in me about something that made me wonder about Mark."

"What about Mark? What did James know?" She asked urgently.

Jack looked at Claire as he held her face and kissed her lips gently. "Now, calm down first, okay darling? It won't help being all uptight about things when I explain. Can you do that, Claire, try and stay calm?"

Claire nodded impatiently. She wanted to know what James had said. Jack started to explain, "James and Mark did some work together last summer. It was just a day or so and James helped Mark demolish some old sheds and take the demolition material to the transfer station, do you remember?"

"Yes, I do," said Claire, nodding with her hair moving up and down.

"Right," said Jack, "so at the end of the trip to the transfer station, Mark suggested stopping for a cool drink, and they pulled up at the river to drink it while they sat with their feet in the water because it was a really hot day, and they had been lugging stuff around over the afternoon. They got on well and talked about a lot of things, and were joking and having fun together like mates do. But James said at one point, Mark got a more serious look on his face, he reached over and took James' face in his hands and went to kiss him."

Claire recoiled, aghast at what Jack had said. "Oh dear, poor James, what on earth was Mark thinking?"

Jack continued, "James pulled away from Mark and made it clear he wasn't interested. Mark, James could see was panicking, and so, Mark started joking and saying, ha-ha gotcha, you thought I was going to kiss you, ha-ha, that sort of thing. James let it go and they carried on home. Mark said he was joking as he dropped James off. As far as I know, they never spoke of it again."

"So, what I saw today doesn't shock you, does it?" Claire asked.

"No, not entirely," said Jack. "It just confirms what James and I thought, but it doesn't shock me, darling, not like it might have if James didn't share what happened when he did."

"I wish James was here, so I could talk to him," said Claire, not thinking about how selfish that might sound. Jack was kind though and agreed softly.

"What do you think you will do?" Jack asked Claire.

She smiled at him with resignation. "I don't know, I have lived a lie without knowing it, now that I do, some of my life makes more sense, in an odd kind of way. But what that means, I don't know. Of course, we need to just carry on for now, with Christmas and the school holidays and everything. I guess we will talk about it at some point," Claire considered as she snuggled into Jack and enjoyed the last of the sun.

"I understand how hard it is, Claire. I really do. I wish that I could help you more. I am here for you, you know that," Jack said sincerely.

"I do, Jack, truly I do, and I am so happy to be with you and for your support," she explained. "You know, Jack, your James was an outstanding young man. He kept that situation with Mark close to his chest, knowing it would hurt my family if it got out. I respect him for that so much because what Mark did was wrong, just as unwanted advances from any person to another are, and James had the right to take it further, didn't he?"

"He didn't want to do anything about it, Claire, but put it behind him. It was awkward and he was embarrassed for Mark and a little himself. He didn't want any fuss and Mark backed off straight away, which was also the right thing for him to do," Jack explained.

"It must have been a huge worry for Mark though, Jack, he said that today, that he thought I would find out from what happened, from his mistake, he called it," explained Claire, suddenly with more empathy for Mark than she initially felt.

Jack hadn't even thought of it until Claire had said the words. Could it be possible that Mark had wanted to take James out to keep his secret? Really, was that likely?

"I don't know, Claire, I hadn't thought of it much, but now I wonder. If Mark was truly worked up over what happened, maybe he had a motive to hurt James, but I don't know," Jack said with some distress. "I don't know what to do now."

Even this morning, Claire would have defended Mark and said it wasn't in him to hurt another human being. She had thought Mark soft about most things, and he wasn't even really much of a hunter. But after what she heard today and had seen herself, she was no longer confident she knew much at all about her husband.

After all, he had gone to extreme lengths to keep his secret life secret, hadn't he? What would he do to keep the secret about what happened with James? Claire wasn't sure.

"I think you need to tell the police," Claire said clearly to Jack. "You can't be sure of what Mark might have done and your beautiful son is gone. You must honour your son, Jack. Get Mark checked out, regardless of what that does to him and our family. You must, Jack."

Jack knew Claire was being selfless and he appreciated what she was saying and her support. Especially after what she had seen and learnt about her husband. He also knew though that they were treading a thin line themselves and a good look at Mark might mean a good look at Claire, and he wasn't sure he was ready to deal with what that might mean.

Jack was in love with Claire, he knew that for certain. He adored her. Everything about her, her motherly ways and even the fact that she didn't have to be the font of all knowledge, unlike Lucy. But to have Lucy find out about them right off the back of James, well that was cruel, even though Lucy could be cruel right back.

Jack felt terribly conflicted, and worse than anything, was his clear understanding that anything done now would not bring back his beloved boy. Nothing at all had the power to do that.

Jack took Claire's hands in his, stroking his finger over hers. "Let's get Christmas over with first, love, then I will have processed things a bit more and the police might have found more out on their own. Let's not have Christmas be a bad memory for your kids and add more pain to mine, aye. There is plenty of time to sort this out," Jack said comfortingly.

Claire knew Jack was making good sense. "Of course, you're right, Jack. Christmas first, then whatever comes after, you can decide," she agreed.

Lucy

Lucy had been glad of the peace, with an empty house after the funeral. Jack had gone off, probably somewhere on the farm, and the girls had gone with their husbands to do some last-minute shopping in town. Lucy was relieved to be alone. She didn't have to hold her tongue or entertain, and she could get on with keeping busy.

She was staking her Delphinium's, now that they were getting taller, and she had been in the potting shed looking after the natives she was planning on planting across the farm. She had dirt under her nails and sweat in her hair and on her body and she was barely managing the scrambled thoughts in her brain. A bee came close, and she carefully swatted at it, not to kill it but to be sure that it wasn't going to tangle in her fringe. Lucy was allergic to bee stings.

Lucy was sorry about her outburst at the funeral, and embarrassed about what she had said about Pippa, and her new car. She knew her mouth engaged faster than her brain could, and it got her into plenty of scrapes. When she had written James' eulogy, what she had planned to say had made perfect sense, but on reflection, Lucy knew it was misjudged and inappropriate.

She didn't give the same thought for her behaviour about Pippa's new car, and she wished she had done. She knew for certain that Pippa, of all people, would have been the first to come forward had she hit James, and she knew how much her accusations would have stung.

But for all that, Lucy could not focus on much other than knowing who killed James. It filled every waking moment, and try as she might to keep busy and distract herself, it was there, simmering and churning in her mind, and she desperately needed to find the answer.

In her desperation, Lucy walked back into the house from the garden, leaving her gardening shoes at the door and stepping onto the cool timber of the homestead's floor, full of new purpose. She had decided to pack up James' things, and while doing so, she hoped she might find something that would help her.

She knew the police had looked, but she wasn't confident about what they were looking for and whether they might have missed something, and so, she felt better knowing that she was able to look herself. Pulling some big plastic bin liners from the kitchen drawer, she marched down to James' room, like a woman with a mission.

It didn't occur to Lucy that this wasn't something that she should decide unilaterally, or that Jack might like to help or be around as she cleared things away. In fact, it didn't occur to Lucy that anyone else needed time to be ready for what she was about to do, at all. No, she just saw a plan in her mind and was full speed ahead.

Opening James' door, Lucy did take a small step backward as she savoured the smell of him and the sight of his things, just like he had left for a quick trip out and would be back shortly. His bed wasn't made, and she smiled at that. She knew that James rebelled strongly against bed-making now he was out of boarding school, where bed-making was compulsory, and there were punishments for failing to use good hospital corners.

James' sheets were rumpled, and the top sheet pushed way down inside the bed at the bottom. He had always been a restless sleeper and so, Lucy wasn't at all surprised to see the mess his bed was in and it made her smile.

Lucy stripped the rumpled white sheets off and made the bed with just the navy-blue bed covers pulled up tidily. The pillows had their cases removed for washing and she lay them neatly at the top of the bed. That done, Lucy moved onto the bedside drawers, with a little trepidation about what secrets she might find.

She hadn't been one for snooping in her children's bedrooms, like many would have expected she would be, and she certainly didn't talk to them about their relationships and sexual habits, and so, she didn't have any idea what James might have in the drawers at all.

Opening the top drawer of the wooden cabinet, she noted it was tidy and there was not a whole lot inside, which probably was to be expected given that James now lived away most of the year. There was a pen, a notepad, a packet of condoms unopened, some old rugby medals and a matchbook from a bar near the university.

In the second drawer, there were a couple of books that Lucy remembered James reading last Christmas when he was home, a university essay in draft and some brochures for different kinds of motorbikes. Something Lucy didn't know anything about, but she guessed that at one time, James was looking to buy one. Although he would have known that if she had any say, he would not be making such a purchase.

Lucy put the books and medals into one plastic bag and put the matchbook and condoms in the bag she was using for rubbish. She put the pen in her pocket and flipped through the notebook. It was largely unused, save for the odd note about an appointment or a date that was important.

James had noted a haircut appointment, one for the doctor at university and in a love heart shape he had drawn, he had written the name *Clara, 7pm, Monday* inside. Lucy had no idea who Clara was, but she knew she couldn't have been around in a serious way, because James surely would have told her that. *Of course, James would have told me*, she confirmed for herself.

On the large dresser across from the bed, James had left his toilet bag, comb, hair products and his favourite aftershave by a designer that made everything from taps to clothes and travel rugs. Lucy squirted some into the air and sniffed it.

The scent filled her senses immediately and it was as if James was in the room, freshly showered and ready to go out on the town. A silent tear fell from Lucy's cheek then and she sniffed hurriedly and swiped at it, refusing to give in to her bubbling emotions.

She packed the things on the dresser in the bag for keeping and went on to the drawers that were rather large and creaked a little when opened. They were largely filled with winter clothes that James wore on the farm and a range of flannel shirts and jeans that were also more farm wear than town wear.

She dug into the pockets of each as she put them into the bag for keeping, thinking that after Christmas, she might donate them. She found a ten dollar note in one pocket, half a packet of gum and a scrunched-up piece of note paper in another that said, *10am, Mark's farm.*

Lucy wasn't sure about when James had been on Mark's farm, but it wasn't unexpected that he had been up at the neighbours and likely did some work with Mark. When James was home, a lot of the farmers offered him jobs, they knew he would appreciate the money, but they also knew he was great at whatever jobs he turned his mind too, and always willing to lend a hand. So, Lucy thought nothing of the note paper and discarded it.

Lucy was feeling purposeful, like she was helping James, as she worked methodically in James' room, and in no time, she had the dresser cleared and half the clothes in the wardrobe also dealt with. She didn't find anything of note amongst them, and continued on searching pockets and folding clothes until they were all in the black plastic bag.

In the top of the wardrobe, James had a collection of things including rugby balls, cricket bats and balls and hats of all different kinds. He had sports medals and school reports, old school projects and university notes. Lucy put all of those into the keeper bag and carried on.

The last thing in the wardrobe after clearing shoes and belts, was a cardboard box with a lid that Lucy didn't recognise. Thinking it was likely more of the same sporting or school memorabilia, she took off the lid with confidence. The box wasn't full by any means, but it did not contain what she expected. There was ammunition, some dirty magazines, which disappointed Lucy for about five seconds, and some photos, some of girls with very little on.

Lucy ditched the magazines and kept the rest. She was a little deflated that she didn't really find a clue to anything that might help her catch her son's killer. She was also a little relieved that she didn't discover some nasty secret that James had been keeping, or that he was doing anything illegal. That, in itself, would mean she could sleep at night, in the confirmation that her boy was as good as she had believed.

Lucy didn't hear Jack come in or notice that the day was largely done, and it was getting on for eight in the evening. Jack didn't exactly rush into the house, but he did notice that Lucy was not around in the kitchen or living rooms. He decided to go and shower, so that he would be ready in plenty of time for church and then worry about finding Lucy. That was until he saw the rubbish bag sitting outside James' room.

Jack couldn't believe it. She was in there. She had taken things from James' room. He was shattered and angry and he strode down the hallway, yelling, "Lucy, what the hell have you done now!"

Lucy was startled but she didn't mistake the anger in Jack's voice and all at once, she knew she had done the wrong thing. It was like a big neon sign flashed 'selfish' above her head and she felt ashamed.

"Jack, I didn't hear you get home. Long day. Can I get us some dinner, dear?" She asked, trying to avoid what was coming.

"Dinner," said Jack, "you think I want dinner? Are you crazy? I come home and find you dumping the remnants of our son's life into plastic rubbish bags and you think that I will just want my dinner. You selfish, unfeeling, ignorant, ahhh Lucy, how could you do this?"

"James isn't even gone a few days and you think what, oh well that's it then, we could use another spare room? Are you serious, Lucy, did you think about me and what gives me comfort, that I might want to spend time in James' room with his things, that I might need some time to process what has happened and heal a little before removing what we have left of our son. Seriously Lucy, did you think, at all?"

Lucy had a strong fight instinct and Jack knew he was pushing those buttons, but he couldn't help it, she was so far out of line.

"Jack," reasoned Lucy, "I did this because at some point, we will need to move on, and dragging it out won't bring James back. He is gone. We know that. I thought well, some of his things could be donated and—"

Jack bit back, "Lucy, do you really think I am ready to see other people walking around in our son's clothes? What the hell is wrong with you?"

Lucy, feeling defensive now, bit back, "Well, I wasn't going to give them away right now, Jack, but I thought well, after Christmas, some families do it tough and maybe then I could give James' clothes to charity to help, that's all. To use James' situation for helping others, Jack."

Jack couldn't talk about giving James' clothes away for a second longer. He was too sad and too enraged. He looked into the room properly, and could see that every scrap of his boy had been removed, the room looking sanitised and like James had never used it.

He was shocked. He couldn't believe what Lucy had done. That room was important, a place to sit with James' memory, a place to grieve and to find peace, and now, it was gone. He was bereft.

Jack looked at Lucy and said in his sternest voice, "Lucy, do not talk to me," and he went to the bathroom to shower and cry while the noise of the water masked his distress.

Midnight Mass

The church looked beautiful with white fairy lights in the trees and over the doors and windows. Like a magical scene from a children's movie, where everyone was happy and nothing bad ever happened. There were masses of excited children and early teens dressed in an array of toga like costumes, with the little ones holding onto cardboard stars covered in glitter. The carpets would sparkle for weeks after their performance.

Pippa had been helping with the costumes for the youngest kids and they had been fashioned from large white pillowcases. She had cut a shoulder out to make them more like a toga and rope belts cinched in their waists, and white shorts or tights were worn underneath.

Each child had a wreath of greenery around their head and sandals on their feet—Roman if possible but some had the more modern variety with no back strap, and two front straps buckled on the side.

Archer and Hunter looked an absolute picture and their curly hair held onto their garland headdresses very well. They both had big glittery stars in their chubby fingers and Roman sandals on their feet, although Archer was complaining that his were hurting, and he had begged to take them off, even before they all left home. Pippa had felt bad, but she also knew that half the problem was that the boys didn't even wear shoes a lot of the time.

Claire's children were dressed in exactly the same costumes as Archer and Hunter and yet somehow, with their locally done haircuts and rumpled pillowcases, they just didn't quite have the style that Archer and Hunter were pulling off. Pippa felt a little sad for them as they stood out from the others, but neither seemed to notice or to care.

Claire came rushing over all-a-fluster, hair not quite as it should be and a mismatched outfit of navy stripes with pink jacket and gold trim. She had her favourite leopard skin boots on again and a big gold chunky necklace with a large cross on it.

"Ooh Pippa, what a fabulous job you have done with the little one's costumes, just fabulous," Claire gushed. "I was just saying to Francis and Flora how lucky they are to be in your designer wear for their singing and how they looked just like little wise men or shepherds. Which are they again, Pippa, I can never remember?"

"They are shepherds or peasants, Claire," laughed Pippa, "but it doesn't really matter, it is just meant to look similar to the things people of all kinds wore back then."

"Yes, yes," said Claire, "people everywhere wore them, didn't they?"

Lucy came towards them then, with Jade not far behind. "Pippa, Claire," she said quietly and then she nodded to Jade. "Nice night for it. I would have had some paper lanterns outside as well, but I guess the fairy lights will do."

No one took her bait, but instead, they all smiled and were kind. "How are you doing, Lucy?" Jade asked carefully.

"We thought your eulogy to James was very good," said Pippa.

"You did very well," added Claire.

Lucy looked at them all with narrow eyes. "Well, someone had to do it and it wasn't going to be Jack, was it?" She said with a passive-aggressive tone. "That useless man can't do anything these days except run away to the back of his farm and bury his head in the sand. Some support he has been."

Claire couldn't help it then and she leapt to Jack's defence. "Lucy! What a horrible way to talk about Jack. He is grieving too. It must be terribly difficult for you both but really, why be so unkind?" She said with greater conviction than usual.

Pippa and Jade looked at each other with raised eyebrows. This was most out of character for Claire, and she would never usually take Lucy on, no one did. "Oh well, Claire, fine for you to comment but you aren't living with the man, look after your own marriage and stay out of mine," said Lucy bitterly.

Claire was deflated then and she tried to apologise but Lucy wasn't interested in hearing it. "I'm going in," she announced, and everyone collectively sighed in silence as she left for the church.

"Gosh," said Jade, "she is really in the angry phase, isn't she? Poor Jack must need a suit of armour for what she is putting out. How sad for everyone with tomorrow being Christmas Day."

"Yes, it is sad, but it is also hard to stomach," said Pippa. "We all know what they have lost but death usually brings you closer, makes you remember what is important, but Lucy isn't really able to do that, is she?"

"I think it is kind of spooky that we are here tonight at this time, the same kind of time that James was killed, and with his grave freshly filled in," said Claire.

Jade nodded in agreement. "To think only a few nights ago, we left here, happy after a nice night and never knew what was coming. To think we all drove past that spot on the main road and none of us saw anything or even knew if James was dead by the time we got there. I feel all icky just thinking about it."

"Oh Jade," said Claire, "my skin is getting goose bumps thinking about it. What if the person who killed James is here, watching us all?"

Pippa looked at them both and was stern. "Come on, snap out of it, it's Christmas Eve and the kids are relying on us to support them and have a nice time. Let's go inside and find some positive energy and thank God for all of the blessings we have between us."

The church was lovely inside. The lighting was softly dimmed and the altar dressed for the nativity with the manger and bales of hay. The older children led on an array of baby animals and Mary came in, riding a real donkey. It was a great expression of the story and included a few laughs as the donkey made itself known in an awkward place and a small dog jumped into the manger.

Then, it was the little kids' moment and they excitedly shuffled onto the altar with their Sunday school teachers whispering instructions all the way. Archer and Hunter were next to Francis and Flora. Archer was smiling a big wide artificial grin with his arms crossed and Hunter was looking at his feet.

Pippa and Duncan had no idea, but during *Away in a Manger*, Hunter had a small solo part and his little shaky voice was like an angel as he nervously sang. Pippa's eyes welled up and Duncan gripped her hand in pride as they watched him.

"No wonder he looked so nervous at the beginning," Duncan whispered to Pippa. "What a little legend!"

Claire's Francis could not have been less engaged, so much so he managed to trip his little sister up as she walked from the altar. Jade wondered if he had secretly done it on purpose, but she didn't say anything in case she upset Claire or Mark.

She did think Francis was a bit of a ratbag and that Claire let him away with too much because she was so busy. Claire had seen what had happened, but she didn't see it with Jade's eyes and just said, "Whoopsie daisy Francis," to herself out loud.

Mark was quiet and didn't react to Francis except with a disappointed kind of grunt. Mark really had limited tolerance for both children and seemed to find them at best a distraction, and really more of a nuisance than much else. He was not particularly interested in them, their schooling or their talents, but he would try to encourage Francis to take an interest in the farm.

Claire knew that after their revelations that afternoon that Mark would have to make an effort, and she wanted him to, her children deserved that from him, she thought.

Nelson watched the scene around him and sat with Jack, who noticeably hadn't sat with Lucy. Their girls hadn't come to church at all, and Nelson worried about Jack and Lucy in the aftermath of their loss. He wondered how things were at home and guessed Jade would have something to report.

He knew what had happened must be tearing them both up and he guessed that until someone responsible was arrested, it would be hard to let go of the anger they no doubt felt. He had asked Jack how he was earlier, and he could tell things weren't good.

Jack teared up and said, "Lucy has been unbearable and has the feelings of a cold fish," so that gave Nelson a pretty good clue about things in their house.

As was tradition, the midnight service finished by 1 and there was no supper afterward, given the time of the night and the festivities the next day. Parents rushed sleepy children into cars and some even changed their little ones into pyjamas before going home, so that they could go straight to bed after brushing their teeth.

Jade grinned at a darling little girl with a gap where her two front teeth should be, shuffling to her car in pink satin shorty pyjamas with fluffy pink Ugg boots on her feet.

"Look Nels," she said excitedly, "just like a mini me!"

Nelson had laughed and said, "Exactly, you will look very much like that in about fifteen minutes if I am not mistaken," and he wrapped his arm around her to head off to their car.

Pippa was with Lucy, and she felt awkward. "Lucy," she said tentatively, "I know you must be really hurting, but please, don't push your family away. You need each other now, no matter how hard it is. Please, Lucy, try to keep close with them, for your own sake."

"Oh Pippa," said Lucy, "like you would ever know what it is to lose a child, you have two sons, mine was my only one. It won't ever be the same. I can't pretend it will. Jack can't pretend it will. You can say all you like about coming together and supporting each other, but at the end of the day, Pippa, James is still dead."

"I am sorry, Lucy, I really am," explained Pippa, "but I also don't want to watch you self-destruct. Don't be too hard on yourself, but importantly, don't be too hard on others. You will need people around you. Maybe it isn't what you want now, but in time, Lucy, you will want to go back to things you did before. All I am saying is don't burn your bridges."

"Burn my bridges? Ha, what bridges? I know people think I am a nightmare, all bossy and loud and full of it. They probably think I deserve what happened. All, there goes Lucy Bossy Pants, couldn't keep her son alive though, could she? Oh, don't look so shocked, Pippa, of course I know what people say about me, I always have!" She said in a resigned tone that Pippa didn't recognise.

Jack came over then, after talking with Claire and Mark. He looked exhausted and older than Pippa had seen him ever before. "Lucy," he said, "it's time to go. Great work, boys," he said to Archer and Hunter as he tousled their hair, "awesome singing, Hunter, you were a rock star."

Hunter beamed and Duncan smiled at Jack, thinking how decent he was to talk to the boys while the loss of his own was so recent and raw. Lucy bundled herself up and said, "Goodnight," as she walked to the car. Jack took a moment to say a proper goodbye and gave Duncan and Pippa big heartfelt hugs before he left.

They both watched him walk to the car and Duncan said, "Poor Jack, I guess he will get the silent treatment all the way home."

"Yes," said Pippa, "but that might be better than what she might say instead."

Lucy

Lucy slumped into her seat in the car, feeling angry and upset. She knew it wasn't Jack's fault, but he was her target all the same. She wasn't wanting to talk much, and she certainly didn't want to rehash the conversation about James' room. It was done, that was it, nothing to talk about.

It did occur to Lucy that it was just a little later than the time that the police predicted James had died and as they started to come upon the spot, she felt compelled to stop.

"Jack," she said, "pull the car over at where we lost James. I want to stop."

Jack was surprised and hadn't expected this but was happy to pull over and slowly brought the car to a stop right before where there were flowers and cards lining the verge in front of the water trough that James had knocked his head on. The grass was well trampled and so, the trough was visible, whereas it wasn't the night James had died.

They sat in silence for a long time. It was like James was wedged between them, tightly wedged and they had no room for thought or air. Jack couldn't stand the tension. It ate him up and he could hear his blood pumping in his ears, faster and faster. Suddenly, he felt hotter, and he loosened the button on his shirt, at his collar as if to cool himself down.

Lucy was stone still and silent. She barely moved, save for her laboured breathing. She stared straight ahead, a haunted look on her face. Her fringe pushed up, so it was sticking out from her forehead in a wild fashion, and her knuckles white from the crushing of her hands together.

It was only then that Jack noticed something else. Lucy was crying. Silent tears flooding her eyes and running like a deluge down her plump cheeks. She didn't move to stop them, letting them fall and puddle on her top.

Jack felt for Lucy. He might no longer be in love with her, but he felt something. She was his wife and she had borne his children and he did care for her. His heart was broken, and it was broken for her as much as for himself.

James had been a surprise baby. They hadn't planned for him and thought their family complete with Anna and Amanda. Lucy wasn't a particularly maternal mother and Jack was content with his daughters, who he adored. When they had found out that Lucy was expecting James, they had been surprised and shocked. They certainly were not prepared and hadn't particularly wanted another baby.

Things changed for the better when they found out that James was a boy. Jack was delighted by the idea of a son and Lucy proud that she was carrying one. Somehow, they turned their shock around and soon, James' pending arrival had become exciting, just as if it had been planned.

By the time he was born, everyone was full of great expectation and there was joy in the family when he came home. The girls immediately adored their little brother, with Anna treating him as her own, and he had been an easy and loving child from the beginning.

Jack smiled as he remembered James' love for baked beans, billy tea and scones with piles of jam and cream. His sneaking the farm dogs' puppies into his bed and the time he fostered a litter of wild kittens and kept hiding food in his pockets straight from the dinner table.

Lucy could not work out why his pockets were always greasy and stained and that had been the culprit as he fed the baby kittens. Jack had finally relented and bought him a store of food from the farm suppliers, so long as he didn't tell his mother who had wanted Jack to 'get rid' of the kittens at the first opportunity.

By the time Lucy found out that they still existed, they were six months old, and she had gone mad about the vet bill as Jack had seen to it that they were desexed to avoid a repeat exercise and even more cats than they could handle. Those three cats had loved James dearly. The last one had died last year and up until then, there was nothing Lucy could do about them sleeping in his room and sharing his bed when he was home.

Lost in his own thoughts, Jack was startled when Lucy suddenly said, "Okay, I want to go home now." Jack looked over to her and saw resignation on her face and absolute sorrow. She was done in, and he knew that sleep was what she needed.

Claire

Christmas had been a strained affair as Mark and Claire went through the motions for their children and tried to hide their discontent from his mother. Claire had found the house tidy when she had returned from seeing Jack on Christmas Eve and Mark had even washed the floors and vacuumed.

It was some consolation to Claire, who had ever present dread whenever she walked into the house and found the mess and disorder never got any better, unless she did all the work.

Christmas Day had been all about the children and they had been delighted by their gifts and the special sweets and chocolates that had been in their stockings. Francis got the subscription to a gaming site he had been wanting and a special controller new to the market.

They had barely seen him, apart from coming away from the screen to be fed and watered. Flora was all about her art and so, her new easel and paints had been a big win and she had loved the blank canvases she was gifted that meant she could do 'real paintings'.

She was also excited by her new mountain bike and Claire was hopeful that she might take up more of an outdoor life, pointing out that her easel could go outside as well as her bike.

Mark's mother had given the children books, a perfectly lovely present, but not something that either of Claire's children particularly enjoyed or valued. They were quickly discarded for other gifts and Claire knew that Mark's mother was annoyed.

She also knew that her mother-in-law would be thinking the children were just as stupid as she was, and it was no wonder they didn't appreciate a good book. Mark had been quiet and on edge, as if he was terrified that Claire would make some wild announcement to his mother about what she had discovered of her husband.

Claire was sorely tempted, if not for the children. She knew that how she managed this situation was important and she wasn't going to traumatise the children with a savage outburst, no matter how much she might have enjoyed the fleeting moment when Mark's mother understood her precious son was not everything she had imagined.

A couple of days after Christmas, Claire had been invited with the children to visit Pippa and her boys who had new puppies for Christmas. It had been a fun distraction and the puppies were delightful. One black and one golden Labrador, all feet and extra skin, the children ran about with them until the puppies conked out with exhaustion.

Archer had explained that his dog was the black one and he had called her Angel because she came at Christmas and that Hunter's dog was the golden one and he had called her Holly for the same reason. Both boys had greeted Flora and Francis with a grunting pup in their arms and the puppies had licked the children all over in delight.

Claire was happy for Pippa and her family, noting that Duncan came in and out and was interacting with the children each time and enjoying the dogs as well.

"Oh Claire," said Pippa, "it's a bit chaotic, isn't it with two puppies and two little boys in the house? We wanted them to have some responsibility and Labradors are such lovely dogs. Duncan wasn't keen on them being house dogs, but he said so long as we didn't get anything bred with 'poodle' in it and they were a bigger breed, he would stomach it. Now, of course, he wouldn't change a thing."

Claire was a little jealous of how lovely it all was at Pippa's. Her home was picture perfect, with lots of white, navy and duck egg blue about, and so was her husband—certainly dishy. The boys were real farm kids, and she was a wonderful cook and kind person who did plenty for the community and those less fortunate. Everyone loved Pippa.

"Pippa, those pups are divine, so soft and their little grunt noises are super cute. Mark would never agree to a dog as a pet in the house, although the farm dogs come in and out at will, and I can't see the point in a pet really, as Francis won't get away from his screen long enough for anything. But I would love one, myself," Claire explained.

"Surely Claire, with all you do for your family, you should be able to have one if you would like too. It might even be good for you all, something to spend time with and take places as a family," said Pippa.

"No," said Claire, "unfortunately, I can see I would have all of the burden, so it's best if I don't have a dog right now."

"That is a shame," said Pippa. "I wish things were easier for you, Claire, it is tough when you have so much on your plate. Doesn't Mark see how much you juggle things? Does he help out much?"

Claire sighed and her eyes brimmed with tears. "Help, Mark?" She smiled bravely. "No, not really. He does what he has to on the farm, and that is it really. He is happy doing some outside work but when it comes to the books, ordering, anything to do with the children or the house, that is all me."

"I am sorry, Claire," said Pippa, "that is a lot to manage. You are very good to juggle it all. I guess I just struck gold with Duncan because he is a very active father, and we work well together."

"Well," said Claire, "Mark is apparently many things and some I know very little about. He certainly keeps his secrets," starting to sob.

"Oh Claire, hey there," said Pippa, "what is it, love, what is making you so unhappy?"

Claire sobbed and sobbed and then blew her nose loudly on a large wedge of tissues that Pippa had given her. Taking a deep breath, she started to explain, "Pippa, Mark has been keeping a secret from me our whole marriage and I found out on Christmas Eve, it was a huge shock, and I didn't see it coming."

Claire then went on to explain what she had seen at the shearers' quarters and how Mark had not denied it and explained he went with men and had been with men their whole marriage. She told Pippa how he had said it was something he needed and couldn't stop. Pippa was surprised, she had no idea about Mark's other life, and she felt terrible for Claire and how distraught she was.

"Claire," said Pippa kindly, "what a shock for you. Such a thing to discover in such a cruel way. You must have been really hurt. Have you talked to Mark since, I mean, about what you know and what it means for you?"

"No, not really," said Claire. "We are going through the motions for the children, but as far as what our future holds, no, we haven't discussed it. I just feel so betrayed, Pippa and then there is the thing with James."

"James?" Pippa questioned. "What about James, does it have something to do with Mark?"

"I don't know if the accident does," explained Claire, "but James knew about Mark and his liking for men. In fact, Mark told me he made a big mistake with someone, and that since then, he's been petrified, I would find out what he was up to. Anyway, well I think, it was with James."

"Why James?" Pippa asked. "Did Mark tell you something happened with James?"

Claire realised then that she had over-stepped, telling Pippa about James because she wasn't ready to tell anyone about Jack. "Oh well, I was so upset, you see, and I went for a big walk and when I got to the back of the farm, Jack was there on his side. I sort of told him what happened, and it was Jack that said about James, and that James had told him that Mark had tried to kiss him."

Pippa was dumbstruck. James was a child compared to Mark and he trusted Mark like her boys would trust Nelson or Jack. Poor James, what a thing to have happen, and then to have to manage himself. It must have given him quite a shock. And what a decent person for not making it public knowledge. So nice to keep it to himself when he could have shouted it from the roof tops.

"Claire, that is such a lot for you to take in, darling," Pippa said. "Are you sure you're okay? Can I do anything? We could take the kids for a night or two, give you time to talk to Mark and plan out what comes next. Duncan won't mind and they are getting on really well. It isn't a problem if that helps you."

Claire smiled at her kind friend. Lovely Pippa, always wanting to help and support others, she thought. "Thank you so much, Pippa, really, but I think for now, the children are best off with us and that we work through it in our own time. I don't want to have too much upset in the house, and we can muddle along."

Pippa smiled at Claire warmly and patted her hand. "Ok Claire, but honestly, if I can help, please let me know, I can't imagine how you must feel about things," she said gently.

Claire was embarrassed suddenly about the fuss she had made and seemed to need a quick escape. She called for the children and bundled up their shoes and hoodies and made for the door. Flora was whining about leaving the puppies and the boys were pouting, but Claire was insistent.

"Come on, Francis, in the car now, say thank you to Pippa and the boys for having us," she instructed.

"Thank you, Pippa, Archer, and Hunter," said Francis and Flora in their best sing-song voices.

"Just lovely, Pippa, lovely cuppa and chat, thank you. Take care," Claire said, waving as she set off down the driveway.

Pippa

Pippa was a bit lost for words after Claire left, and she sat at the table, watching the boys with the pups, taking time, thinking it over. She certainly thought that Mark was a dark horse and doing that to Claire was disgraceful. She had nothing against gay men at all, but she did not agree with disrespecting a marriage like Mark had done. That wasn't fair on anyone, and now, Claire and the children would pay the price.

She wondered then if Duncan had ever suspected anything like that with Mark. They had known each other since childhood and gone to the same boarding school in the city, along with Nelson. Duncan always said Mark was more of a loner and didn't seem to have a lot of friends, but then, Duncan and Nelson were joined at the hip, so they couldn't have been more different in that regard.

It occurred to Pippa then that Claire had inferred when talking about James that maybe Mark was connected to James' accident. At least that was what she thought she understood. Pippa wondered what that meant exactly, and whether the police would be involved, but she didn't get the impression that Claire was intending on calling them.

As she mulled over the events of the afternoon, Duncan returned from across the farm and came to sit with her at the table where she was perched on their deck. The pups and the boys were lying exhausted in the grass, and she could hear their little voices talking to the dogs about rabbits and hunting. Duncan laughed and remarked on how cute they were, but Pippa was still locked in her head and barely heard him.

"Earth to Pippa," Duncan joked as he patted her hand.

"Sorry, darling," Pippa smiled as she patted his hand right back, "I was a bit distracted as I have had the saddest and most surprising conversation with Claire this afternoon."

Duncan looked at her then with raised eyebrows. "Oh dear, that sounds a bit ominous."

"You know Mark pretty well, right?" Pippa asked.

"I know him as well as anyone knows Mark, I guess; he isn't really an easy guy to get to know. He keeps largely to himself," he explained.

Pippa laughed a little sarcastically at Duncan's innocent comment. "Well, it would appear that way, but apparently, he has a whole other life that Claire has just discovered."

"What!" Duncan exclaimed. "What does that mean exactly?"

"Well, it turns out that Mark has male lovers."

Duncan nearly spat his cool beer across the lawn in surprise, and started to cough. "Mark, Claire's Mark has male lovers," he said, letting out a big sigh. Pippa continued on to explain what Claire had said, about Mark disappearing, going to find him, then finding him with a man and the conversation she and Mark had after that.

"Wow," said Duncan, "that is so unfair on Claire and the kids, no wonder the poor woman is upset. What a shock for her, and right on Christmas as well."

As the details sunk in, Duncan suddenly remembered something from years ago. "Pippa, you know years back, before Claire was around but after we left school, there was a brief rumour about Mark. It was really brief though, and then it just faded away and I just haven't thought about it again. But after today, well, perhaps it was true back then as well."

Claire then explained the James connection to Duncan and the story Claire had told her about Mark saying he made a big mistake and Jack telling Claire that Mark had tried to kiss James. Duncan was more shocked than before.

"That's a bad show, Pippa. James is his neighbour's kid, good God, what in the hell was Mark thinking?" Duncan said in disbelief.

Pippa agreed and then went on to explain that Claire was now seemingly wondering if Mark had anything to do with James' accident. Pippa said, "That while Claire didn't say it, she is clearly thinking there might be motive for Mark to hurt James, after his rejection."

Duncan was upset at the thought. Not because he didn't see the logic but because he was devastated to think that a wonderful young man like James might have been a victim because of the actions of a selfish man like Mark now seemed to be.

"Pippa that is just not right, even if there is an inkling of truth to it, it's not right at all. Mark needs to explain himself and fast," said Duncan animatedly. "I am going to call the police, Pippa, I just can't let it lie, it might be the answer for Jack and Lucy, and they need to know what happened to James. Let's hope it isn't Mark who is responsible, but at the very least, he can man up about what he has done."

Pippa agreed but was anxious just the same. She understood the world was complicated and complex and she knew that Mark's situation wasn't straightforward. She thought about Claire and the kids and the scandal they would face, and she thought about how she might feel if it were Duncan who had a second life and may have hurt someone.

But when all that boiled down, Pippa knew Duncan was right, if there was something to be answered for, it needed to happen, for Jack and Lucy, and for everyone's sake. Otherwise, the village would forever ask questions of each other about whatever had happened the night James had died.

As Duncan was ending his call to Sam Dorsett, the inquiry head, Jade pulled into the driveway and tooted as she came towards the house. Nelson was in the car beside her. The boys and the pups ran up to meet them and Nelson went straight out onto the lawn with them to run about and see how the pups had learnt to sit on command.

Jade made her way to the table on the deck and Pippa handed her a cold glass of wine in exchange for a large box of cherries, freshly picked from the trees on Nelson and Jade's farm.

Duncan came back from the bedroom where he had made his call, commenting to Jade on the lovely cherries and thanking her before telling Jade and Pippa, "The inquiry head was going to look into things with Mark." Duncan then went out to the lawn where the boys were entertaining Nelson with the pups, one of which was dragging off the end of Archer's shorts.

Jade looked at Pippa with an inquisitorial gaze. "What's up, love?" She asked. "Why did Duncan say they are looking into Mark and does that mean looking into him for James?"

Pippa sighed heavily and again recounted her afternoon with Claire. The more she said, the wider Jade's eyes became and the more concerned her tone for Claire.

"Bloody hell, Pippa," said Jade kindly, "that is a whole lot for someone to deal with, isn't it? Poor Claire and after all she did for that man, around the farm. She must feel used and betrayed, the poor mite!"

Pippa agreed and explained to Jade that she thought Claire was still in shock. Sort of going through the motions and trying not to think about it all. Then she outlined what Claire had said had happened with James, just as Nelson had said to Jade and Jade to Pippa on Christmas Eve. Mark was the missing piece to the story Nelson had and now Claire had explained how Mark had tried to kiss James and then laughed it off. And how Mark hadn't fully admitted who it was, but said that he had made a big mistake that scared him, because he thought the person would tell and Claire would find out.

"And so that's what Duncan was doing, calling the police, to let them know that Mark might have had a motive for hurting James," concluded Jade.

"Exactly," said Pippa. "Let's hope it isn't anything to do with Mark at all but yes, given what we know, Duncan thought it was best to inform the police."

"Couldn't agree more. Absolutely the right thing to do," Jade confirmed as she took a large swallow of the cool wine.

Lucy

Christmas for Lucy and her family was a low-key and sombre affair. She had tried to make a nice meal for everyone on Christmas Day and the girls had helped with the preparations, but no one really enjoyed it. When it came to getting around the Christmas tree for gifts, everyone had put on a brave face.

Dutiful smiles and thank you's were exchanged when gifts were opened, but it wasn't the same and Lucy felt very much like they were pretending or in a low-budget soap opera.

The low point was when Jack called out James' name for a small gift that Lucy had missed removing from the pile that had been beneath the tree since before James died. After that, everyone retreated into quiet contemplation and the celebrations were complete for the day.

Since then, Lucy had busied herself in the garden and with cooking and baking. What wasn't eaten, she put in the freezer or gave to her in-laws. And when she had filled every tin and freezer, she moved on to cleaning. She cleaned the windows, the cupboards, the laundry and even the cobwebs from the outside sheds.

Each day, she took a break and drove herself to the place where James had died. The flowers had largely died, and she had collected up the cards and mementos that had been left and put them in a box in the wardrobe in James' old room.

She wanted to put a small cross on the grass at the site just near the tank, even though someone had kindly put a very basic one there almost straight away, but she hadn't found the strength to make it yet. She wanted something fitting for James and not the typical white road marker type that was standard for road deaths.

Lucy had also been onto the local council to get the old trough removed from the roadside, so that another accident like James' could be prevented. At first, they had not been particularly obliging but in the end, when she explained her son had died because he had hit his head on the trough, they agreed to take it away. Lucy was relieved and she had fist pumped the air in celebration, such as it was.

The girls and their husbands had gone home earlier than planned. Lucy was not in the mood for company and the girls could not reach their mother. Try as they did to engage her or spend time talking about James, Lucy was detached and more focused on cleaning and cooking than spending time with her girls.

In the end, they gave up and said tearful farewells to Jack as they left to go home to the city. They promised to return in a few weeks, but Jack knew that it was unlikely, given Lucy's state of mind, and he accepted that for the girls' sake.

Jack spent as much time outside of the house as he could. Lucy was unpleasant to be around and he either got the complete silent treatment or a mouthful, depending on her mood. She still put a meal on the table each night, but apart from that, Jack may as well have been on his own.

Lucy had moved into the spare room beside James' and had made it plain by her actions that her husband was not welcome in her bed. Jack got the hint, especially when Lucy chose the room with two single beds in it, rather than the room with a queen bed just next door.

One morning, just before New Year, Sam Dorsett called into the farm to talk to Jack and Lucy. He brought Joanna, the young constable with him. Lucy was in the kitchen and by chance, had just sat down to a cup of tea and so, she pulled another couple of cups from the cupboard and poured as Sam and Joanna took a seat. Jack had brought them in and was sitting at the table also, but he wasn't offered any tea. Something both police officers noted with interest.

"How are you both doing?" Sam asked of Jack and Lucy. Lucy said nothing.

Jack took up the conversation. "Oh, you know, Sam, these things take a lot from you and it's taking us some time to find our feet again. The girls have gone home to the city and it's just Lucy and I here now."

Sam looked earnestly at Lucy and Jack. "Well, as you know, we haven't had a lot to go on with our investigation and things really have stalled since Christmas. We are working hard to keep the lines of inquiry live but so far, we don't have anything to report."

Jack nodded in understanding. Lucy was less accepting and launched pure venom, "Well that just isn't good enough, Sam, it really isn't. Our boy is gone and you're telling us you have no answers. Well, I won't have it, Sam, I can't. Just bloody find who did this before I do!"

Jack's cheeks reddened with embarrassment and Sam shook his head to signal that Lucy wasn't an issue. "I understand, Lucy, I really do. It is frustrating and we feel that, but I promise, we are still working hard to find out what happened to James, and when we do, you will be the first to know."

Lucy quietened down and sat at the table, sulking with her arms folded. Jack then suggested a walk outside with Sam, leaving poor Joanna to manage best she could through small talk with Lucy. Sam was glad of the reprieve and keen to understand what was on Jack's mind.

He noted that the man had lost some weight and was well-tanned from the sun, suggesting he had been spending a lot of time out of the house. He suspected that things were not particularly happy in the home, and he understood what a handful Lucy was, even when things were going well, so imagined it was tough on Jack with James' loss so raw.

Jack leaned against the outside shed and Sam shared his weight with a fencepost a few metres away. He let Jack take the lead and didn't push the conversation. Jack started to talk, and Sam took out his notebook to be sure and record what Jack had to say.

"Sam," explained Jack, "there was an incident between James and Mark Green, our neighbour last summer that I think you should know about. See Mark, well, I know now, Mark has relationships with men outside his marriage. I think he got the wrong idea about James and last summer, he, well, he tried to kiss James while they were taking a break from doing a job on Mark's farm."

"They had dumped some rubbish and driven to the river and Mark took James' face in his hands and pulled it towards him and tried to kiss him. James, well, James liked women, you know, and so, he rejected Mark. Mark then tried to make a joke of it, but James was adamant it wasn't a joke."

"Okay," said Sam.

"Well then," said Jack, "Christmas Eve, Mark's wife caught him with a man, you know, and Mark told her he had made a mistake last summer and thought the person would tell her. So, what I wonder, Sam, is if Mark wanted James to be quiet about what happened, is that a motive to hurt him?"

Sam let out a thoughtful sigh and scratched at his chin. What Jack was telling him was almost exactly what Duncan had told him when he rang the station the night before.

"So, this Mark, Claire's husband, is he?" Sam asked.

"Yeah, yes he is," said Jack.

"Ah ha," said Sam, "the husband of the woman you're having an affair with, right?"

Jack nodded. "Yes that is right."

"Hmm," said Sam, "it's a tangled wee web, isn't it Jack?"

Jack was embarrassed and annoyed now. "While it may be, Sam, the man may well have had a motive to hurt my son, and you haven't found anything better. So, please can you look into Mark, I think it might be worth doing," pleaded Jack.

Sam agreed. It was something, and they needed to look more deeply at the relationship between Mark and James, especially as two different sources had mentioned it. Sam wasn't convinced of anything yet, but he was willing to give it a go.

Although he did think about Claire, and how it would be for her if this were true. Jack was thinking of Claire, also knowing that she supported looking at Mark completely. *That's his Claire,* he thought warmly, *would do anything to do the right thing by James, even if it did hurt her own family.*

Claire

Claire had been into the village to get haircuts for herself and the children at the Wild Cut Salon. Jessa McDonald, aunt of the pastor at church, had owned the place for thirty years and she was still the only stylist. It was basic and Jessa hadn't exactly kept up with the times, but she was fast and inexpensive and so, a lot of the locals, who didn't mind basic, were very loyal customers.

Francis and Flora had their cuts first. Francis with a number two and Flora with a good lop off the straight cut bottom of her locks and a skim across the tops of her eyebrows to shorten her fringe. She giggled when Jessa touched the bridge of her nose while making it straight.

While Claire had her haircut, she had given the children $10 for an ice cream each and a bag of sweeties to keep in her handbag and they were happily licking melting ice cream outside the shop.

Jessa was putting the final touches to Claire's haircut, all the while muttering away to Claire about the terrible business with James, and how the police had been next to useless. Claire had nodded and been told off for moving her head, so she then agreed, loudly remarking that it was such a shame, and yes, it would be good if the police could hurry along and get someone for it.

Jessa had agreed with Claire and said she was all for stringing whoever did it up by their ankles, but that she supposed that wouldn't happen with how everything was so soft these days. Claire had muttered her agreement, too scared to nod, for fear of being told off again.

Haircut complete, Claire paid Jessa and booked again for six weeks' time. The children had finished their sticky ice creams and piled into the car, the heat of the day making it unbearably warm before the air conditioning got going.

As they drove, Flora told Claire all about Mrs Halifax at the shop, saying "Mummy, did you ever see Mrs Halifax without those warts on her chin? Do you think she is like a witch or maybe she kissed a toad once, Mummy, what do you think?"

Claire was mortified to hear Flora speak of poor Mrs Halifax in that way. "Flora, I think Mrs Halifax is a lovely lady with an unfortunate problem on her face and it isn't nice to talk about it," said Claire in her best schoolteacher voice.

"I know," whined Flora, "but how did she get them, Mummy, that's all I want to know."

As Claire searched her memory banks for a plausible explanation, they made it to the driveway of their farm and Francis yelled excitedly, "Mummy, look, there's police cars at our house! Do you think they have found a burglar?"

Flora's eyes got very wide, and she started to cry. "I hope they didn't take my easel," she said, with big tears dropping onto her summer dress.

Claire felt panicked and she didn't want Flora's distress to escalate. Taking a calming breath, Claire said, "It's okay, whatever is going on, we will find out together, and I am sure Daddy is helping the police with whatever they need. Don't worry, it will be alright."

Confidence was never Claire's strength, and she was pleased that she managed to calm Flora and get the children out of the car before anyone went to pieces. Taking a few steps towards the house, Claire and the children stopped as Mark came out with Sam Dorsett.

Mark couldn't look Claire in the eye, and she knew why Sam was there. She moved towards Sam and Mark, and Sam said calmly, "Claire, Mark is going to come with me for a chat and the other officers here are going to search your house. A copy of the warrant is inside on the table."

"You are welcome to wait outside or if you prefer, you are free to go elsewhere while we conduct the search. We should be finished in a couple of hours or so, but if you like, I can call you when we are done."

Claire whispered in response, "Just call me when you're done, Sam, I can't stay here while you do this. I will visit a friend and wait."

Sam smiled at Claire reassuringly. "No problems, Claire; that sounds sensible. I will make sure you know when you can come back home. We will try and be quick as we can, and to leave things as tidy as possible."

Claire almost laughed out loud then, *as tidy as possible, compared to what,* she thought, *the abomination that you found on arrival, well someone has a sense of humour!* But as soon as she finished her thought, she heard Flora and Francis both crying, like forlorn little strays.

"What is the matter?" Claire said, surprised at the fuss.

Francis spoke up first, "Mum, why is Dad in the police car, is he in trouble?"

"If he is, Mum, will we still live in this house, or will you get a divorce?" Flora asked between sobs.

Claire looked at her children, almost seeing them and their feelings for the first time. She hugged them both to her and said quietly, "I promise everything will be okay. Daddy will have a good chat with the police and then, they will let him come home. It will be okay. Don't worry, and here," digging in her handbag, "have a sweetie to make it all better."

Claire put the children back into the car and drove off calmly down the drive. She had no idea what might be coming for her and the kids when they got home, or if Mark would be home or not. Seeing her beautiful children so distraught had shaken her, and she remembered how important it was to keep them calm and hopeful.

They had a lot to come in their little lives, and she knew now that nothing was going to be easy, given who their father was and the lie that was her marriage.

Mark

Mark was beside himself in the back of the police car and by the time they walked into the interview room, he was worse. He had no idea why Sam had brought him in, and he was perplexed about the search warrant and what they might be looking for.

Mark had already talked with Sam about the night James was killed, so he didn't think it could be that, but then, a lot had changed since then, he remembered. Sam was calm and even in his tone when he spoke to Mark. He didn't shout or even raise his voice from a clear, deep constant, even when he was clearly not happy with what Mark had to say.

They sat with Joanna, in the interview room and Mark had waived his right to a lawyer. The interview was being recorded and Mark was reminded he couldn't rely on gesturing to answer questions and had to use his voice in all instances.

The questions had started out routinely and they were all questions Mark had answered before. Where had he been on the night James was killed, when, what time did he travel home, did he see anything, and did he know James was shooting rabbits that night? Mark gave the same answers he had previously, explaining he saw nothing, got home about 11.30 or close to midnight and never saw James.

Not satisfied with his explanations, Sam ramped up the pressure and suggested to Mark that he had a motive for harming James. Mark, taken aback, had no answer. Sam pushed again, reminding Mark of his 'big mistake' and commenting that he must have been petrified that James would give up his secret.

Mark denied having made any mistake and that there was a secret to give away. He played dumb, nearly as well as Sam played bad cop. Sam wasn't finished, however, and he went in for the money shot.

"Mark," said Sam, "you like to be with men, don't you? To have your way with them and discard them like old shoes. Is that what happened, Mark, could you not cope with James' rejection? Was it too much for you, for your ego, or were you just out of your mind with the thought that James would tell, and everyone would know your dirty secret?"

Mark insisted Sam was wrong, that he didn't understand, and that he had never touched James.

"Never touched James." Sam laughed. "Mark, you didn't just touch him, did you, you tried to kiss him, Mark, to do one of the most intimate things."

But Mark was having none of it. "You are wrong, Sam, dead wrong, it was nothing more than a joke, a prank, of course, I wouldn't have kissed James, I'm married," screamed Mark.

Sam smiled. "Marriage mean that much to you, does it Mark? So much that you have looked after those marriage vows and been faithful and loved your wife? So much that you would never so much as look at anyone else, no matter how tempting? Never once thinking about having someone else or the feel of them with you—"

Mark interrupted, "Stop it, Sam, just stop, you're making me sick. I am not like that. I am not, I never did anything to anyone, stop it, Sam."

"So, you're a reliable, faithful man then, Mark, ha, is that it? Faithful to your wife and family, to your God and good and honest and righteous? Is that right, Mark, is that you?"

"Yes," said Mark quietly.

"Really," said Sam with surprise. "That's really you? Well Mark, I am surprised, given I know that your wife caught you on Christmas Eve with your trousers around your ankles and a shearer in your—"

"Stop, stop," said Mark as he started to cry. "Okay, okay, so you know then, you know what I do with men."

Sam wasn't letting up then, he knew if Mark had done anything to James, he was close to breaking. "So, you are a liar, Mark, you lie to your wife, your kids, your mother. Do you lie to yourself too, Mark? Ha? Did you tell yourself that you never tried to kiss James, did you, did you tell yourself over and over that it didn't happen, it was a prank, a joke, a laugh?"

"Is that it, Mark? See, funny thing that because no one has ever said to me that you are any kind of comedian, that you are a prankster or anything that even closely resembles someone with much of a sense of humour. So why, Mark, why on that one occasion, would you think that it was okay to joke about kissing James?"

"Why would you do something so risky like that? I think it wasn't a joke; you were dead serious, you lusted after that young man and you got yourself a little too excited, the day was hot, and you were close to him, and you just misjudged and before you knew it, you had his face in your hands and you could smell him and you wanted him and you—"

But before Sam could finish, Mark was up, out of his seat, thrashing about the room, raging with arms flying, sobbing and breathing through clenched teeth and then he said, "Alright! I bloody wanted him. I wanted him so bad, I had no control. I saw myself in my mind's eye as I took hold of his face and I lost all reason and yes, I tried to kiss him, I did and then I saw, I saw the look, the look in his eyes, the fear and the repulsion and he pulled away and I was caught."

"What could I do, confess that I fancied the pants off him. Of course, I couldn't do that, I had too much to lose, so I laughed, and I made a joke, and I kept making a joke until I saw him relax, saw him believe the joke and then I breathed for the first time since that stupid moment."

"And then when the opportunity presented itself, Mark, you killed him," said Sam in a voice with no emotion, but pure conviction.

Mark was rubbing his hands through his hair and rocking back and forth after sitting back down in his chair. He was folded in on himself and he had long forgotten his manners, wiping the snot from his nose on his sleeve. Mark steeled himself.

"Sam," Mark said calmly, "I did not kill James."

Lucy

Lucy scrubbed the dirt from under her fingernails, rubbing the skin on her hands raw in the process. The water was too hot, and she was so numb in her grief for James that it didn't register. She had been in the garden again and while it looked an absolute picture, it was becoming her obsession.

Lucy always had something to obsess about, while it was the garden now, in times gone by, it was recycling, exercise, baking bread and even match-making. Obsession fitted her personality. Just as her bossy boots ways and her constant judgement were her trademarks.

Jack had not been around much during the long days over the summer and Lucy noticed but wasn't particularly of a mind to bother. She liked having control of her own life and her time and it meant she could spend as long as she liked in the garden, without having to answer to anyone.

Lucy knew she should care more about Jack and how he felt, but she was consumed by her own thoughts and didn't have much room for Jack or the girls for that matter.

Sipping on a glass of elderflower cordial she had made herself, with ice and mint, Lucy collapsed into a chair at the kitchen table with a bit of a thud. She was wearing a large basketball type shirt that had belonged to James and some yoga pants with flat sandshoes that were comfortable and Velcro fastened to avoid laces getting in the way when she was gardening.

Her fringe was sticking out from her face and the rest of her hair had been hastily tied back in a rough ponytail when she got out of bed that morning. Lucy couldn't remember if she had washed her face or brushed her teeth. In fact, she wasn't entirely sure what day it was until she passed the clock with the date on the face in the hall.

As if like autopilot, the minute Lucy stopped working and sat still, her mind turned to James. Her beautiful son, his curly hair and cheeky grin, his kindness and his strong drive to help and make a difference. It was so unfair. Lucy had loved him so deeply and so hard and while she wasn't great at showing it, she had felt it fiercely.

She understood that bond between a mother and her son, that invisible umbilical cord that while cut, was never severed. She felt the pull of grief when she let herself and she pushed away the pain of her loss, most of the time. That was why the gardening was her new obsession. It kept the pain at bay and allowed her some reward when a flower bloomed, or the scent of the garden filled the air at dusk.

Like always recently, Lucy was thinking of James and turning the events of the night he died around and around in her head. With no one coming forward and no results from police inquiries, Lucy was sick to her stomach and starting to get angrier and angrier.

While she had never thought the police did enough locally, she could not accept that they were not doing more to find James' killer. Sighing heavily, Lucy drained her glass and planted it firmly back on the table.

Suddenly, Lucy's quiet reflection erupted in movement, and she was up out of her seat and running outside to her vehicle. She took off down the driveway at breakneck speed, kicking up the dust with her fat tyres and travelling faster than she knew she should.

Lucy's mind raced and she kept whimpering to herself, making small squeaky sounds like an animal in pain. It couldn't be, couldn't be, please no, she thought as she drove erratically down her road towards the turnoff where the main road joined it.

Lucy knew she was driving recklessly but she couldn't stop. She had to get there. Get to where James was hit. She had to know. She turned onto the main road, making the turn wide as she took it at speed. She could see where she was heading now, where the makeshift shrine to James had sprung up. There were all kinds of flowers starting to fade past their best, and cards, fluttering in the afternoon breeze gently.

Lucy drove on past and found a place to turn around. She had spent weeks trying to remember that night and now, it was like she was playing a movie in her head. The picture was clear and sharp, in contrast to the numbness Lucy had felt ever since that day at church.

Lucy remembered she was last to leave the party, locking up as Pippa had left. She was tired and while she thought about it, she didn't change to go home, so was still dressed in her elf costume. She had set off nicely and turned the radio up a little to sing along, something she did often in the car, particularly if she was driving alone in the dark.

She remembered being happy and pleased (smug even) with how the night had turned out, despite being a little annoyed at Jack. Retracing her drive, Lucy started heading back towards the intersection of the main road and her road and just before it, on the same side, was James' shrine.

Driving on the main road was like clockwork to Lucy, and she didn't really need to think too much about it. Muscle memory guided her hands and feet while she watched the road ahead. She remembered that on the night, she could see Pippa's lights in the distance, turning off onto her road, but apart from that, the road was dark and deserted.

The movie in her mind played on and try as she might, Lucy could not switch it off. She recalled now that at a point on her drive that night, she had shifted her foot slightly, still wearing the elf shoes with their little bells on the end. Her foot didn't respond as she expected and one of the little bells on the end of her elf shoes was caught in the pedal of the accelerator.

Lucy was annoyed at herself for failing to change into her sensible shoes, and being confident she could continue, she let her eyes leave the road to try and see why the bell was snagging. She thought she was driving at about 25km per hour at that point, because she had lessened the pressure on the accelerator pedal and the car had slowed. She couldn't be certain, however, of her exact speed.

And then, the soundtrack played in her ears. The picture was of her foot, the bell snagged on the pedal. The noise was unrelated. It was familiar. It was then Lucy knew for sure, knew in her heart that she was responsible, that it was her that had hit James. Lucy, his own mother, the one that accused others, the one that behaved terribly to Jack, the one that was responsible.

Lucy could see now that as she had looked down to the snagged bell, she had heard a noise, a thump. It was the kind of noise she had heard many times on country roads, including the main road. It sounded exactly like she had hit a rabbit or a possum.

So much so, that until that very moment, in her basketball shirt and with her crazy fringe stuck out, the moment when she stopped directly beside James' shrine, she had thought, perhaps wished, it was. She couldn't breathe; now, it was confronting her, the truth, the horrible truth.

She could see the whole picture now. It was her, Lucy. She had killed James. Stopped, beside the shrine, Lucy opened the car door, gasping and retching, her mind racing and rejecting its reality. She vomited into the road, shaking and crying silent tears. The trauma of retracing her steps gifted Lucy her memory and gave her the truth she had so craved. She had killed her boy. Her own son.

Claire

Sam had dropped Mark off at the house well after dark, and Claire was thankful that the kids were fast asleep. She had battled with herself over what she might do when Mark came home. He was a rat and she played what she had seen in the shearers' quarters over and over in her head. But when he came inside, looking somehow smaller and less of a man, Claire didn't send him away.

Mark was exhausted, and he looked scared. Claire wondered what he was scared of really. After all, he didn't have to do much in life that was difficult, he was more or less given the farm by his parents, and he was more of a play farmer than the real thing.

That was left to Claire. *It's me who should be scared,* she reasoned. She was the one with the husband who liked men, who could have given her diseases and who didn't have the security of a stable marriage anymore. And according to Mark, she was stupid.

Dropping into his lounge chair that was so moulded to his body, it almost held him, Mark looked at Claire. "I am so sorry, Claire," he said, with tears rolling down his cheeks in a very small voice.

Claire might have laughed at him, but it was so pathetic, she couldn't even bring herself to do that. "What exactly are you sorry for, Mark? Are you sorry you got caught, sorry that you probably have to tell your mother, or are you sorry that your mates might find out? See, I know you are not sorry for hiding your secret from me, because you have done that all our married life, so that is a choice, Mark, not a mistake, not an indiscretion and certainly not the right thing to do!" Claire said calmly.

Mark looked at Claire. "Are you leaving me?" He asked quietly.

Claire hadn't expected the question, well, not quite like that, just matter-of-fact, resignation. "I don't know who is leaving who," she answered, "but I don't think it is a simple choice. We have to think of our children first, Mark, it's them who will lose more than anyone, losing the family they know, maybe their home."

"It isn't about me, Mark, it certainly isn't about you. We must do what is right for the kids. So, I don't know who is leaving or even when, but I do know this, it is time you grow a backbone, man up and start being the kind of father our children deserve."

To Claire's surprise, Mark agreed, "You are right, Claire, of course you are. I do need to do more with the kids and be more involved. I know I have left a lot of that to you, but I will change. I will make them my focus. They can stay on the farm with you, Claire, I can move out, take the cottage closer to my mother and set up a home there."

"Right," said Claire, "and how does that work when your special friends come over, in the house, near your mother! You must be insane to think that will work. She would be over in a flash, looking to see who is calling, muscling in to meet your gentlemen; that is if she ever decides to forgive you for her shame."

"You have to know that this isn't something your mother will ever understand, with her Ten Commandments and her old-fashioned values and beliefs. She would just about crucify you herself, if she could."

Claire wasn't really wanting to be cruel, but this was something she knew plenty about. Mark was the golden child. He could do no wrong in the eyes of his mother and Claire was his only problem, in her mind. She hadn't wanted Mark to marry Claire, sulked on the wedding day and was nasty about Claire's dress and her family.

She didn't consider her good stock, looked down at Claire's hardworking but relatively unsuccessful parents, and she scoffed at Claire's parenting style and the way she kept the house. Claire was categorical about the fact that Mark's mother would nearly die on the spot once he told her what he was. It would not go down at all well—ever.

Mark was tired. "I'm not thinking about my mother, Claire and for what it is worth, I am not thinking about men either. I want to do what is right for you and the kids, and that is my only thought. I know that my mother will struggle with what has happened, she will huff and puff, but she cannot fix it or change it. I know for God's sake because I tried to change and look how that ended up!" He said, frustrated. "I didn't choose this, Claire. I didn't choose to need the things I do."

"Oh, shut up," said Claire in exasperation. "Poor you! You might not choose to be attracted to men, but you absolutely chose to trap me in a sham of a marriage. Don't kid yourself, Mark, about how this isn't your fault. You knew exactly what you were doing when you married me."

"Now, I know what you were doing too. It was nothing more than a front for a life you wanted but didn't think you could have or weren't brave enough to confront. You have been a coward, Mark, I suspect all your flipping life, hiding away like a scared boy who didn't want to tell the truth about something uncomfortable."

"You're pathetic. A snivelling yellow-bellied liar who didn't give two hoots about his family in all this. You are so selfish; I can't even begin to fathom just how much," as her face reddened and she raged inside.

Claire got up and put her mug of cold tea in the sink. She started to put the leftovers from dinner away and filled the sink with hot water to start the dishes. Mark stood up from his chair and came over to the kitchen, picking up a dish towel to start drying what Claire had washed.

Claire laughed at the irony. *Twelve years of marriage and this is the first time Mark has dried the dishes.* If only she had figured him out earlier! They did their chores in silence, finding a rhythm and getting the job done in half the time it would normally take Claire on her own. Mark even filled the jug ready for their drinks in the morning.

The fight seemed to leave Claire during the time at the sink and she didn't want to talk again that evening. It was pointless anyway because they had no real plans yet and she didn't feel it was necessary to continue going over the details of what had happened and why.

"Sam is happy I didn't hurt James," said Mark. "He took a statement about where I was that night and about the thing that happened with James when we were at the river and that was it. He said he doubted we would need to talk again and offered me a ride home."

"Well, that is good for you, I guess," said Claire. "At least you are not locked up and I don't have to explain that to the kids." She shrugged.

"Thank God; that would really do my mother in," Mark said with a grin.

Claire didn't want to, but she did see the funny side, and so, she smiled back.

Pippa

Pippa and Jade were relaxing in the quiet with three sleeping dogs at their feet. Hunter and Archer had been in bed for about an hour and the bottle of wine Pippa and Jade had shared over dinner was just about empty. Pippa got up to make some tea and the Labradors both stirred in their beds, checking to make sure there wasn't something to eat coming their way.

Two car doors slammed outside as Duncan and Nelson came home from the Beef Breeders Association meeting that had been held that evening over a light dinner. Duncan came in first, followed by Nelson and both looked a little weary. Duncan went straight to his wife and squeezed her bottom while she poured hot water into a large floral teapot.

"I'll have one of those, darling," he said, before turning to Nelson, who said, "Thought you would never ask."

Pippa laughed at them both, their farmer shirts and moleskins making them look like boarding school brothers. "I suppose you're both starving as well." She smiled as she filled a plate with healthy wedges of cake and several shortbread biscuits that she had baked that afternoon.

"Ooh lovely," said Nelson, taking the biggest piece of cake in his giant farmer hands. Duncan followed suit, but took a large piece of shortbread instead, dunking it into his hot tea that was steaming in a large mug.

Without waiting to swallow his mouthful, Nelson launched into the events of the meeting and most particularly, the things that were not on the agenda. "Something going on at Mark and Claire's," he said between bites of cake. "Sam took Mark away in a police car, reckon it's to do with what happened to James."

Pippa and Jade looked at each other with wide eyes. "Poor Claire," they said in unison.

"Claire will be distraught," said Pippa. "She would never be caught up in such a terrible thing."

"What about Mark though, aye?" Duncan said. "He can be a bit of a loner, you know, kind of sticks to himself mostly, not one for much socially. Maybe he hit James?"

"No, do you think so?" Jade asked. "Surely if he had, Claire would know, wouldn't she?"

"But how would she?" Pippa explained. "Remember she stayed back with us to help clean up and Mark left separately a bit earlier, so unless he told her, she might not know."

"I wouldn't be surprised if that is true, Pip," said Nelson. "Mark was never one to say much, so that would stand to reason, I reckon."

"Whatever happened, it must have been quite a drama having the police take Mark with them," said Pippa. "It will have upset the kids seeing their dad taken away like that."

"Pippa," said Jade, "we should make a point of seeing Claire tomorrow at church if we can, just to check that she is okay."

"Absolutely," said Pippa. "Claire is so good at pitching in to help others, if she needs us, we need to be sure to make her feel she can ask for help."

Pippa thought quietly for a moment. She was thinking about Lucy and how she was doing. "I wonder if Lucy knows about Mark being looked at," Pippa pondered. "Have you seen her, Jade? The boys and I have seen her at James' shrine a couple of times. She just sits there in her car. I worry about her."

"I've seen her too," said Nelson. "It breaks my heart just seeing her car parked at the spot where James died. She must spend ages there just sitting and thinking. I worry that she might need some help."

"I know," said Pippa. "I think about how I might feel if it was one of the boys that was hit and killed. I honestly don't think I would live through it. I just can't imagine that pain, just knowing that you will never see your child again and haven't been able to protect them. I know it would be agony for me."

Duncan piped up then, "I think about Jack and how he is doing a lot. He was close to James, and I know he was super proud of him. We all know Lucy is not the easiest person to be around, especially if she is under pressure or in a crisis and so it makes me wonder what it is like at home, just the two of them, without anyone else in the house to break the silence or the atmosphere. Poor Jack, I bet he is going through hell."

"You two need to check up on him more," said Jade. "He is a decent man, despite his challenging wife, and I imagine it would be pretty lonely for him, without James around. Come on, Nels, please can you have a chat with him at church or tomorrow some time, I would hope someone would do that for you."

Nelson was feeling pretty bad about his not having paid Jack more attention over the past couple of weeks. He had meant to do more, but it was a busy time, and it was easy to forget others had different challenges at different times.

"I will, Jade babe, I promise. Jack will need a friend or two, and I know Duncan and I can do that for him," said Nelson, taking a large shortbread biscuit from the blue floral plate Pippa had placed on the table in front of him.

Lucy

It was a beautiful summer morning and Lucy was up early, walking around her garden, and pulling out the very rare stray weed, and dead-heading her rose bushes. The flowers were waking up and pointing their heads to the sunshine and the foliage was lush and a thousand shades of green. Spider webs were glistening in the morning light and a monarch butterfly was darting over the flowers.

Not yet dressed for church, Lucy was in her pyjamas and her Velcro-strapped sensible garden shoes. Her fringe was splayed over her forehead in a random manner with no two strands pointing in the same direction. Her face was tanned and a little weathered from the time she had been spending in the outdoors and her fingernails held dirt beneath them, too stubborn for the scrubbing brush to eradicate.

Since realising the truth about what had happened to James, Lucy had developed an increasing calm about her. She had a sense of purpose, and while she was absolutely horrified at what she had discovered, she also felt more in control.

She had prepared herself for today and what she was going to do, and she was not afraid. She was devastated about her role in James' death, but she was not afraid about what might happen, because in reality, she no longer cared. She didn't matter. Her pain or excuses were irrelevant, she had killed her son, and that was all that would ever matter for Lucy, for as long as she lived.

After collecting eggs and feeding the farm dogs, Lucy went inside to the kitchen. She flicked on the jug and started to make a coffee. She wasn't hungry but she appreciated the small buzz that the coffee would give her, on such an important day.

Perhaps it helped with her courage, or maybe it was imagined, but whatever the case, Lucy hugged the mug of bitter liquid close and allowed herself a moment to relax.

Since she remembered what had happened when James died, Lucy had prepared herself for what she knew was coming. She wrote letters to her girls to explain what had happened. She baked and cooked, making sure the tins were full of Jack's favourites and that his parents had some extra meals in their freezer.

She cleaned the house, but not her car. She would have but then she thought about it more. Would it look like she was trying to destroy evidence? Lucy had wondered. Would people think she was dishonest, because she couldn't help but think they would.

Lucy hadn't been able to bring herself to talk to Jack. It wasn't that she wanted to hide anything from him, but she just couldn't seem to make herself say the words. Every time she thought she might tell him, she couldn't, the words stuck in her throat like a lump of dirt, too awful to be uttered.

She wondered if Jack could sense something was wrong, and to her, it seemed obvious that was the case. But Jack didn't really seem to notice much at all when it came to Lucy lately, and he completely missed any sign that she was struggling.

Lucy felt he had been even more distant since he came home to the shock of her having cleaned out James' things. Somehow, he just couldn't move past that moment, his despair and his anger at what she had done.

Lucy dreaded the moment Jack would know. She was certain that the minute he found out what had happened, his anger would bubble over. He was never a violent person or for that matter, someone that got manifestly angry very often, but Lucy knew this would be the time.

She knew that he could never forgive her for what had happened, for how stupid she had been and for not even realising at the time what she had done. Lucy knew that this was the end of her marriage.

After showering, where she sobbed quietly at the horror she had created and the day ahead, Lucy dressed in a pair of wide-legged navy pants and a crisp white linen shirt. She didn't bother with her jewellery or her watch and laced up a pair of flat shoes that were navy with white tips.

Her fringe was damp from the shower and sticking out from her face and she did try to flatten it down but quickly forgot and ran her fingers through it, sticking it out again.

Jack had showered also and was dressing in the moleskins and white shirt with little anchors on it that Lucy had bought from a fancy store in town. He slid into his good going-out boots and combed his hair. He didn't speak to Lucy, but then, he didn't need to as they always went to church on Sunday morning, and he had no idea that this would be any different to any other Sunday.

Lucy watered her house plants and nursed a cup of tea, waiting for Jack to come out of the bedroom. She changed the tablecloth and put the old one on a quick wash. She filled the sugar bowl and busied herself refilling the tea caddy and the salt grinder.

Nothing was out of place, in need of filling or without a wipe. Jack's tea sat, getting cold, on the bench. Lucy expected it would stay there if he didn't come into the kitchen in the next minute or so. It was getting late, and they needed to get going to make it to church in time for the first hymn.

"Righto," called Jack as he walked quickly from the bedroom. "I guess you're starting to jiggle your foot like you do when you worry about being late, so let's just get in the car, shall we?"

Lucy nodded but said nothing. She climbed up into Jack's Ute, and brushed some dust from her pants in disgust. For the life of her, she did not understand why they didn't use her car when they were going out, it was cleaner and more comfortable.

Then Lucy realised there were lots of things they did that they never really thought about. Quite automatic but undeliberate decisions that they made routinely without a word or a thought.

They rode in silence, the tension hanging in the air between them like a thick cloak. Jack's radio didn't work and so, there was no noise but the grip of the tyres on the road and the hum of the engine that slightly changed with each gear shift. Lucy looked straight ahead, and so did Jack.

Turning onto the main road, they could clearly see the shrine to James that remained on the grass in front of the place where he had died. At exactly the same time, Lucy and Jack turned their heads as they drove past, looking at where they had lost their son and the fading flowers and ribbons shifting slightly in the breeze. Lucy's heart hurt, and so did Jack's. They said nothing.

Lucy fiddled with her Bible the rest of the way, feeling unsettled and less confident than her usual, bossy self. She was used to being in control, managing the inadequacies of others and keeping order wherever she went. She was not used to this new feeling, the one that she had had since remembering what had happened to James. That feeling was unfamiliar, it was terrifying, and she struggled to keep it under wraps.

It was just starting to feel more humid as they arrived at the old stone church and Lucy sighed, hoping it wouldn't be sweltering inside with all the warm bodies and the chatter. The church was charming but not particularly well-ventilated and she often felt hot and got flushed when she was there with a good crowd of people.

Jack seemed to be completely unaware of the warmth. He didn't really fuss over much, Lucy thought to herself, noting how different they were in that way. Lucy knew she was a fusser.

She was the mother licking her handkerchief to wipe her kids' faces before they got out of the car, she was the one who insisted on hats in winter and summer, and she always ensured the children were well-fed and in bed at a sensible time.

Jack was not that parent. He was relaxed, more patient, adaptable and not at all bothered by last-minute changes or messy moments. Knowing this about Jack made Lucy more content. She knew that Jack was calm in a crisis, didn't catastrophise and would have a pragmatic response to almost anything.

He balanced her flaws, and she was grateful for that. Glad that her daughters had the benefit of his pragmatism and his common sense. Lucy knew that she was high maintenance and not always the most enjoyable person to be with. Jack, on the other hand, was completely pleasant nearly all of the time.

Lucy and Jack left his Ute and walked together, but without talking or touching, towards Pippa and her family and Jade and Nelson. The men shook hands, all dressed in moleskin pants and boots and well-pressed shirts. The women hugged each other warmly.

Jade was dressed in a green pants suit that was incredible against her complexion and Pippa had a long floral skirt and blush pink shirt on with some strappy sandals. Lucy felt frumpy in comparison, but comfortable at the same time. She wasn't one for trying to be anything but herself and neither Pippa's nor Jade's outfits would be her cup of tea, although she did like the look of them.

"How are you doing, Lucy?" Jade asked kindly. "I have been meaning to call by, but I wasn't sure."

"Thanks Jade," said Lucy, more confident now that she had started to speak. "I am doing well, given what has happened. It is very difficult, but needs must, I suppose."

Pippa gave Lucy a warm smile and wrapped an arm around her shoulder. "We are here, Lucy, you know that. Anytime if you want to talk or not talk and just sit, whatever you need, we are here for you."

"I know," said Lucy, her eyes filling with tears. "Everyone is so kind and I really don't deserve it."

"Nonsense," said Pippa. "Lucy, you do more for this community than anyone and we are all very appreciative of that and want to ensure you are looked after now that it is a time when you need support. So, let's not talk about deserving or not, there is no question that you are."

Jade nodded in agreement and smiled at Lucy. "Pippa is right, Lucy. We want to help and are so sorry about James, really, we are."

Before Lucy could answer, Claire arrived with Flora in tow. The little girl was dressed in clean but rumpled clothes and her hair was not quite brushed through.

"Hi lovelies," said Claire in her usual bouncy way. "How are we all? Isn't it hot? I feel like I need another bath and it's just gone breakfast." Claire laughed. Pippa thought Claire was extremely chipper given that Mark had been in the police station yesterday, but she kept that to herself.

"How are you, Claire?" Jade smiled. "Everything going well with you, and what about you, Flora?"

Before Claire could collect her thoughts, Flora was off responding to Jade. "Well, I am okay," she said, "but I cried yesterday when the policeman took Daddy away. But he is back now, so he isn't in jail, and I am glad about that."

Claire blushed with embarrassment. She was hoping not to have to discuss the events of the day before and here was Flora jumping into it, boots and all. "Oh, now Flora, it was just a misunderstanding now, wasn't it? I told you, Daddy wasn't in any trouble, the nice policeman Sam just wanted to talk to Daddy and then he gave him a ride home."

"Oh," said Jade. "I can understand you being upset, Flora. I am really glad your daddy is back home now." She smiled.

Claire sighed and looked at the three women with a face of resignation. She felt she had no choice now but to explain what went on, even though she didn't want to expose Mark and his other life.

"Sam came over and wanted to question Mark about some time he spent with James last summer, and then he asked him about the night James, well, you know. Anyway, Sam brought Mark home late last night and said he didn't think he would need to speak with Mark again."

Lucy looked at Claire. "That is good, Claire," she said. "I am glad Mark is okay and back with you all."

Claire smiled back and blushed again. "Thanks Lucy," she said quietly.

"Well," said Pippa, "I think we should go inside and try and find a spot where there is some air coming through. We will fry in this heat if we don't."

"Sounds like a plan," followed Jade as they made their way into the church.

Lucy dropped back to speak to Father McDonald. She wanted to ask him for something, and it would have been awkward with the others in earshot. He had been kind and agreed to her request. She found Jack and they went into the church together. Lucy insisting that they sit on the aisle to get the best of the air flowing though the open doors.

The service was about keeping one's faith and the pastor had a great many examples of tests of faith and how faith prevailed. He quoted from the Bible, and they sang three somewhat sombre hymns. The room got hotter, and hotter, and it was stifling when Father McDonald finally asked if Lucy would like to come forward to speak with the congregation.

Jack was puzzled. What was Lucy up to this time, was his first thought. Lucy walked slowly and deliberately down the aisle to the microphone and Father McDonald kindly stood aside. Lucy was shaking but calm.

"I don't want to keep you long on this very warm day, but I do have something I would like to say to you all. I know that at Christmas time, in my grief, I was out of place when I suggested someone in this church had something to do with the death of our son, James. I am sorry about that, more than you can ever know."

There were nods and kind looks from the pews at that point. "The thing is that now that some time has passed and I have gathered my thoughts, I know what I said was untrue. None of you is responsible for what happened to James." Lucy then took a very deep breath. "You see, I am."

There was a collective intake of breath and disbelief at that moment. Some questioned whether they had heard Lucy correctly, while others were stunned.

"I know I have shocked you," Lucy went on, "and I am sorry for that. I didn't realise until recently that I was responsible. However, with the passing of time and some calm reflection, I was able to recall exactly what happened that night as I made my way home, and I am absolutely certain that it was me that knocked James down."

Jack was horrified at what he was hearing, and he wasn't sure what had possessed Lucy to say such a thing. He knew she was upset, but this was further than he would have thought Lucy would take things.

"Jack," said Lucy, "I can see your mind racing. Please let it rest. I know I killed James. I didn't mean to, and I didn't see him, but I know it was me. Now please, don't think of me, our girls will need you and that is where you need to focus. Sam is waiting for me outside and I will go with him and face up to what I know to be true."

"I pray for you, Jack, and the girls, and for all I have hurt and accused. I am deeply sorry. I will never forgive myself for what happened to James, and I certainly don't expect anyone else to."

Lucy then walked down the aisle, crying gently and without speaking to anyone, she walked out of the church to Sam.

Jack ran out of the church after her. "Lucy," he yelled. "Lucy, please say it isn't true. Come on, Lucy, of course you didn't hurt James."

Lucy looked at Jack with tired eyes. She turned to Sam and said, "Let's go and get this done, Sam. I am ready to face the music."

Six Months Later

The time after Lucy's announcement passed quickly. Initially, there had been the immediate shock of what she had confessed to the congregation, and of course, Jack, who could not have been more surprised and bewildered in those early days. It was like the world swallowed him up, and he lost a piece of himself with all of the trauma and despair he had suffered.

Lucy made a statement and was charged with a driving offence resulting in accidental death. She pled guilty. The community supported her, far more than she had expected or dreamt would be the case. She became a shadow of her former self, but the character references were sincere and kind and on sentencing Lucy, the judge acknowledged just what a community support she was.

Lucy received a non-custodial sentence and the judge explained that on the facts, Lucy had not been deliberately deceitful and that she had taken appropriate action on becoming aware of her responsibility for James' death. He acknowledged that Lucy had already experienced the worst possible result of her actions and that there was nothing the court could impose upon her to improve upon that.

Lucy felt relieved in one way and cheated in another. She wanted her punishment for killing her son and being so stupid, and yet, the judge was also right in that nothing anyone could do to her now would ever hurt her as much as losing her boy. And the truth of that was plain, when shortly after her sentencing, Jack left Lucy for Claire.

Jack couldn't look at Lucy, much less live in the same house. He tried his best, but he just couldn't get over what had happened. He was heartbroken and beyond repair. He didn't want to use what had happened to excuse his behaviour over Claire, but in the end, his love for her was the thing that was important to him, and he chose her.

Pippa had tried to stay close to Lucy and to support her through her ordeal and Lucy was a grateful friend. Pippa didn't find her easy, and sometimes, it was a struggle to carve out the time and sympathy she knew Lucy needed. But, over the rest of the summer, they sat together in their gardens, talked about James and life generally and shared recipes and dishes that they made with the bounty of the season. Pippa was a good, kind friend and Lucy valued her.

Jade sometimes visited Lucy also and spent a lot of time with Pippa and the boys, while Duncan and Nelson were busy on their farms. She wasn't close to Lucy like Pippa, but she absolutely felt for her and the shell of her life that remained.

Jade wasn't judgemental and she didn't think Lucy deserved any more pain for what had happened. She also understood Jack and what he needed, and tried to be a good neighbour and support to him where the opportunity arose.

Duncan and Nelson wrapped Jack up in typical country folk support, offering help around the farm and a lift, when he was moving out of the homestead and into the cottage he had spent a lot of time in with Claire. They lugged boxes and pieces of furniture and towed trailers and Utes, loaded with possessions. They also knew about Mark.

Mark had come clean to his mother and as Claire expected, it was met with great drama and despair. She had called him a sinner, blanked him, raged at him and for some time since, had never mentioned it again. Mark had thought it was better than expected and was grateful that Claire was a support over that period.

He acknowledged how much he had betrayed her and how he valued her support and kindness. He also turned his relationship around with the children and became the active and engaged parent Claire had always known he could be. Francis was thriving and Flora had become her daddy's girl, and Claire was delighted.

The rest of the community had mixed reactions on hearing about Mark's affairs away from home. Most ignored what they had heard and just continued on as normal. The surprise for Mark were the ones who sought him out. It had surprised Mark that others in the district had struggles and challenges about their own sexuality, and he was really glad that he was able to help them.

Even if his advice was mostly about what not do to and to avoid hurting others at all costs. In some ways, his lifestyle becoming public knowledge had helped to grow community understanding and tolerance and he hoped that it had made a difference for others who might have the same fears he did.

Inevitably, Claire left Mark. It was Claire who moved into the little cottage on Jack's farm in the immediate aftermath of Lucy's confession and Mark's revelations. Jack lived with Lucy in the homestead until sentencing and then he could no longer take it and, just until the children were more comfortable with him and having a new adult in the mix.

The children were distraught to begin with but over time, especially as Mark made more of an effort to be a decent father, things found a new normal and for the most part, the children grew into their new arrangements. Claire still helped Mark out with the farm, and they hadn't gone down anything formal in terms of legal separation.

Claire had been with Jack along the painful journey of Lucy's conviction and sentencing. She had helped him write down his victim impact statement that categorically stated he was certain that James' death was nothing more than a horrible accident. She comforted him and helped him with his relationship with his daughters, through their distress at what their mother had admitted.

Francis and Flora both liked Jack. He was at ease with them and there was no discomfort or awkwardness in how they interacted. Perhaps it helped that they had known him in some way all of their lives, or maybe it was that Jack was just a kind patient man that didn't react to the normal ways of children in good times and bad. Claire was happy. Happy that Jack was accepted by the children, the things in the world most important to her.

Of course, Claire didn't share everything with Jack and most of all, she didn't share her biggest secret with anyone. Just as she had committed to long before, she kept silent about what had happened when she drove home the night James was killed.

She knew one thing for sure and that was how much Lucy's admission had altered the course of her life. If it wasn't for Lucy, the truth may well have been revealed at some point and Claire would have been in a far different position.

Now, she understood the irony well; she had Lucy's husband and Lucy had taken her punishment. Perhaps most of all, however, Claire learnt the value of sensible shoes.